MURDER AT
THE PODIUM

ALEC PECHE

GBSW Publishing

ACKNOWLEDGMENTS

Thanks to GMM for your suggestions for the angles of this story.
You prevented my writer's block!

i

Prologue

Barb Jordan had flown to Dallas to present data to health care executives on how they could make improvements within their hospitals. She was nervous about speaking to this room of one-hundred conference attendees. Her co-panelist, Stacy Johnson, began speaking about ten minutes ago pausing to grab a sip of water. Barb was expected to take over in another seven minutes and so she was half listening to Stacy and half imagining the audience naked to calm her nerves.

She looked over at Stacy and noted that her face was pale, she was sweating, and had paused mid-sentence in her speech. Oh no! Maybe the woman had the flu hitting her at the wrong time.

Barb leaned over and said softly, "Stacy, are you feeling okay?"

Before she could respond, Stacy slumped to the floor, clutching her stomach.

Barb and several members of the audience surged forward to render aid. Someone called 9-1-1. First the woman vomited, then she moaned, mumbled some words, and then she lay back not moving and lifeless, as members of the audience began cardio-pulmonary resuscitation. Paramedics arrived and she was soon loaded in an ambulance. The woman was young and so CPR continued all the way to the hospital even though it felt futile. The hospital continued the effort for another twenty minutes before calling it quits and she was pronounced dead.

Barb was stuck back at the conference room where the smell of Stacy's vomit was beginning to make her feel queasy. The police had grilled her incessantly about what she knew of Stacy, the exact sequence of events. Fortunately the session was taped and so there was video footage of the incident. Mostly, Barb was freaked out about how quickly the woman she had spent two months discussing this lecture with had died. Her stage fright had completely and forever deserted her. If it ever reappeared, she would pause and think of Stacy for a few seconds. She would also never drink water from a glass at one of these conventions as that appeared to contain whatever had made Stacy so sick. Her nurse's mind was sorting through a list of poisons trying to think of what might have been colorless, tasteless and oh so deadly.

Chapter One

Jill and Nathan were checking into the Dallas hotel attached to their conference center, looking forward to a week in Texas. The trip was part business, part pleasure. They were starting off with a wine making conference, then Jill's friends and teammates for murder investigations would arrive for a long weekend of fun devoted to cheering on the Green Bay Packers as they took on the Dallas Cowboys for a traditional rivalry of National Football Conference opponents.

At the conference, Nathan was a featured speaker lecturing on the intricacies of a wine label and the impact on consumer spending with the right label. He was a rock star speaker having been stopped by several people while they were in the hotel lobby. Many of his clients, for whom he had designed wine labels, Jill included, were attending the conference.

As they crossed the lobby and Jill looked around at people, she realized she was playing one of her favorite mental games imagining the story of their lives. This time she did a double-take and squinted at a woman coming her way. Sure enough, when they got closer, Jill recognized a friend from her past.

"Barb Jordan! What are you doing in Texas?" Jill exclaimed.

"Hey Jill, long time no see. I haven't seen you in what - five or seven years? I'm here for a healthcare conference. This hotel is where the meeting is being held. What are you doing here?"

Barb asked, looking questioningly at Jill and Nathan.

"I'm also here for a convention, but not yours. I'm attending a convention devoted to wine making which is also being held in this hotel."

"Wine making, huh? I remember that was a passion of yours. Do you have a winery now?"

"I do. Let me introduce my boyfriend, Nathan Conroy. Nathan, this is an old and dear friend that I met perhaps a decade ago. She is actually a Facebook friend as well. Hey we were just checking in. Let us take our luggage to our room and then how about if I meet you in that lobby bar in say ten minutes and we can catch up?" Jill asked pointing to a bar off the lobby.

"That sounds like a great idea. I just had the strangest experience of my life and I'd love to pick your forensic pathologist brain - a co-panelist dropped dead of what appears to be poisoning during our presentation. I'm still shaken up by the experience."

"OMG! What an unsettling experience! Let me drop my stuff off in our room and I'll be down to chat."

The two women parted ways with Barb heading right to the bar and Jill arriving perhaps twenty minutes later. After ordering a glass of wine she settled in to chat with her old friend.

"Although I am anxious to hear about your experience this afternoon, tell me what you're doing now - where are you working, how's your daughter's bar doing, and why were you giving a speech at this hotel?" asked Jill.

It was typical of Jill to launch a barrage of questions at anyone new crossing her path. While Barb was an old friend, they hadn't spoken in several years.

"I'm working for Golden Star, which is the largest group

purchasing organization in the United States. I've hospital accounts assigned to me and I'm responsible for helping them improve a variety of metrics. Some of those metrics are supply costs while others are quality indicators. It's a real interesting job and I'm very happy with what I'm doing. Given my track record in assisting hospitals with improving their operations, I was asked to co-present on a panel with a woman named Stacy Johnson. I'll tell you more about her in a moment but let me take a minute to brag about my kids and grandkids. Kelly continues to operate a bar close to the University of Wisconsin campus. I'll help serve beer on special weekends when she has an overflow of customers. My son is working for the state utility company and he's given me two grandkids to spoil."

"And how about your partner? Are you still with J. B.?"

"Wow Jill, you have a good memory. Yeah, J. B. is still my partner. Other than Stacy dying on me while we were giving this panel discussion, I've no complaints in life. What are you up to?"

"I left a state crime lab about five years ago to operate my own winery. I bottled my first vintage of Moscato wine last year. I also built a chemistry lab on my property for the perfection of fermentation processes and to be used for forensics. I work as a part time consultant offering a second opinion on the cause of death and I have a private investigator's license as well. I average one case a month and that has been an exciting second career. I've been dating Nathan for about two years. I met him when I needed a wine label design and he's the best artist in the industry in my humble opinion."

"Really? Your wine career combined with the forensic pathology sounds fascinating! Could I interest you in weighing in on what may have happened to Stacy, my co-presenter?"

"Tell me more about the case - the sequence of events,

Stacy's age, her behavior before your panel started - stuff like that," Jill requested.

Barb gave her a lengthy explanation of all she knew about Stacy and the incident that day.

"So it sounds like there was something poisonous in her water glass. Did you drink from your water glass?"

"I didn't sip from my water. I was working on getting my nerves under control by imagining everyone in the room being naked," Barb admitted.

"Did you notice if she grimaced when she sipped her water? Did you see any indication that the water tasted different than she was expecting?"

"I had my head down and I didn't look over at Stacy until there was an extended silence at the podium."

"What'd you see when you looked at her?"

"She was leaning heavily on the podium and grimacing as though in pain. I figured she had a sudden attack of the flu and was about to vomit. Then she just crumbled to the floor. She vomited and then I was afraid she'd aspirated her vomit as she seemed to stop breathing. Someone began CPR, then the paramedics arrived and took her to the hospital. She was only in her mid to late thirties so I hoped they could restart her heart, but whatever poison she'd drank in the water had to be potent because she didn't survive perhaps two mouthfuls. The police were here and questioned me for a long time and they bagged the water glass. When she fell to the floor, the podium rocked and the water tipped over and crashed to the carpet. I think the crime scene team cut out the carpet where the glass landed, so I guess their lab will have an answer as to what was in Stacy's water."

"Did they take your water as well?" Jill asked.

"Yes and I will be completely bummed if my water was

poisoned too. It's bad enough watching your fellow panelist die after drinking the water, but to know that I was also supposed to die is beyond scary. Who did I make angry enough in my life for them to want to kill me?"

"Was it announced in the program who was going to speak first, you or Stacy?"

"Yes it was in the program that way."

"Sounds like the police have quite an investigation to follow and some really good leads. I know what I'd be looking for if I was a consultant on the case, but I'm not," Jill said and then she transitioned the content of their conversation. "How about you? Are you happy with your job or do you have plans to retire anytime soon? What are you up to in life?"

"So I ran for alderman of my local city and won the election. I like my job, but I think it's time to retire and enjoy my kids and my life. The elected position is very part time and carries a small stipend so it's not something I would switch jobs for. This panel presentation was going to be my last hurrah on the job prior to retiring. Jill, you seem very happy with where you are at this point."

"I am happy. My personal life is great. I love my winery and my consulting job. My mother is in good health. As the saying goes, life is good. Do you remember Angela, Marie, and Jo?" Jill asked.

"I've remained Facebook friends with them so of course I remember them. Why?"

"Nathan and I are here for a wine industry convention, but in a few days the gang is arriving and we have tickets to the Green Bay versus Dallas game. How long are you in town?"

"My convention ends in two days and then I was going to visit a few clients in the Dallas area before heading home Saturday. I would love to meet up with you guys for a meal and drinks," Barb said and then she dug through her purse and handed Jill a business card. "Here's my card with my cell phone number on it; let me know when we can meet."

"That sounds like a plan and here is my card as well," replied Jill. The two friends shared a hug and parted ways.

Chapter Two

Jill joined Nathan in their hotel suite after her conversation with her friend. For the next several days she would be playing sidekick to Nathan's power standing in the world of wine. She was looking forward to following in his shadow, while they socialized with the denizens of the Texas wine industry. She planned on being a sponge, absorbing all she heard or learned about the wine industry. This was the fortieth meeting of the Texas Wine and Grape Growers Association which was a much smaller organization than the California Grape Growers and she had already met some controversial wine growers from the great state of Texas. Jill grew the Muscat grape and it also favored the hills region of Texas. Unfortunately it was about a five to six hour drive from Dallas, and she wouldn't have an opportunity to tour any of those vineyards.

"How'd your meeting with your friend go? Are you getting involved in the investigation?" Nathan asked.

"We caught up with each other's lives and then we discussed what happened during her presentation today. By the way she also knows Jo, Marie, and Angela and was excited to hear that they would be visiting in a few days. As to whether I am involved in this investigation, the answer is no. It was such an unusual murder; we couldn't resist discussing the case."

"That's good; I'm glad you're not taking on the case," Nathan replied. "Texas is different than California. To me it has a feel of a wild frontier at times coupled with brass arrogance, and a willingness for any citizen to own at least one gun and carry it with them at all times. California has a flamboyant edge while Texas has a vibe of 'don't mess with me'. You also don't have Deputy Davis here for protection. I'd rather focus on our convention and your friends' arrival than looking over my shoulder trying to figure out if someone is going to kill you."

"I'm sorry that my investigative cases cause you such distress. I would tell you not to worry, but I know that my telling you in no way reduces your anxiety about my safety so I'll just say nothing and thank you for caring for me and loving me despite my fairly odd and recently dangerous occupation."

Jill had wrapped Nathan in an embrace while she was speaking and they enjoyed each other's company, taking time for hugs and kisses. Eventually, much to his dismay, Nathan pulled away, knowing that he had to make his way to the convention; business before pleasure, as his dad would always say. He felt the urge to return to the convention and socialize with people from the Texas world of wine. He knew that an artistic rival of his from Italy would be at this convention and he was interested in meeting her for the first time. He had not lost any customers to her and he didn't like the artistry of her wine label designs, but winemaking and wine labels were very personal and unique for the winery owner.

Hand in hand they approached an outdoor patio where the reception was located. At least ten Texas-based wineries had sponsored the reception by providing their wine to the attendees. Nathan commented quietly on the quality of each wine while Jill focused on the two Moscato wine offerings. The reception was on an outside patio overlooking the grounds of the hotel and convention center. Upbeat Jazz played through the speakers surrounding the patio. The temperature was in the mid-70s with some humidity so Jill was comfortable in the short sleeves of her casual dress. Other than Nathan, Jill didn't know a single person attending the convention. She knew she appeared to be Nathan's significant other rather than someone from the wine industry. She suffered through a few conversations wherein someone explained a wine industry concept or word to her. Rather than taking the time to set them straight about her own winery she just smiled and continued to listen to the conversation. That behavior was so unusual for her that during a break when Nathan and she were alone, he asked her if she wanted to be introduced as the owner of Quixotic Winery.

"Actually Nathan, I'm amused by the condescension of some of your friends and colleagues. I had to bite my tongue when one of them explained what a portable wine bottle machine was. I was dying to tell him that last year's harvest had produced five-hundred bottles at my winery. I'm not capable of acting like a passive airhead, but I'll admit I'm having an amusing time in my acting role tonight."

Nathan wasn't sure what to make of Jill's comment so he asked her, "Do you want to leave now?"

"No, but don't be surprised if I introduce myself as a winery owner sometime tonight. That will be when you know that the airhead is permanently retired from the stage," Jill said graciously.

Nathan watched her for a few more seconds before someone new walked up to him. Then he shrugged and decided to take her at face value. They stayed for another hour at the reception with him passing his business card out to at least thirty people interested in some way in his work. Jill passed her own business card out to one particularly obnoxious investor in a winery that had presumed to tell her about the sugar content in wine. Since he so obviously did not understand the chemistry involved in wine production, Jill decided it was time to set him straight based on her expertise in both chemistry and vineyard ownership. Nathan, taking his cue from Jill, introduced her as a winery owner from there on out.

An hour later, they drove to a small but renowned Texas Barbeque restaurant. Jill hesitated calling it a restaurant as they shared picnic tables with other customers and had a choice of soda out of a can or beer in the bottle to accompany their meal.

"You know I'm not fond of barbeque, but I have to admit that this is pretty wonderful food. I'll have to hit the hotel's fitness center tomorrow to get in a run before the convention starts."

"If you like, we could go outdoors and run around this area," Nathan suggested.

"The hotel is in a city center area that means a lot of car traffic and stop lights that get in the way of a smooth run so I would rather retreat indoors to a treadmill. You know me, just about anything is an excuse not to run and I am afraid that the wait at two stoplights would be all the incentive I need to end my run."

"I'll probably take to the streets then and sleep in since my first presentation is at eleven. Knowing you, you'll be at the 7:30 breakfast and 8am plenary session."

"You bet!" said Jill with a grin. "I paid my registration and flew all this way; the least I can do is come away smarter on the subject of growing grapes. I'll even do you a big favor and shower and change in the gym's locker room so I don't disturb your beauty rest."

"Wow, I'm honored you would go so far just to make sure I get rest. What do you say we head back to the hotel and put the bed to good use?" replied Nathan with a hug and a kiss.

The evening ended on a pleasurable note and Jill's natural alarm clock had her up the next morning for her gym workout.

Jill got her workout in and attended several sessions designed for the new vintner like herself.

She planned to attend Nathan's session and then they would go to lunch. Jill hoped to get an afternoon nap and then there was another reception to attend with Nathan followed by dinner somewhere in Dallas. The next day was expected to be a repeat and then the following day, her friends would arrive. She planned to miss the final two days of the conference, preferring to spend time with her friends. What a relaxing yet educational couple of days. After the long day, and mellowed by some great food and wine, she drifted off to sleep.

Chapter Three

Jill was just sitting down to breakfast when her cell phone ring tone rang out.

"Hello?"

"Is this Dr. Quint?"

"Yes, how can I help you?"

There was a pause, and then the male voice said, "Hello, Dr. Quint, my name is Adam Johnson. I am the husband of Stacy Johnson." There was a pause as though the speaker was waiting for Jill to recognize the name immediately. When she didn't, he continued, "My wife was murdered at the Dallas convention center two days ago and I was given your name by her co-presenter, Barbara Jordan."

"Ah yes Mr. Johnson. I'm so sorry for your loss. How may I help you?"

"I'm here in Dallas to speak with the police and take Stacy home. I was trying to understand what happened and spoke with Ms. Jordan for about half an hour. At the end, she mentioned you and your background and I wondered if you could meet with me to discuss my wife's death."

"Sure I can meet with you. Are you staying at the convention center hotel?"

"Yes, I have Stacy's room," Adam replied in a pained voice.

"How about if we meet later at the lobby bar? For a hotel bar, it has some remarkably quiet tables."

"I appreciate you taking the time to meet with me on such short notice and I'll see you in two hours."

Jill went on to provide him with a description of her appearance so he could identify her at the bar. She'd looked at the convention schedule as soon as Adam Johnson identified himself. She'd had a feeling that he wanted to meet in person. There was a seminar starting in half an hour on organic pest-control which was a topic that Jill was highly interested in. The subsequent seminar was on increasing vine production and she knew based on industry statistics that she already had highly productive vines and so would pass on that educational seminar to meet with Mr. Johnson.

Two hours later she found herself shaking hands with a thirty-something man, who was tall to Jill's five foot three stature, with perhaps a hint of Swedish ancestry. He was pale skinned and likely handsome when his face wasn't wearing deep grief.

"Hello Mr. Johnson, I'm Dr. Quint, please call me Jill," she said as she sat down at a quiet bar table.

"Hello Jill, and please call me Adam. Thank you for meeting with me on such short notice."

Jill had found that sometimes family members didn't know how to breach the subject of a suspicious death once they met her for the first time. So she began the conversation.

"Barbara Jordan is a friend of mine and she described the details of your wife's death. As you know, I'm a forensic pathologist. Do you want some help understanding something with your wife's death or perhaps something the police said to you?"

Jill liked to break the ice with these statements as often clients that hired her felt awkward negotiating a contract with her. It was bad enough talking about the death of a loved one without the business of hiring her getting in the way of a crucial conversation.

"Frankly I don't know what I want," Adam replied. "I'm horrified about my wife's murder and worried for our three children that are at the present staying with my mother."

Jill thought that the second part of his sentence was intriguing. Why was he worried about his children in regards to his wife's murder?

"Why are you worried for your children? Did the police give you some indication that you or they were also targets of whomever murdered your wife?"

"I don't know that the police are thinking that far ahead. Let me tell you about my family. Stacy and I have been married for nearly ten years and our kids are ages 7, 5, and 4. She's a nurse and I'm a petrochemical engineer. We're both native Texans and her family is from the southern region of the state near the border with Mexico. My family is from the Houston area. Stacy has not been in contact with her family throughout our marriage. I've never met them and the little I know about them was provided by Stacy before we married. None of Stacy's family members attended our wedding."

Now Jill was brimming with curiosity as to who this family was. She had never started out a meeting with a potential client with this strange reference to a family that the surviving spouse knew nothing about. When there was a pause in Adam's explanation, she got in her question.

"What's special about Stacy's family?" asked Jill clearly puzzled.

"They are somehow related to Mexico's Sinaloa Drug cartel. As soon as she turned eighteen years of age she changed her name, began wearing blue contact lenses and had facial plastic surgery. One of her high school girlfriends had an older brother in law enforcement and he assisted Stacy leaving the family."

The air went out of the bar area where Jill and Adam were seated. Jill didn't pay attention to the Mexican drug wars, but she knew that the drug gangs could be as ruthless and murderous as ISIS. This was a group she didn't want to fool with. She paused to think about potentially turning down her first client in her career as a consultant. If Adam wanted to hire her for private investigator services as there seemed to be no doubt by her or anyone else on the cause of death, she would have to discuss that with Nathan and her team. All of their lives might be at risk if they came to the attention of the Sinaloa Cartel.

"I'm convinced that the Sinaloa Cartel is behind Stacy's death and I'm worried about the health and safety of our children and I need to do something but I'm not sure what," Adam said, sharing his thoughts out loud with Jill.

"The police are focused on finding Stacy's killer. I think they think I'm just a paranoid husband of a murder victim and Stacy did such a good job of hiding her identity twenty years ago that they can't link her to the drug cartel now."

"How about DNA testing? They could match Stacy to some of the captured Sinaloa cartel members. Isn't the cartel's El Chapo in custody? I thought they did DNA testing on him to be sure they had the right man," Jill suggested.

"I'm not sure who Stacy is related to in the cartel. It could be El Chapo, or one of his henchmen, or even one of his wives, she mentioned a name, but it's been ten years and I don't remember. I don't know if we need the permission of the Mexican authorities to do DNA sampling against any of their leaders. I'm also afraid that making such a request would alert the cartel of our existence."

"True, but if they're behind finding Stacy and poisoning her at this conference, then they likely already know of your existence, right?" Jill reasoned.

With Jill's statement, Adam's brows furrowed and his sad face became consumed with desperate worry.

"Crap, I hadn't thought of that, but you're right. I'd better hire security and send the kids to my sister. Let me do that and then I would like to meet you later to finish our conversation. Do you have time to meet again in say three hours?"

"I can, but I'm not really sure what you want to discuss with me. It seems that Stacy's death by poison is not being questioned by you or the police. So you don't need me for a second opinion on the cause of death. That leaves my investigative services and I have to frankly tell you that the cartel scares me. We can discuss that later, now just go ahead and make arrangements to protect your children."

With the conversation at an end, they parted ways and Jill watched the back of Adam Johnson as he hurried off, cell phone at his ear, talking presumably to whomever was taking care of his children at the moment.

Jill was conflicted about the case. She genuinely wanted to help Adam, but she wasn't sure her forensic knowledge was of any help. Furthermore, just the words 'Sinaloa Cartel' scared her. Maybe she could wait and see what the police uncovered in their investigation. Jill and her team were increasingly being threatened in each recent case by the murderers. As she accepted each previous case, she and her friends hadn't expected to become targets. If she went to work for Adam Johnson, it would be with the knowledge that the cartel was involved and that they had a long and bloody reputation for killing people. A quick internet search revealed that the State of Texas estimated that about ten deaths a year were due to the drug cartel. She wondered how many other deaths were attributed to the cartel in other states. They weren't in just the border states either; they ran narcotics into Chicago and other major cities.

Chapter Four

Jill returned to the grape growers' conference and attended a seminar on starting a tasting room. She was strictly gathering concepts at this time as she wasn't planning a tasting room for at least another year. Later that evening, she and Nathan were trying another uniquely Texan meal experience; this time it was Tex-Mex. Her mouth was on fire from the hot chilies in the sauce of the enchiladas and salsa. Adam hadn't set a time up and so she was in standby mode. She had been giving thought as to how she could help Adam and had come up with a few meaningful ideas. She'd also been thinking about how to break the news to Nathan and her team. She was fairly confident that they'd want to decline the case out of fear of the cartel. In the end she decided there was no good way to break the news to them.

"Adam Johnson called me this morning and asked to meet with me this afternoon," Jill told Nathan, deciding it was time to let him in on Adam and his problems.

Nathan just looked puzzled and asked, "Who is Adam Johnson?"

With an 'oh', Jill realized that Nathan had put the death at Barb's convention two days ago out of his mind; so she added, "He's the husband of the woman who drank the poison water at the seminar two days ago."

"Oh, right. I thought you said you weren't involved with that case?"

"I wasn't, but apparently the husband met with Barb to

hear from her what happened and Barb passed my business card on to him. I skipped the seminar on increasing vine production and met with him."

"Okay, got it. What did he say that has made you uneasy? I could tell that something was on your mind, but I thought it was something you heard in one of the seminars. I should have known better. What's up?"

"You know me so well. I have been brooding over what he told me since we met. There's no controversy over his wife's death. She was clearly poisoned and the police have identified the agent. Adam thinks his wife's murder is linked to the Sinaloa Cartel and so far the police aren't in agreement with his suggestion."

"The Sinaloa Cartel? Are you talking about a Mexican drug cartel? Jill, you need to stay away from this murder case; those drug cartels are very violent. They'll make all your previous killers look like amateurs. You can't get involved with this case," Nathan stated emphatically.

"I know what you mean since my heart started pounding the moment he mentioned who he thought the murderers were. I don't know if Angela, Marie, and Jo would even help me on this case if I took it or if I would even ask them. Adam was supposed to call me back today after he made arrangements to step up the security on his children and so far I haven't heard from him. This may all be a moot point."

"As this isn't a cause of death case, what could you do for Adam? Investigate the cartel? Why aren't the police doing that? You really don't want to investigate the Sinaloa Cartel."

Jill could tell that Nathan was very dismayed and he didn't want her to have anything to do with Adam. "Adam mentioned that when he and Stacy got married that she confessed that she was related to someone high up in the cartel, but at the age of eighteen, she had left that life and with the assistance of plastic surgery and a couple of new identities, she disappeared from sight of the cartel."

"Before you talk about the case, let's discuss the cartel. I'll admit I don't know anything about their behavior in the United States, but in Mexico, they routinely kill politicians, judges, and police officers. They have a reputation for slaughtering small villages in the way of the drug trade routes. They have automatic weapons, machetes, and who knows what other weapons. This isn't a single madman or even two; there are thousands of cartel members. I'm sure if I did some research, I could tell you other bad statistics about these guys. You need to refuse to get involved in this case."

"So tell me what you really think," Jill said with a sigh. "All of those same thoughts were running through my head - the danger to me, you, and my friends. Then the flip side of me wonders what I could do to help this grieving husband with children to protect. Since I wouldn't cross into Mexico to investigate, how would the cartel even know about me? If I did electronic research, do they have the sophistication to detect my interest? Perhaps I could just advise Adam for his conversations with the police and he could say he did the research and found the leads. He likely already has the eye of the cartel on him so it wouldn't put him in any more danger. At the moment, though, I don't even have a guess as to how I could help him."

"So is that your way of saying you haven't ruled out helping Adam?"

After a pause, Jill replied, "I guess you're right. If I did decide to help him, then I would go it alone - no contract, no payment, no involving my friends in any of the work. I might even set up a false name to operate under for this case. I would also do some investigation on the cartel's behavior in the U.S. to get a better assessment of my risk."

"I'd really prefer that you decide not to assist Adam Johnson, but if you do assist him, I'll watch your back," said Nathan heaving a huge sigh.

"Have I told you I love you recently? You're a really special man and thanks for your support," Jill said as she moved in close to hug Nathan.

The next morning, Jill was up early for the 8am conference start while Nathan planned on attending after eleven. He wasn't an early riser and the conference was oriented to vineyard owners which he wasn't and so he didn't want to waste his time attending seminars that had no useful value in his work life.

Jill received a call from Adam shortly after nine with a request that they meet. They agreed to meet in the same location as they had the previous day around eleven. Jill was curious as to what she could do for the man. Other than a little internet research, she had drawn a blank on how she could help him. After their discussion the previous night, she wanted to be upfront with Nathan as to what she was doing with this case so she texted him to let him know of the scheduled meeting. She then went back to her seminar, titled 'fermentation in steel versus oak barrels'.

At eleven, she walked into the bar and found Nathan there getting her a Diet Coke, and Adam occupying a table, coffee cup in front of him. Nathan and Jill locked gazes briefly and Jill decided the message was *I'm not happy with you getting involved in this case, but if you're in, I'm your back-up.*

Jill walked over to Adam's table and waited for Nathan, with two drinks in his hands, to approach before pulling out a chair for him. She introduced the two men.

"Adam, when I mentioned your possible connection to the

Sinaloa Cartel, Nathan indicated he preferred that I have no further contact with you. To be frank, you would be my most dangerous client ever, even though I have had attempts on my life several times in past cases. Perhaps I am jumping the gun, and you don't need my help."

With a pained look at Nathan, Adam began, "I need someone's help and if not you, Jill, perhaps you can direct me to someone else who provides investigative services. After our conversation yesterday as you know I ran out to make arrangements to make sure my children are well protected and safe. That took me most of last night. When I contacted the police this morning for an update on their investigation into Stacy's death, I wasn't pleased with what I heard which was essentially nothing new to the investigation in the last twenty-four hours. I read once that every hour you get away from a murder investigation the odds increase that the killer won't be found."

"Adam, I have many questions about the case but let me start with asking you why you think I could help with the investigation of your wife's death?" Jill asked. "Have the police followed up on your connection to the cartel?"

"If they have, they haven't told me. I don't know if they have any suspects yet."

"That's surprising! I thought they captured Stacy's presentation on videotape. Can't they go back and look at the tape to see who placed the glass of water in front of her?"

"That's just it, the videotape began rolling when the first speaker introduced Stacy to the audience. The water glass was already at the podium."

"How about the service hallways that staff use to bring supplies into the various conference rooms - do any of them have cameras for security purposes?"

"I didn't ask and they didn't mention it, but surely they'll have thought to look for those cameras," Adam said.

"Yes, I think they would have looked at that footage and gone from there. Let me return to my earlier question - what do you think I can do for you?"

"I feel like I'm not getting much information from the police and I don't know how to investigate the case. I feel like I need a translator between me and the police. As for why I am asking you, it is because of the recommendation from Ms. Jordan. My wife had great respect for her and so I respect what she said about you. My other option is to hire someone that I find from doing a search on the internet."

"You might be better served to hire someone with an investigator's license from this state," Jill suggested. She wanted the case on one level as she had never investigated a cartel. On the other hand, it might be bad for her personal safety and Nathan's to take on this case.

"Haven't you worked in other states where you don't have an investigator's license? I looked you up before contacting you and I know you have solved cases in Colorado and Wisconsin," replied Adam.

"Yes, I have solved cases in those states and in my line of work, I have found that my medical degree was more important than an investigator's license but I do have a PI license issued by the State of California. Adam, what are your plans over the next couple of days? Have they released Stacy to a funeral director for you yet? Are you joining your children?"

Adam opened his mouth to respond then paused to gather his thoughts and replied, "The detectives said she would be released tomorrow to the funeral home. I need to return home and plan a funeral and I also need to spend some time with my children. I don't know what I am going to do about a funeral service. Our friends and family will expect one, but I want the children to remain safe from the cartel. I'll see if I can plan something very small and private for the children, my parents and me. I then could have a larger reception or something for our friends and co-workers. I don't know yet, I'm going to bounce some ideas off of my parents as to what is best for the children."

"Where do you live?" Nathan asked.

"Odessa. It's about three hundred and fifty miles from Dallas. It's a town that has a lot of oil industry companies. Stacy worked from home helping hospitals all over the south so it didn't matter where in Texas we lived. The kids are with my parents in Houston."

"Sounds like you have no reason to remain in Dallas. The police can keep in touch by phone, and you have a lot of work to do figuring out the memorial and how to protect your kids on potentially a longer term than just the next few days. So as I understand you, you want me to separately investigate this case from the police to bring you and your family resolution."

"I'm not sure what I want," Adam said hesitantly. "Do I need to sign a contract or something with you?"

"Let me think about our conversation for a few hours then I'll let you know. I'm mulling over a few options in my head including whether I want to take on this case. It's a very intriguing case and I would love to help you find resolution with Stacy's murder, but my team and I have come close to being killed in prior cases with villains that appear to be amateurs when compared to the Sinaloa Cartel. I just need some time to think about the ramifications of your request."

Actually Jill knew what decision she wanted to make, but she had others to consider. Nathan as the person closest to her would be at risk. Even if she didn't have her teammates work on this case, were their names discoverable? Would the cartel sit in the background waiting for the perfect time to kill her and not just during the time she worked on this case? She wondered who she could ask for advice on the cartel's behavior. Then it came to her - she would ask Leticia Ortiz from the San Francisco FBI office. Surely they understood the cartel's behavior, perhaps had a dossier describing their patterns of behavior.

She and Nathan were soon standing up and shaking hands with Adam. They left the bar with a plan to return to their convention. There was a major closing session by a speaker that interested them both and then they had the remainder of the day free as well as the following one with Jill's teammates arriving from Wisconsin in the evening.

As they were walking toward the ballroom for the lecture, Jill said, "I'm going to call Leticia Ortiz and get her read of this cartel. I want to take this case, but not if it exposes you, Jo, Maria, and Angela. If by simply knowing me will put you guys in danger; even if you don't work on the case, then I'll have to pass on this investigation."

"Jill, you know that something else is going on here, don't you?"

Jill drew her brows together and asked, "What do you mean? Did you get an odd vibe from Adam or something?"

"Or something. I think you should investigate Adam before taking on the case."

They arrived at the ballroom for the convention wrap-up and Jill noted she had about ten minutes before the start of the session. She said to Nathan, "Let's select our seats and then I'll step out to make a call to Agent Ortiz."

Nathan shrugged and continued into the ballroom for seat selection. After finding seats, she left her briefcase on the chair next to Nathan and stepped out to make the call. Moments later she listened to the phone ringing while composing the message in her head for the agent.

She was startled from her thoughts when she heard Leticia's voice, "This is Special Agent Ortiz, how can I help you, Jill?"

"You know I think I have overstepped my welcome with the FBI if you have my number in your phone contact log. Thanks for taking my call. I wanted to talk with you about the Sinaloa Cartel."

"Jill, I keep you on my contact list as whenever you call, I know my day is about to get more interesting. Why do you want to know about the cartel? You need to be more specific with your questions as I could spend an hour briefing you on their behavior and history."

"Leticia, I am thinking about taking a case that will likely involve the Sinaloa Cartel," Jill replied giving Agent Ortiz the highlights of her potential case with Adam Johnson. Then she continued, "You know that I have recently been hunted by some of the murderers involved in my investigations. These individuals didn't have the reputation of the cartel for violence. If I nose around in their business and their connections, will I become a target? Do I have some protection being a U.S. citizen on American soil from their behavior?"

"Jill, as a matter of policy I need to tell you to refuse to take this case. I would tell you this if you were investigating the ninety-two year old actress Betty White, as you have a poor track record for coming into violence with your recent cases."

"Come on Leticia, I could come to that conclusion myself. Tell me about the cartel's behavior - will they be average bad guys or something far worse? I know in Mexico that they have wiped out entire villages, but according to the FBI, have they been known to target individuals or kidnap family members inside the United States?"

Jill heard a sigh on the other end of the phone then the Agent said, "I'm not a cartel expert, let me contact my counterpart in the El Paso office as they are likely closest to the cartel and are far more intimate with its behavior. I'll give you a call later today, okay?"

"Thanks Agent Ortiz," and they ended their call. Jill was able to return to her seat in the ballroom just as the speaker was being introduced.

Nathan looked at her and asked, "Everything okay?"

Jill nodded and whispered back, "Agent Ortiz is going to gather some intel and call me back this afternoon. That leaves us free to enjoy this speaker," and with that they both tuned in to the speaker for the next hour.

Later that afternoon, with the conference over, Jill and Nathan headed to North Park Mall to do a little shopping. Nathan was nearly as bad a clothes-horse as Jill was and she liked to get the flavor of a city by visiting its local shopping mall. This mall contained a Nordstrom, a Macy's, a Niemen-Marcus, and a Dillards. She was looking forward to watching the southern belles go about shopping. While Jill was a diehard Packer fan, she had secretly enjoyed the vice of watching the Dallas Cowboys Cheerleaders reality show. From a dance perspective, the women trying out for the squad were amazing athletes, and the attention the cheerleading squad leaders paid to finding the perfect women to fit their brand was interesting watching as well. The only thing she knew about southern women came from watching that show.

Strolling around the mall, she actually found herself doing a double-take; a woman in her 50s or 60s was sitting on a bench outside of Niemen-Marcus with what appeared to be fresh bandages from a face-lift. She had to give the woman kudos for going out in public with her face in disarray. Perhaps she was tired from recovering at home, or simply the store had an irresistible sale.

Jill's cell phone rang and she looked around for a quiet place to sit and take notes suspecting that Agent Ortiz was her caller. Nathan was two steps ahead of her and directed her to a quiet table in front of a restaurant.

"Hi Agent Ortiz. What do you have for me?"

"Hey Jill, it's a mixture of good and bad news. There have been cartel associated murders across Texas, but they're killing strictly their own drug runners, buyers, and sellers. There have been no kidnappings or murders of anyone not touching illicit drugs. South of the border, it's another story and if you traveled there, you would last two days at most."

"How about Northern California, does the cartel reach there?"

"Since I have been the Special Agent in Charge, there have been no cartel suspected murders. I can't comment on the situation in Los Angeles or San Diego."

"Okay, this situation sounds like a reasonable risk to me. Do you have any sense of their computer skills? Has anyone tried to hack into a cartel computer system? I read somewhere that it's a five billion dollar operation; surely they have computers to manage the complexity of that operation?"

"Certainly some U.S. government agencies have tried to hack into their systems as a means of tracking their leaders, and intercepting shipments. It was how they captured El Chapo the first time by using cell phone records. Why?"

"I just wondered if I do a bunch of computer research, do they have the technology in place to determine that I am looking into their organization on the internet?"

"I don't know the answer to that. Do you plan to take this

case on? What's wrong with letting local law enforcement do their job? Are they looking into the cartel connection?"

"I am going to take this case on. I don't know how much good I can do the husband, we'll see, but I feel relatively safe taking on this case and even perhaps using some of my team members - I'll leave it up to them. As for the locals here, I haven't spoken with them yet and perhaps, they already have the case solved. Agent Ortiz, thanks for your help. I feel better equipped to handle this case."

Shortly, they ended the call and Jill returned to Nathan's presence beside her at the table.

Looking at him, she said, "I'm going to take the case. I believe I am safe from the cartel as long as I stay north in the United States. I'll give Jo, Marie, and Angela the facts about the cartel and let them make their own decision to participate or not."

"When are you going to have time to do any work? I thought the weekend was all planned out."

"It is all planned. We'll do some work now but I think the bulk of the investigation will occur after we all return to our respective homes. Between now and when they arrive, I'll send a contract to Adam, do some research on him, and meet with the police. I think the remainder will be handled from California."

Nathan didn't say anything, just turned a skeptical eye on Jill as she grinned. An hour later she had a contract sorted out, an appointment with the police lined up for the following day, and two new outfits purchased at the mall. They headed back to drop off their purchases in the hotel room before walking the few blocks to the Dallas Museum of Art. They spent the rest of the day touring the museum and sculpture garden and catching an outdoor music concert at Warren Park then tried their luck at one of the many food trucks parked nearby.

Nathan was meeting a potential client late in their hotel's bar so Jill took the opportunity to drop an email to her friends about the case and begin work on developing a profile on Adam and Stacy Johnson.

Chapter Five

Jill enjoyed vacation time with Nathan. Unlike their daily lives wherein she needed to think of his or her schedule, staying in a hotel usually equated to undivided attention for each other. Long nights, private conversations, shared showers or baths and doing touristy things always reminded her of how lucky she was to have Nathan in her life. With that thought in mind, she started the day with a more than usual sunny disposition. Her friends would arrive that evening, and now she had a few hours on her own before Nathan woke up. While she liked the together time, she also cherished her early mornings when Nathan usually was asleep since he was a night person. Despite dating for almost three years they had never managed to synchronize their biological clocks. Jill quietly dressed, grabbed her laptop and headed down to one of the hotel's breakfast options to begin work on her new case.

She had a meeting with a detective Castillo later that morning. When she identified the case and her private investigator's license to the detective, she almost heard the groan in his voice. She thought about the approach she would take establishing her legitimacy with the detective.

After ordering breakfast Jill checked her email and noted that Marie had responded to her email, while Jo and Angela had not. No surprise there, she would have been shocked if Jo had replied as she was usually several days behind with reading her email. Next she got to work investigating the Johnsons.

As Adam stated, Stacy's history seemed to start when she

was eighteen and try as she might, she couldn't find anything else on her from high school or earlier. Jill was able to verify her nursing education and licensure. She worked for a health care system in their hometown and for most of the last decade by the same large purchasing organization as Barb Jordan. She had given a large number of presentations on wound prevention and treatment. At various times in her life she had supported programs in her kid's schools, sport teams and scouts. Just an average American life. Jill stared at her picture looking for scars from plastic surgery, but she didn't see any and Stacy likely had the work done nearly two decades prior when she changed other aspects of her identity.

She moved on to Adam and found a more thorough history beginning with his middle school years athletic feats to a recent lecture he gave on fracking for shale gas. Of the two, Jill would likely find Stacy the more interesting lecturer. He also had an extended family whereas Stacy had none. She avoided researching their children at this time. Somehow that felt like she was exploiting children. After spending perhaps a half-hour, she could find nothing of concern in Adam's background, so she moved on to creating a list of questions for her meeting with Detective Castillo.

After her interview, she would return to the hotel and drive with Nathan to visit a couple of wineries that afternoon. There appeared to be at least twenty wineries in the Dallas metropolitan area. Nathan had a meeting with one owner and after that they would decide which wineries to visit. In the early evening they would be meeting their friends at the airport and would head out to dinner once they dropped their luggage off at the hotel.

Jill determined that Dallas Police Department Headquarters was just under a mile from her hotel. After checking to make sure there was no rain in the forecast for the next two hours, she set out at a brisk pace. The six story glass and brick building appeared to be big enough to house all the major services a large police department like Dallas must provide. She wondered if the crime lab was located within and how far away the Medical Examiner's office was. Depending on what information she gleaned from her meeting with the detective, she might want to schedule a meeting with the person who had conducted Stacy's autopsy. As she approached the front door, she was startled by what appeared to be bullet holes around the front entrance. She'd thought she was in a safe neighborhood.

As she approached the reception area, she noted two armed officers in the lobby. "Hello, my name is Dr. Jill Quint and I have an appointment with Detective Castillo."

The receptionist replied, "If you'll have a seat, I'll contact the Detective and he'll meet you here."

Jill hesitated, then asked pointing to the entrance, "Are those bullet holes by the front door? I walked over here from my hotel by the convention center and so I wanted to make sure it was safe for me to walk back."

"Yes ma'am those are bullet holes. Two months ago an assailant fired shots at this lobby and planted bombs in our parking lot."

"I assume your police department located the perpetrator and arrested him?" Jill asked feeling both a need to stay away from the glass enclosed lobby and happy that her assessment about the neighborhood had been correct.

"Ma'am, the gunmen died during a twelve hour stand-off with this department."

"Oh" and on that note, Jill looked around for seating that was far away from the glass enclosed entrance. The receptionist was obviously miffed with her as she hadn't heard about the gunfight, but she couldn't remember it playing out in the news in California. In fact she couldn't remember ever hearing about a gunman firing on a police headquarters. It seemed like a stupid thing to do, given all of the armed officers in the vicinity of or inside any police building. Then she thought back to a prior case in her own hometown where covert security operatives had fired upon her Sheriff's station after she had taken refuge inside causing extensive damage to the building. Maybe it happened with greater frequency than one expected.

Perhaps five minutes later and at her appointed time, a man in plain clothes entered the lobby from an elevator bank and looked quickly around the lobby spying her and heading in her direction.

"Dr. Quint?" said the man. He was likely about Jill's age, tall and lanky with a gun holster. His face was blank and Jill wondered what his real thoughts were about her request to meet with him.

"Hello Detective Castillo," Jill said as she stood and shook hands with the detective.

"May I see your driver's license and private investigator license as well," yep, Jill thought, he was all business giving nothing away.

Jill quickly handed over the requested documents and he used his cell phone to take a picture of both. She was impressed with his actions and she had a feeling that he would file away her face and information looking at her connection to the murder of Stacy Johnson. He handed the documents back to her and directed her to the elevator bank.

Shortly they arrived in an interview room in the detective division. He had a pad of blank paper and nothing more. She had been hoping he would have Stacy's homicide file in his possession while they spoke. Rats!

The detective remained silent waiting for Jill to begin the conversation. Jill was impressed with his technique so far, he had volunteered zero and she was going to be forced to dig for every morsel of information from him.

So she began, "As I indicated on the phone, Stacy's husband engaged me to investigate his wife's death."

"Do you have a copy of the contract that I can review?" asked the detective.

"Yes," and Jill passed him a copy of the contract that Adam had signed. In her past experiences she had learned to carry with her several copies of the contract to share with various agencies, law enforcement, health services and public records all required proof that she had Adam's permission to obtain private records typically only available to the spouse.

The detective read the contract and then looked at her as though silently instructing her to continue.

"I would like to review your report of the murder, any reports from the medical examiner and crime lab. I'd also like to view your murder board." Jill lobbed the ball back at the detective, interested to see what his response would be. She'd looked up Texas privacy rights and knew that she legally had the right to her first two requests, but there was no law that could compel the detective to share his murder board with her.

"Why should I share that information with you?"

Again Jill was unable to read any emotions from his face or his word inflexion.

"Because under Texas State law you are compelled to share the first two items with me as Mr. Johnson's representative. You're not required to show me your murder board, but if you're willing, I would like to view it."

Moments after Jill finished explaining her reasons for the

information, the detective stood up and said, "Follow me and I'll walk you through the murder board and I have copies of the requested items for you at my desk."

With this last comment, Jill was both chagrined that she was so predictable and delighted with the cooperation from the detective. In the resulting tumult of emotions she was rendered speechless; and found herself silently following the detective down a corridor and entering a large room with cubicles. They rounded the corner into an open space containing a cubicle with Detective Castillo's name on it. He approached his computer and moved the mouse and the murder board appeared on screen. At the top of the board was a picture of Stacy Johnson. Jill stood there for a few minutes studying the contents of the board. When she looked over at the detective, she found his eyes on her, an eyebrow raised.

Jill was beginning to think that they had done the most communicating with the least amount of words.

"Cause of death is poison and mode is homicide. Suspects include husband and Sinaloa Cartel represented by El Chapo's picture. The poison hasn't been identified and you haven't discovered any camera footage that shows the glass being placed on the podium. Do you have any reason to suspect the husband or is he there because the spouse is usually considered a suspect until he or she is eliminated?"

"You are correct in that we have no evidence to suspect Adam at this time. As far as we know he was four hundred miles away in their hometown. However, at this point in the investigation we haven't done enough due diligence to rule him out."

"When do you expect your crime lab to identify the poison and do you think that will help identify the murderer? Since it is poison, perhaps you should have some female suspects on your murder board as that is the typical poisoner."

The detective just smiled with her last comment and handed her the paperwork that she had requested.

"Do you have any further questions for me?" asked the detective.

"I may after I read your information in the reports. May I have one of your business cards in case I need to contact you further? I don't intend to take up a lot of your time or otherwise get in the way of the investigation. Unless it's urgent, I'll communicate by e-mail if you don't mind."

The detective handed her his card and motioned her toward the exit to the homicide division. Clearly he was ready to escort her to the lobby. Jill was itching to ask him one more question.

"Are you usually this cooperative with private investigators, Detective Castillo?"

"No, but when you requested the meeting I did a quick internet search on you and was impressed with some of the cases that you have been involved with. Furthermore, you appear to be a magnet for murderers and sooner or later your very presence on this case is likely to bring the murderer to my attention so you become just another tool in my detective's toolbox."

"Are you saying that I have a target on my back, that I naturally attract murderers?"

"So it would seem."

Jill paused for a moment, and then ended with, "You might be the most perceptive detective that I've ever worked with."

Jill left police headquarters with the reports in hand for the walk back to the hotel. Dumbfounded by Detective Castillo's assessment, she couldn't concentrate on the next steps of the case. Especially concerning was his comment that by her simply being on the case, she would attract the murderer's attention and he could take it from there. She didn't know whether she should feel flattered, miffed, or scared. Mostly she felt miffed but she knew she should be scared as no one would want to attract the attention of the Sinaloa Cartel. With her emotions raging, she was so distracted that she arrived back at her hotel without remembering the journey by foot.

Entering the hotel room she found Nathan comfortably ensconced in the hotel room's sofa, laptop open and in use. He looked up as she entered and asked, "Hey babe, how'd your meeting go?"

He hit a few keys on the laptop shutting it down for the time being, setting it aside and patting the space next to him for Jill to come and join him.

Taking her seat next to him, legs stretched out and aligned with his, she briefed him on the meeting.

"With the detective's view of this situation, are you reconsidering staying with the case?"

Jill looked over at Nathan, one eyebrow raised and said "On the way back to the hotel I tried to talk myself into being scared about the cartel. Unfortunately since we have all survived multiple attempts to kill us, I feel too lucky to die at the hands of a murderer from one of our cases."

"Too lucky to die? You know that kind of arrogance will get you killed eventually."

"Actually, I'm trying to make a statement about the great protection I have around me starting with you to everyone from the FBI to the Palisades Valley Police Station. I've awesome and smart protection around my teammates and me. Detective Castillo also gave me a vibe that he would come to my defense at a moment's notice. In fact his analysis was so clear and accurate, that he might be able to step in front of me before the murderer throws a cup of poison my way."

Nathan leaned away from Jill and gave her the squint-eye, "Throw a cup of poison your way? Besides looking out for guns and knives, I also have to watch for anyone approaching with a red solo cup?"

Jill had the grace to look chagrined and replied, "That is if you wouldn't mind..."and then she ducked as a pillow flew at her.

"If I asked you to drop the case, would you?" Nathan asked.

Jill looked at him trying to read his thoughts and then she gave up and shrugged.

"Since I seem to be putting your life in danger every time I make the decision to put my life in danger, I would have to abide by your request and call Adam Johnson and decline the case. He hasn't paid for my services yet so now would be the opportune time to do that. Are you asking me not to take this case?"

After a lengthy pause, Nathan said, "No I won't ask you to do that."

Jill leaned over and gave Nathan a long silent hug, then followed with a few kisses. She looked at her watch and said, "We probably ought to hit the road if you're going to make your appointment with the client."

Chapter Six

Jill and Nathan spent an enjoyable afternoon visiting his client and then going on to an additional four wineries. They both loved visiting wineries; he liked to assess the wine label and marketing materials compared to the location, the people, and the owner if he met them. Jill knew someday she would build her own tasting room and so she was collecting best practices from all the wineries she visited to put into her future design. Then there was the wine, they both loved tasting wine. The problem lay in drinking and driving. Where possible they looked for a private location to taste the wine with the plan of spitting rather than swallowing. The wine tasting public assumed that anyone spitting wine out didn't like the flavor; Jill and Nathan thought they kept their taste buds sharper by avoiding swallowing the wine and raising their blood-alcohol level. As Jill had visited numerous California wineries she was enjoying the architecture of the Texas wineries. Since land was cheap, the vineyard tasting rooms were larger and more spacious.

After a pleasurable afternoon and no further conversation about the Sinaloa Cartel, they navigated their car to the airport to meet Jo, Marie, and Angela. Their plane was on time and soon hugs were given close to the baggage carousel where they were waiting for their luggage. They had rented a full-size sport-utility vehicle to accommodate the five adults and their luggage. After everyone was checked in and unpacked, they walked to a restaurant about a mile away as the new arrivals wanted to stretch their legs after being cooped up on an airplane. It was only about a two and a half hour flight, but it was more about being unable to move unless you inconvenienced your fellow passengers.

After catching up on everyone's lives and admiring pictures of Jo's new granddaughter, they moved on to the case. Jill had sent a brief email to them summarizing the case and so they had a vague outline.

"When you said she was poisoned in front of a room full of health care people while giving a speech, I was appalled," Jo said. "I mean who likes to stand in front of a hundred people and give a speech? Then to drink poison from a water glass and then have your last moments be vomiting in front of those same hundred people is terrible. First I would feel queasy over having to give a speech, then I would feel terrible and embarrassed that I had to vomit in front of those people, then I guess you sort of lose consciousness when your embarrassment and misery is at an all-time high. Poor woman."

Everyone at the table nodded in agreement and Nathan added, "I had to give a speech to the wine growers convention that we were at, and I made sure that I put the water provided to the speaker well out of reach - I walked to an attendant and asked him to take it away. I didn't want to absent-mindedly reach for a sip of water. In the future, I'll bring my own bottled water with me when I am giving a speech."

Jill went on to describe her call with Special Agent Ortiz and the meeting with Detective Castillo. Nathan hadn't heard the full play-by-play of that meeting and, like her girlfriends, enjoyed Jill's chagrin at having been so easily understood and slightly appalled by the comment that she would bring the murderer to law enforcement's attention, simply by being on the case.

"The detective's assessment should inspire the three of us to quit as your teammates," Jo said.

This is exactly what Jill was afraid of and really who could blame her friends for feeling that way?

"But since we love you and wouldn't leave you with just Nathan to face these horrible people, we'll stay on the job as long as you do," Angela declared while Jo and Marie nodded agreement.

Marie looked over at Nathan and said, "It's not that you aren't a great protector of Jill, it's just that you need our help."

"Jill is lucky to have attracted such loyal and crazy friends as you three," Nathan said sincerely.

Nathan's comment necessitated a group hug.

"I'm back to the start of this case, given what you know now are you guys interested in working on the case? Specifically are you willing to put up with the risks of coming to the attention of the Sinaloa Cartel?"

"Even though I'm a new grandmother, I for one feel that if we stick together we'll solve the case faster which will take you, Jill out of harm's way sooner. So I'm in," Jo responded.

Angela put her hand in the center of the table and soon Marie, Jo, Jill, and with a little nudging, Nathan were putting their hands on top of Angela's with the affirmation from the Three Musketeers of 'all for one and one for all'.

The group declined dessert and soon walked back to the hotel. They stopped in to assess if the hotel bar was crowded and noisy or whether they could sit and map out a work plan while having the advantage of the bar to aid in their creativity. Fortunately, there was a large table and it was a relatively quiet night. Nathan reserved the space while the women went to their respective hotel rooms to gather pen, paper, and laptop computers.

Fifteen minutes later, libation of choice in hand, they sat at a table working out their plan for the case. Nathan was usually not involved in this phase of a case, but circumstances placed him in the case at the start. Besides he had his own read of Adam and he would be interested in what Marie found on the man.

"I'll start with reviewing the finances of the cartel and of the Johnsons," Jo declared. "Since the cartel is based in Mexico and the Johnsons are private citizens, this could be a very short search. I'll take a look at the employers of the Johnsons as well but I don't know if my financial skillset will be much help on this case."

"I'll do my usual people search on the Johnsons and the cartel," Marie added. "I briefly looked at Facebook this morning and was happy to see that the cartel didn't have a Facebook page. Sure they're mentioned in a lot of posts and I heard El Chapo was on Twitter, but at least they don't have a cartel page."

"I'll make an appointment to interview Adam Johnson and Barb Jordan," Angela proposed. "She is still here in Dallas isn't she? Is she coming to the Packers-Cowboys game?"

"Barb should still be in the area - she was going to visit a few clients and no she isn't attending the game. She would love to have dinner or at least a drink with us."

"I would like to borrow your car so I can go interview Adam in person, see him in his own home," Angela said. "I'll set up an appointment for tomorrow. I can't imagine that he has returned to work, so it shouldn't be a problem."

"It's a five hour drive, one of us should go with you," Marie noted.

"I'll go with Angela," Nathan volunteered. "I didn't like Adam, but maybe if I give him a second chance, I'll warm up to him. I'd visit local wineries along the way, but there're none in that region of the state. I guess oil and grapevines don't mix."

"Wow, thanks Nathan for volunteering," Jill replied. "I'm going to try and see what I can find about the poison. I have the autopsy report from the medical examiner and perhaps based on the findings, I can speculate on the poison. Sounds like we have a good plan going forward, but Angela and Nathan's trip tomorrow cancels some of our Dallas sightseeing and I feel bad about that."

"Actually, I think that we could take in one sight tomorrow. I don't have much work so far on this case and since I am the money person I want to visit the US mint in Fort Worth. However since Nathan and Angela have the car tomorrow and I think Fort Worth is some distance from Dallas – I mean we can't walk there I'll save that excursion for the following day. What's within walking distance of this hotel?"

Jill drew a quick map of the Dallas region with a few ideas on what they could see within walking distance. In the end they decided on the JFK Memorial, where the last American President to be assassinated in office occurred. Depending on their available time, they might hit the same museums, parks, food truck area that Nathan and Jill had visited a few days earlier. With the next day planned and research efforts related to the case assigned, they closed up their laptops and concentrated on each other. Jill spoke of her thoughts regarding the future tasting room, Marie described her training for sprint triathlons, Angela caught them up on several mutual friends, and Jo was planning a vacation with her partner Jack in the winter in Mexico as she described her new focus was beyond Cabo San Lucas. After multiple trips to that region of Mexico she was looking for new cities to explore. Finally as one, they all turned on Nathan with inquiring eyes. He searched his mind for something to share.

"Ladies, I live a simple quiet life and can't think of anything to update you with."

"Nathan, I find that hard to believe. I think the last time we chatted with you, you were designing glasses for beer. Whoops, I meant wine of course you're a wine label designer," Angela corrected herself. "How's that going? What kind of unique designs have you come up with?"

Before he could answer Angela's question, Marie asked, "Have you spoken with Nick or Henrik recently?"

Then Jo asked him, "How's Arthur doing with Trixie?"

"The wine glass design is fine but a small part of my portfolio, yes, fine."

At the look of their frustration with his brief answers he elaborated on his short comments.

"The wine glasses are being used by five clients and if you give me a moment, I'll bring the glass pictures up on my tablet."

Jill hadn't only seen the designs, she had copies of the wine glasses in her cabinet, and once her friends viewed the designs they were soon asking Nathan for copies of the glasses. They were very unique and added a level of sexiness to a glass of wine. The lower stem area was full of curves yet the top of the glass was appropriate to a wine breathing. Nathan promised them he would mail copies of the glasses to them.

"Tell us about your conversations with Henrik and Nick," Marie urged.

"Henrik has decided to plant a vineyard on his property in Germany," Jill said. "Nathan and I flew out to spend a long weekend with him about two weeks ago. He is such a nice person and he has been so helpful with our work that I wanted to say thanks in person. While we were there, he picked Nathan's brain for a winery name and spoke with both of us about which grape to grow. I wasn't any help since I only know grapes that suit California's climate, but Nathan arranged a tour while we were there of some vineyards within about seventy-five miles and so he hooked Henrik to some good sources close-by. In the end, he decided to grow mostly Riesling grapes, but he also is devoting a small amount of land to a hard grape to grow in Germany just for the challenge."

Looking at Nathan, Jo asked "Did you design his label and help him name his winery?"

"I gave him some ideas. I thought he should name the winery something very modern that implies that he has used the best science to create an exquisite grape flavor. Germans admire engineering feats and so he could approach it from that angle. They also value tradition, but as a new vintner he'll be able to stand out better if he avoids tradition yet still appeals to the German people."

"That's really fun to be in on the early stages of a new venture," Marie noted. "I wish him luck."

"Actually he would like to see all of us back at his estate. He asked if we would consider a long weekend in early December. Apparently the German craftspeople go nuts over the holidays and it is an exciting place to shop. He offered to send his plane to California to pick up Nathan and I with a stop in Wisconsin to pick up you three. What do you think?"

"Fly on a private jet, enjoy Henrik's house, and shop? Count me in!" Jo said. "In fact that sounds like such a great idea, I would be happy to move up the visit to two weeks from now as we could hit Oktoberfest."

"That's a brilliant idea!" Angela said. "Marie and I are always looking for new beers to add to our beer app. In my photography business, I'll be finished with senior pictures and it's before the rush of Christmas family portraits, so it's a good time to take off."

Marie had been looking at her calendar and nodded agreement that she could take a long weekend in two weeks.

"I'll give Henrik a call in a few hours and check his availability. My guess is that he'll be happy to host us sooner rather than later."

"How about Nick, do you think he could join us?" Angela asked. "Last I heard they were on good terms."

"Henrik mentioned inviting him over the same time we're there. He can just take a train or drive. They've had a few dinners together and seem to be good friends."

"And Jo your final question about Arthur and Trixie," Nathan remarked with a grin. "Let's just say the war is still on and Arthur appears to have secured his empire at my house. When Trixie visits, it's very clear who the alpha cat and subservient dog are in the equation."

"Trixie behaves in the subservient manner in order to get fed fabulous food created by Nathan. When she's with me at my house, then its treats and dog food. At Nathan's, having to tolerate Arthur is just part of her plan to get more table scraps."

With the final comments about the pets, they were ready to call it a night and head to bed. Maria, Angela, and Jo were on a lower floor and got out of the elevator first. The elevator continued to Jill and Nathan's floor and soon they were strolling, hands casually clasped together, to their hotel room.

Chapter Seven

Angela and Nathan were on the road to Odessa. Angela was driving, as Nathan hadn't really woken up yet. True he was dressed in jeans and a polo shirt and had taken time to shower and shave judging by his scent and smooth cheeks, but she knew him well enough not to say anything for several hours. She was listening to the NFL channel since the rental car had satellite radio stations, and Nathan sat beside her with his eyes shut. She was glad for the company and knew that he would do the five hour drive home. Adam Johnson was on bereavement leave from work and would accommodate the interview whenever they reached town.

Angela expected the drive to be relatively bland. Texas was flat in this part of the state and after Fort Worth, the next large city she would pass would be a hundred and fifty miles later, and then another two hundred miles to Odessa. Maybe she would play a game with herself. Count the number of Wisconsin license plates that she passed or passed her, or maybe the number of oil rigs. New to Interstate 20, she would stick with the license plates; she imagined that some parts of the state had oil rigs as far as the eye could see which would make counting hard. She counted five Wisconsin plates in the greater Dallas area - even if you were coming for the Packers game it was a little too far to drive. Once she'd reached the Interstate, she hadn't seen a Wisconsin license plate all the way to her first break in Abilene. She gassed up the car, used the bathroom, and settled back in to continue the drive, noticing that Nathan had barely stirred at the drop in speed, or the noise she made with the gas nozzle and getting in and out of the car. Perhaps he had a long conversation with Henrik and stayed up late on the phone.

Three hours later she dialed Adam Johnson's number on the outskirts of Odessa. Nathan had been awake and a good conversant for the past hour or so and he had taken notes for Angela of the questions she would ask Adam. Shortly they pulled up in front of a two-story brick house in a nice neighborhood. Adam opened the front door and invited them in to a family room. On the mantle of the fireplace were several family photos of Stacy and the children.

"How was the drive? I generally find it boring and flat."

"I think that about sums it up," Angela replied. "It wasn't on my bucket list and now I know why."

They exchanged a few more pleasantries and then got down to business. Angela began with the list of questions that they discussed in the car. Nathan had met Adam before but had kept his thoughts to himself. He thought that of the four women, Angela was the most perceptive, perhaps that was a result of her studying so many faces in her photography business.

"Tell me about Stacy's family. When did you meet her and when did she mention her family ties?"

"We were both students at the University of Texas - she was in the nursing program and I was in engineering and we met in a humanities course as freshman. We continued to date and married a few months after we graduated. We decided that with our degrees whoever was offered a job first, the other would find a job in the city we moved to. I found a job first and we settled in Odessa. Stacy worked at the Medical Center of Odessa, but once the children were born, she wanted a nursing job that she could work at from home and so she was hired by Golden Star. She was happy working with them and delivered perhaps four speeches a year around Texas, and the surrounding seven states."

"Over the course of your marriage did she ever speak of fear that the cartel would find her?" Angela asked. "Was she nervous at any time or did she feel like someone was watching her?"

"She told me about the cartel after I proposed marriage, but even in college I didn't have a feeling that she was looking over her shoulder, worried that someone was after her. She was relaxed and easy-going. At the christening of our third child she looked a little sad and I remember asking her what was wrong. I figured the problem was that we had decided to be happy with three children and perhaps she was rethinking that decision as our last child was christened. Instead she said she wished her mother had been there to witness the ceremony. My wife chose our third child's name and so I think it is somehow related to her mother's name, but that is all I know about any connection to the cartel since our marriage."

"What's the child's name?"

"Maria Camilla, we call her Cami for short."

"What a pretty name and unusual. My day job is that of a photographer and I do photos for a lot of families and some schools, so I can tell you that it is an unusual name for a girl at the moment. Did Stacy mention anything else about her mother or any other family members throughout the course of your marriage?"

"That was her only mention in the thirteen years we were together."

"You weren't curious and didn't ply her with questions about her family?"

"When I proposed marriage and she explained her family connections, she asked at that time that I never mention her family again and so I didn't."

Angela decided to switch directions and asked, "Tell me about Stacy's relationship with your family, friends, and co-workers."

"I can't think of anything to tell you - she had a good group of girlfriends and they traveled somewhere together every year. She volunteered at our kids' school, was an active member of a bible study group at our church, and was a ranked tennis player at a local tennis club. Stacy was very active and loved by all."

"And your marriage? Life was going well for your relationship with your wife?"

Adam looked a little affronted at the question, but answered, "Yes, we loved each other as much as the day we were married and our children as well. We both wanted more kids, but realistically knew we couldn't afford more."

Angela continued with questions that she and Nathan had discussed on the journey to Odessa, but really she gathered little new information. So she ended the conversation with a final question, "Can you think of anyone besides the cartel that we should consider as a suspect for murder? Anyone that seemed mad at her? Think back a few years as people can remain angry a long time."

Leaving the question sitting on the air in Adam's family room produced a long, thoughtful moment of silence and at the end he uttered a single word.

"No."

Nathan and Angela stood up preparing to leave. Angela had noticed a restaurant that was close to the house. After saying their goodbyes they got in the car to drive to the restaurant. They were hoping for a decent lunch and planned to pick the server's brain as to whether she or he knew Stacy or Adam. In a town of 100,000 people, they were making a guess as to whether Stacy was a regular at any of the local restaurants, but maybe they would luck out by picking one close to Stacy's home.

They sat at a café style booth, menus in hand. The food was Southwestern and American. Angela loved spicy foods and ordered a spicy vegetarian fajita and Nathan did likewise with his spicy fish tacos. He cooked many nights for Jill and she liked bland food, so his only opportunity to satiate his spicy taste buds was when they dined out or he dined without Jill.

When the server arrived to take their order, Angela eased into a conversation about the Johnsons.

"We're just passing through this town- we came to pay our respects to Adam Johnson."

The server looked at them blankly, poised to take their order which they quickly gave.

"Ok, this entire day has nearly been a waste of time," Nathan said in frustration. "I wish we had traveled by air to Odessa. Even with security screening, we would have been tied up traveling for no more than two hours; instead we have a ten hour drive round trip. Arrgh."

"Oh well, we've seen a part of Texas that we'll never need to see again the rest of our lives," replied Angela with her usual dose of optimism. "Consider that item checked on your bucket list."

"It wasn't on my bucket list," grouched Nathan.

Angela just looked at him cheekily and said, "Well it should have been. It's probably been labeled the best road for napping in America!"

With the last comment by Angela, Nathan let go of his frustration with the non-productive day and laughed, then he asked, "So what did you think of Adam?"

"I felt sorry for him losing his wife while having to raise three young children. I lost a friend to cancer two years ago and she left behind seven children, some in college, some in kindergarten and everything in between. In her case, her death was expected so the husband had time to prepare the children, but still it was very hard. I think his young ones will have a hard time understanding the situation for a while, but they'll manage."

"Any other impressions?"

"Yes, but why are you asking?"

"When Jill and I met with him in Dallas, there was something I didn't like about him. Ever since I've been trying to figure out if he is hiding something or if I am mad at him for exposing Jill to the cartel's violence."

"I've found over the years working for Jill that people are rarely themselves in the days following the death of someone they love. Sometimes overwhelming grief has changed them, and other times it's because they are guilty as sin of murder and so the weird vibe is them hiding that secret. I haven't come across a magic formula for detecting which is which at the beginning of the case."

"Angela, thanks for the feedback and I'll keep that in mind," Nathan said as their server approached with their plates of food.

A second server followed her with their drinks and as she placed them in front of Jill and Nathan, she said, "It is so sad about the Johnsons. Cindy mentioned you were in town to pay your condolences."

Ha!, thought Angela, you never knew when a random information drop would bear fruit!

"Yes, we just spoke with Adam," Angela said. "Have you

stopped by to chat?" She wasn't one to tell lies and it was true that they had paid condolences to Adam; it's just that it wasn't the reason they had stopped and spoke with Adam.

"I didn't know the Johnsons that well. I was their server for several years and they stopped in perhaps once a month. On occasion, they would have their children with them. Poor little tykes with no mother now."

"We never met Stacy, we just know Adam, but we assume they had a great relationship," Angela wanted to kick herself for fishing for information by using such an awkward and stupid question.

The server looked at her strangely then said, "You mustn't have seen them recently, they seemed unhappy with each other the last time they were here. Oh excuse me, it's rude to speak ill of the dead," and she turned away to leave.

Angela put a hand on her arm and said, "You sound like someone who cared about them as a family and you're disappointed that your last memory is of them unhappy with each other."

The server just nodded and left.

Angela and Nathan seemed to mutually agree to change their conversation as they weren't sure who was listening and so they moved on to the planned long weekend with Henrik. Aware of the long drive ahead of them, they finished lunch, paid their bill, used the bathroom and were soon back on the Interstate heading back to Dallas.

"I guess we should've attempted to interview some friends of Stacy while we were here, but I'm not sure what my angle of interview would have been given her secret identity. I can't imagine she told anyone other than Adam about her connection to the cartel."

"I don't get involved with your cases in great detail, but on the surface I have to agree with you that I'm not sure what the goal of interviewing her friends would be. If the cartel was on Stacy's trail, then the last thing you would want to do is jeopardize her friends."

"That's a good excuse for not staying here longer," Angela agreed.

Chapter Eight

Marie, Jo, and Jill decided to camp out on Jill and Nathan's sofa with room service for food to power their brains. They would work all morning then have lunch on the way to the President Kennedy Memorial and spend the afternoon walking and sightseeing. The next day they were going to tour the mint and have dinner at Jill's niece, Michelle and her husband's house in Fort Worth as both were in the same area. Her niece was a full time student and was working, her husband was working the night shift, and in order to devote all of Sunday to tailgating and the game, they hadn't been able to hang out with Jill and friends other than this dinner and the Sunday festivities. Jo handled large sums of money in her role as a Chief Financial Officer and was looking forward to seeing what the money looked like newly minted. She could look at an MRI machine and understand that it represented four million dollars, but there was something far more exciting about looking at bundles of hundred dollar bills.

"I started researching the Sinaloa Cartel, figuring that it wouldn't have much of a social media presence, but it actually does and there are a lot of brutal pictures, so I'm going to put that aside and concentrate on the Johnsons instead," Marie announced. "Then I'm going to move on to Golden State - wasn't that the name of the company that Stacy worked for?"

"Golden Star, not State," Jill replied. "Sounds like a plan. Let's chat in an hour or so with our respective search results. "

The three women quietly worked taking notes as they

went. No one was paying attention to the time and they were startled when Jill's phone alarmed, announcing their hour was over.

"Let me go first as I suspect I've the least to report on," Jo said. "I can't find any private information on the Johnsons other than they haven't filed for bankruptcy or divorce. I viewed their marriage license and the birth certificates of their children which leads me to exactly no-where. Golden Star seems to be well managed and large with no concerns as to their success. The Cartel is interesting. I have no official financial statements from them; instead I used various sources like the FBI, Mexican Government and thank you Google for translating the documents into English from Spanish for me. They appear on the surface to be a prosperous company with the various product lines of drugs, human trafficking, transportation, etc. There seems to be no effort by the Mexican Government to break up the cartel. They have too many well placed bribes and corrupt officials to really govern the group. On our side of the border, we have several federal agencies trying to curtail the cartel. The U.S. government put a reward on El Chapo's head with each jail break, but no one is snitching on him. Basically that is all I can find on my targets. Is there something more to research?"

"That is essentially the same conclusion I came to when I briefly researched the cartel," Jill agreed. "Good to know the little information we do about the Johnsons and I can't think of anything else to have you help with - Marie, do you need Jo's help?"

"Not yet."

"Ok, then I'll take a walk and hang out at a café to watch the world. Send me a text when you're ready to leave for the memorial," and with that Jo exited the room.

"So what did you find in your search, Marie?"

"On the Johnsons, nothing unusual - family pics, sports comments, tributes to various causes. The cartel has many pictures so it is hard to sort through it and much of it was violent. Half the time I stared at the pictures because they're so appalling and other times I couldn't look. People riddled with bullets mostly. Yuck. There are separate pages devoted to El Chapo. I need to think about how to approach sorting through their information. It's a combination family and corporation. On the surface I don't see any connection to Stacy in appearance but then we know she had some plastic surgery. There was also the problem that El Chapo has gone through four wives, although I just concentrated on the first two given Stacy's age. Still I didn't end up with any leads to follow. I'll continue to chase some leads, but I'm not hopeful yet. What have you found?"

"Kudos to the detective for being so open and sharing with me. I have all the scene notes, their search for something on camera, her autopsy reports, tests run on her vomit, etc. There are still tests pending as they haven't identified the killing poison yet which isn't surprising. Once you move beyond say the top five poisons, unless you have luck, it seems like it takes weeks to months to get back results. There are fingerprints on the glass, but they aren't in the database and they are not Stacy's. Only about one-third of U.S. residents have their fingerprints on file and if this is a foreign resident the odds lower more as to whether fingerprints are available. They did a grid search of the conference room and didn't find anything. The only odd item in the police report is the crime scene entry log."

"What's that?"

"Every crime scene is supposed to keep a log of who enters

the crime scene and why. If law enforcement doesn't tightly control the crime scene, then during a criminal case they can be charged with failure to control evidence and interject into juror's minds that some mythical character entered the crime scene and tampered with the evidence."

"That makes sense," Marie agreed. "So what is the problem with this crime scene and have you seen that before?"

"I have not reviewed that many crime scene documents and every law enforcement agency does it different so perhaps I just don't understand what I am looking at. They have a sign in log of everyone that enters the scene. One of the crime scene staff in one of the pictures is not on the sign in log. I know that because they are wearing numbers on their protective clothing and this one person has no identification visible in the picture. I'm sure it is just an oversight."

Jill continued, "I reviewed the report by the forensic pathologist and I can't think of anything I would have done differently."

"Does the pathologist suspect any particular poison; is there mention of what it could be?"

Jill paused a moment looking through the report to verify that she had seen no reference to a particular poison then said, "No."

"So really we haven't found any leads worth pursuing so far. I wonder how Angela and Nathan are doing. I don't think they will have arrived in Odessa yet," Jill noted looking at her watch. "Perhaps we should start exploring the city now since we have run through most of the leads. Given that the police have no suspects, I am guessing that the murderer hid their identity well and we'll not solve the case before this weekend is over. With that in mind, I think I might schedule one follow-up meeting with the detective on Monday before we leave and just blow off the rest of the investigation until we get to our respective homes."

"Jill, you're not really blowing off the investigation," Marie pointed out. "We've run out of leads unless Angela and Nathan find some new threads to follow in the investigation. We're also waiting on more findings from the medical examiner and you'll pick up the case from there, correct?"

"Yeah, you're right," Jill said with a sigh. "Let's go out and sightsee in this great city of Dallas!"

Thirty minutes later, Marie, Jo, and Jill were walking toward the John F. Kennedy Memorial. In 1963, it was a moment that changed the world with the assassination of an American president. Not just any American president, but the couple - President Kennedy and his wife Jacqueline were viewed as Camelot. Like many icons of their time, the world was left wondering about his potential. The three friends had visited President Kennedy's grave at Arlington National Cemetery where the eternal flame marked both the President's grave and some of his most memorable words. By contrast, the site of his assassination was in many ways much more depressing.

"This is a strangely sad memorial," Jo said. "It represents the death of a single human being, but it's been projected to reflect the death of an era in America in the 1960s. Unlike many historic sites, I don't feel the need to ever come back here again. Maybe I'm not suited to sites of assassination."

"I have to agree with you," Marie said. "I don't know that I've been to any other famous assassination sites, but this one is definitely not my cup of tea. I must have been to the site of President Lincoln's assassination but I don't remember it. Instead I remember all of his famous speeches that are carved in the marble at the Lincoln Memorial. So in a way I guess this is like President Lincoln's assassination in that the Memorial site is so much more inspiring than the assassination site."

"I'm not depressed but let's move on to some other interesting areas of Dallas," Jill said. "If you walk toward the Dallas Art Museum, we'll come across some food trucks that Nathan and I ordered food from a few days ago. I think it's a great place to break for lunch."

Half an hour later the three friends were sitting with extremely different dishes from wildly different food trucks watching the people traffic in the park next to the Dallas Art Museum. They had seen at least five Green Bay Packer jerseys in the park which meant that the fans had arrived early to enjoy the city prior to the game on Sunday.

Feeling guilty with their easy day, they arrived back at their hotel around six. Angela and Nathan were expected to arrive at any moment. Once they had the opportunity to refresh and relax the group planned to drive over to the Fort Worth stockyards for Friday night entertainment. There was a rodeo to watch and then they planned to hang out in the restaurants and bars of the area. Later they would take in a mechanical bull and some line dancing somewhere in the stockyards. Normally it wasn't something that any of the group sought out in their home states, but when in Texas, one felt compelled to try Texas culture.

Saturday was a day to explore the Dallas area some more. Jill marveled at the instruments used by physicians in the Civil War for patient care and amputations at the Civil War Museum. Jo was satisfied when she looked at twelve million dollars in brand-new twenty dollar bill bundles at the United States mint in Fort Worth. Angela and Marie were content with visits to the other museums of the Dallas area and the many sculpture gardens. They'd been unable to make their schedules work so they could have dinner with Barb. At dinner later that night at

Jill's niece, Michelle's house, they enjoyed an excellent meal. Michelle had inherited her parents DNA for cooking and her husband manned the Mojito bar to keep the drinks flowing. Michelle shared with them the green and gold jello shots she had made for the game the next day. They would share the jello shots as an icebreaker with fellow Packers tailgaters. They made plans on how to meet in the enormous parking lot at the Cowboys stadium and left to return to their hotel.

The next day they woke up to a brilliant Sunday and game day. Angela attended Mass at a historic downtown Catholic Church. As Lombardi once said "Think of only three things: God, your family, and the Green Bay Packers in that order." Once she returned, they headed in the rental car to tailgate in the parking lot at Texas Stadium. They met Michelle and John on a feeder road for an outer parking lot and were able to park the two cars side by side. There were several other Packer fans in their lot and so they had a great time talking about their favorite team. Michelle had a cooler filled with beer and wine coolers, a small barbeque, and six foot folding tables and lawn chairs. Soon burgers and brats were grilling, beers bottles tapped in celebration, and everyone was pleasantly buzzed by the friendship, food, drink, and atmosphere in the parking lot.

All too soon they were cleaning up their supplies, and preparing to enter the stadium. They walked through the usual pat-down of security and entered the mammoth stadium. It looked like a spaceship from the outside and had been nick-named Jerry's World after Cowboys owner Jerry Jones. Angela had read somewhere that the arches holding up the roof were one-quarter mile long. Because the Cowboys sold standing only tickets to their games, the huge stadium averaged about eleven thousand more spectators than Lambeau Field, home to the Green Bay Packers. Nathan hadn't been to Lambeau for a game, but the four women as well as Michelle and John had attended a home game and were underwhelmed by the soullessness of this stadium. Yeah the big screen was cool, but over time they found themselves watching the screen rather than the action on the field.

Three and a half hours later, the final score was 38 to 25 in favor of the Packers. The defense had holes in it at times, but in the red zone, they were able to stop the run and thus had forced the Cowboys into lots of field goals. After returning to their cars, they enjoyed a few cold beverages while waiting for the parking lot to clear enough to drive away.

Finally, they could see their way clear. The occupants of the two cars parted ways with Michelle needing to return home to study and Jill and crew looking for a place to snack, people watch, and just spend a lazy evening chatting. Mid-day the next day they would be boarding their respective planes for the return flight to home. They would next be together when they had their long weekend at Henrik's or when they vacationed in the United Kingdom.

The next day the friends lingered over breakfast and then the Wisconsin trio left for the airport. Jill had asked Detective Castillo if she could have a test tube sample of the water that Stacey drank as well as a second test tube of the vomit that the crime scene techs had bagged in the conference center. He had managed to fulfill both of her requests and so she and Nathan would be stopping by police headquarters on the way to the airport. Jill knew her boarding pass was a TSA pre-check and therefore she would not have to pull out the test tubes separately for security screening. She would hate to be stuck explaining and need the DPD officers stationed at the airport to ease her transit.

It was early evening when they arrived back in the

Palisades Valley to a joyous reunion with their pets. After a lingering goodbye kiss with Nathan, Jill was soon heading home in her car with Trixie, the dog's head out the window catching the air. The air had cooled off and she could safely leave the dog in the car while she ran in to the grocery store to get some food as she had emptied her refrigerator of most food prior to their trip. They arrived home, Jill to unpack luggage and groceries, Trixie to reacquaint herself with the squirrels of her backyard. After a salad for dinner, she sat on her couch with a glass of wine and thought about poison.

With her laptop, Jill began reviewing her favorite toxicology textbooks. She was searching for a fast-acting, colorless, and tasteless poison. Those three attributes really helped narrow the possibilities. She reviewed the police report and noted approximately twenty minutes from Stacy's first sip of water to her collapse at the podium. From Barb's description of Stacy's death, it seemed like she drank a bit of water and then collapsed and died within moments. Jill had puzzled over what kind of poison reacted like that and had been unable to think of anything that worked that fast; that Stacy wouldn't have spit out at the podium with the first sip. When she noted the multiple water sips in the narrative of the police report, the number of poisons used for the murder multiplied in her head. It was one of the reasons she had asked for samples of the water and the vomit.

Among the instruments in her on site lab was a mass spectrometer analyzer which she had used in prior cases to determine trace elements of compounds. She had also used it at various times for her vineyard when she was experimenting with natural pesticides. It was the most expensive instrument in her lab and she purchased it used when the manufacturer introduced a new, faster model. As she didn't run many tests on it, she was happy to have the slow speed but accurate analyzer. The results of the analyzer would be compared against a library of mass spectrometer results to identify the components of the poison and if that didn't yield anything she could move on to manual interpretation. The analyzer could also look at radio-isotopes. It was starting to get late and she had just traveled from a time zone that was two hours ahead of California, looking up at the clock she thought she was prepared for the next day of chemistry lab work and headed for bed.

Chapter Nine

Jill woke up to another sunny California day, and while she was excited to analyze her two test tube samples, she needed to do a quick three mile run with Trixie and cool down from the run by walking her vineyard to make sure no strange plant disease had attacked while she was gone. Heading into fall, her vineyard required little work at the moment. Once the leaves finished dropping, she would need to work long hours pruning her plants, but that was a favorite activity for Trixie and herself. Since they spent long hours outdoors, the dog could play as much catch as she could handle, while Jill always found it to be a time of reflection. She would remind herself of all that she was grateful for in the last year, take stock of her life, and set goals in her mind until the next year's fall pruning.

An hour and a half later, she had run, inspected her vines, and showered. Now it was time to get to work on the case. She had given Adam Johnson a general timetable of the work she did while she was in Texas and back in California. As a courtesy and to stay on Detective Castillo's good side, she had also provided him with the same information. While she had been reviewing the various poisons last night she developed a short list of the top contenders for the poison that killed Stacy Johnson. There were other poisons that could be involved with this case but given that the substance had to be clear and tasteless and cause Stacy to exhibit the symptoms she had at the podium, she was hopeful after an hour or so in her lab she should be able to identify the poison.

Jill gave thought to the use of poisons and the Mexican cartel. Did the cartel have members amongst it who were specialists with poisoning or was that a service they hired out for? She would have to do more research in regards to the homicides connected to the cartel. Certainly any pictures of cartel murders that she had seen were gun related.

Ricin was the first potential poison on her list. It came from castor beans and a very small amount ingested caused death. The murderer would have to have some experience working with the bean to extract the deadly pulp or waste product of the bean. Some other poisons were dioxin which was tasteless and could kill in a single drop placed in a glass of water, or maybe something more exotic like polonium which was reputed to have caused the death of a prominent Russian dissident.

Her phone rang and Jill picked it up off the table saying, "Hello."

"Dr. Quint, this is Deputy Davis."

"Hi, Deputy Davis, what can I do for you? It's quiet at my house at the moment so if you're looking for an opportunity to brush up on your shooting skills, you'll have to wait as there are no bad people trying to kill me at the moment."

"Ha ha. At the end of your last case, I asked if you would do me a favor and tour some youth I am working with through your lab and talk to them about death and murder. You know - scare them straight."

"Yeah, like I told you I would love to help. When do you want to bring them by?"

"How about right now?"

Jill thought about what she was about to do with her two test tubes from Texas and thought *'what the heck - might be a perfect time to talk to teens about murder'*.

"I'm at the start of a new case and I was just about to

process some samples, it's likely a perfect time to bring them by. When should I expect you and how many kids are there?"

"We'll be there in about fifteen minutes and I have six boys and two girls."

"Okay, you know which building houses my lab, so just come in when you arrive."

"Thanks Dr. Quint." said the deputy with true appreciation running through her voice.

"Even if you hadn't saved my life a few times, I would do this for you, if I can steer kids in a better direction, then that is a good thing."

They ended the call and Jill took Trixie with her to the lab. She would count on her bark to alert her to the deputy's arrival. She looked around her lab and straightened a few things up. Her murder board was blank at the moment as she hadn't filled in the details of the case yet. Perhaps she would take the kids on a walk-through of the current case. Better that they become crime scene techs or forensic pathologists than street thugs; she figured she just needed to grab their interest to ignite a spark in them. She went to work printing a picture of Stacy, as well as pictures from the scene. As the crime was in another state and the kids would not have name recognition of anyone involved in it, she thought it would be fairly easy to keep the case private yet share it with the kids. She collected the police report as well, so she could go over the details with them while she filled out her murder board. She heard Trixie bark and then the wheels of a vehicle arriving outside of her lab. She walked outside to greet the new arrivals.

Deputy Davis was in uniform and the kids exited the van looking around her property. After a quick handshake, the Deputy had each kid introduce him or herself to Jill adding the personal fact of their age. Jill was amazed at how much older the kids looked than their actual age. Even the toughest of the lot had a hard time not warming up to Trixie. The dog had sized up the kids and then taken a ball over to drop at the feet of what Jill would have called the hardest looking kid. When the kid didn't respond and throw the ball, the dog moved closer, picked up and then dropped the ball on the kid's shoes and then sat back expecting the kid to throw it.

Jill had watched the interchange and said, "Antonio, this is Trixie and she won't let you enter my lab until you throw the ball, so you may as well chuck the ball."

The tough teenager was having a hard time maintaining his bored expression while throwing a ball for the dog, to Jill's amusement. The kid threw the ball then they turned and entered Jill's lab. Deputy Davis hadn't told her anything about these kids; she didn't know if they had spent time in the Juvenile Justice system or not. She would make a pitch that they choose a law enforcement career and then see if she could excite them with helping her work on her current case.

Jill had them sit down on chairs and opened with a lecture on lab safety. She had a variety of chemicals used in her lab that she didn't want the kids to touch, so she started by having them lean in to smell a container of sulfur dioxide. They reeled back and two of the kids exited for fresh air.

"Sorry to make you guys uncomfortable for a few moments, but I do that to demonstrate lab safety. I have substances and chemicals that will blister your skin, make your eyes water, and lungs spasm. Don't be curious about things or you'll get hurt. I want to see each of you nod that you won't touch stuff. I need to know you'll stay safe while here," and Jill got the nods of agreement she was looking for.

She went on to describe her background and those of other personnel in law enforcement and a crime lab. She tried to demonstrate that her and Deputy Davis' side of the law was so much more interesting than spending time behind bars. She saw she was losing a kid or two which she expected. She then moved on to her murder board and her two test tubes along with the circumstances on Stacy's death. The kids and Deputy Davis were asking questions about the crime scene. She knew some of the kids had been excited by the gruesomeness of murder, a few were turned off, and a few were using their brains to solve the whodunit. While they were talking, Jill had been filling in her murder board. They were running out of time as the Deputy had to get the kids back to wherever they had come from soon, so Jill wrapped it up.

"I don't think the cartel did this woman," Antonio said as they were leaving.

Jill stopped him before he exited the door to her lab and asked, "Why not?"

"That not their style," commented the slouching teen.

"What do you mean 'their style', Antonio?"

"The cartel don't like you, they take you out with a gun. This was too much work; they don't have that kind of time to waste. If she needed to die, just park on her street and shoot her when she leaves the front door."

Deputy Davis paused on her way out and said, "Thanks Dr. Quint, I'll give you a call later. And by the way I agree with Antonio's line of thinking, I don't think the cartel is involved."

Jill watched the van leave and thought of what a satisfying time she had talking to the kids. She was intrigued with Antonio's comments. It had been a question in the back of her head but she hadn't articulated it into the front of her brain so to speak. Like Deputy Davis, she agreed with Antonio's reasoning. Now what was she to do with that line of thinking? She recalled that Detective Castillo had the cartel on his murder board but didn't put much weight on that selection. So Adam was the only person to think that the cartel was his wife's murderer. Interesting.

She re-entered the lab and started her analyzer running so she could compare chemical compounds. Then she picked up her phone and called Nathan.

"Hey babe, how are you?"

"Doing well, how about you?"

"I was about to call you to make dinner plans tonight. How's your day going in the lab, find the poison yet?"

"I've just begun work on identifying the poison as I had a very pleasant interruption this morning."

"Oh really! What happened?"

"After the sovereign citizens nearly caused your house to burn down in the last case, Deputy Davis asked me if I would do her a favor and spend time with some at-risk youth that she was mentoring. I said yes but when she didn't contact me immediately I admit I forgot about it. She called me this morning and asked if she could bring some kids over."

"Did you say yes?"

"Of course I did and it was most instructive."

"How so?" Nathan asked.

"So I'm starting this new case and at the time of the call I'd not laid out the murder board yet in my lab. So after giving the kids a tour of the lab and telling them about the various occupations related to crime scene investigation, I took them through the current case. I could tell a couple of the kids were bored stiff, but I think I might've made a positive difference for a few others."

"I bet that was a unique experience for both you and the kids. Did you learn anything about the case while laying it out for the kids?"

"Actually I did. I had been bothered by something but couldn't put my finger on it until one of the kids, just as he was leaving, told me I had the wrong suspect."

"I wish I'd been there to watch this whole thing - you and a bunch of juvenile delinquents with Deputy Davis serving as referee. I can't believe that one of the kids didn't do something stupid in your lab as you have some dangerous things there."

"I thought of that before the kids arrived and so I gave them all a whiff of sulfur dioxide. It stinks like rotten eggs and after several of the kids ended up gagging, they got my point and kept their hands off my stuff."

"Good strategy and again I'm sorry I missed it."

"I set up my murder board in front of the kids based on the evidence we had collected so far. As the kids were leaving, one of them told me I had it wrong - that this murder was not something the cartel would do. He said something like, 'If the cartel wanted you dead they would just shoot you in your driveway. They wouldn't bother with poison.' I had to agree with his reasoning."

"That's an insightful teenager! What did Deputy Davis think?"

"She agreed with the kid."

"So what are you going to do now?"

"At this point, El Chapo's picture will remain on my murder board representing the cartel. I'll have to give some thought into other suspects. Of course, there's the husband, but why would he hire me to dig into the case if he poisoned her? How'd he get into the convention center conference room to put that poison in the water? He's not on screen but then I've not found the person that placed the poisoned water on the podium. So my approach hasn't changed from this morning. I'm still looking for the poison hoping that will point me toward a suspect.

How's your day been?"

"Not as exciting or fruitful as yours has been. I've mainly caught up on correspondence that arrived while we were in Texas last week. I made a few appointments to meet with the various vineyards that I met at the convention who think they want to hire my services."

Jill heard a timer go off in the background on one of her analyzers and so she knew she needed to bring the conversation to an end and get back to her lab.

"I'm going to be working in the lab all afternoon. How about if I come over to your house at seven tonight for dinner? I actually stopped at the grocery store on the way home yesterday so I could bring over a loaf of French bread if you're in the mood to whip up a pasta dish."

"I can do that and I'll plan on seeing you tonight. Stay safe and I love you," Nathan said.

"Love you back and see you tonight," replied Jill.

Jill walked over to the analyzer with the dinging timer to examine her results. She had a printout of chemical composition. This was a sample of water from the convention center. Jill had filled a test tube before they left Dallas to know which minerals were naturally occurring in the convention center's drinking water. Practically every water system in the country had a different set of metals, minerals, and impurities related to the soil and the wells located in that city. She now had her baseline of what her analyzer should find in the test tube sample that Detective Castillo gave her from the crime scene.

After a second analyzer bell, she walked over to view the results of the water from the glass at the podium that Stacy Johnson sipped from.

"What the heck?" Jill said to herself. She went over to

where her three test tubes lay, one marked 'hotel water fountain', the second marked 'vomit', and the third with the label 'podium glass'. She must have mixed up two test tubes. She pulled a sample out of her third test tube and again put it in the analyzer, set the timer, and went back to studying the murder board. Sometime later she jumped when the timer went off and she walked over to study the results.

She picked up the phone to call Detective Castillo. She was pleasantly surprised when he answered his phone.

"Detective, this is Dr. Jill Quint."

"Yes?"

"I just finished my first analysis of your podium water and I think there is a problem with the specimen."

"How so?"

"Before I left Dallas I collected a water specimen from a convention center drinking fountain. It is an exact mineral match for the glass of water at Stacy's podium. I've run it twice with the same outcome. There was no poison in the glass of drinking water."

"Yes, I know. I got the same result back from our crime lab about an hour ago."

"Would you have shared that with me if I hadn't called?" Jill asked.

"Probably, like I told you, you seem to be a magnet for murder, so it makes sense to keep you close to this case."

Jill had to think about that. In the end she couldn't decide how she should feel about the detective's comment. So she shifted to her next question.

"Where do you think she came into contact with a poison?"

"Perhaps it was a natural death," Castillo proposed.

"Do you really think that was a death by natural causes?"

"You tell me, you're the doctor."

Jill wondered what the detective was up to. He was answering her questions with a question.

"As you know, I didn't examine the body, but based on the findings of your medical examiner and based on observation of the film recording of Stacy's death, I think she was poisoned with some agent."

"I agree."

"Then why the runaround detective?" Jill asked exasperated.

The detective ignored the question and asked one of his own, "What are your next steps, Dr. Quint?"

Jill paused and thought for a moment about what she had so far in this strange case.

"I'm going to analyze the contents of the vomit. As it's likely to contain a variety of substances including what Stacy Johnson had for breakfast and any medication or vitamins she might've taken, it'll take me several hours to days to sort through the analyzer results for the vomit. What are you working on, Detective, to find Stacy's killer?"

"I'm waiting for results from our medical examiner on the testing she did on Stacy's stomach contents."

Again the detective hadn't told her any more than she suspected. Since they were having such a strange conversation she thought she may as well throw Antonio's comment at him to see how it stuck.

"I had a group of potential future thugs in my lab today and I discussed this case with them. The toughest thug of the future thugs suggested that this is not a murder by the cartel because essentially they would not waste time on the whole poison scheme. They would take the easy way and just shoot Stacy in her driveway."

She could hear the detective laughing on the other end of the phone and she waited for his next noncommittal comment just so she could grind her teeth.

"Dr. Quint, you do have a way with words and I can almost picture the teenage boy who made that remark to you."

"How do you know it was a teenage boy?"

"Because I'm a detective and most potential future thugs are presently teenage boys. By the way, I happen to agree with your teenage boy. This is too elaborate a murder plot to be at the behest of the cartel. All of the suspected cartel murders inside the state of Texas have used a gun as the murder weapon."

Finally, Jill had dragged some useful information out of the detective. Now if she could only keep him talking.

"When I was last in your office, you had two suspects on your murder board. Are you now strictly focusing on Stacy's husband, Adam Johnson?"

"No. At this point in the investigation it would be foolish to focus only on Mr. Johnson."

Great, after that one breakthrough sentence from the detective, she was back to sorting through his cryptic comments. She decided to change course and asked him, "Has any other new information come across your desk?"

"No."

Chapter Ten

Jill ended her call with the detective and returned to processing the vomit specimen. She mechanically prepared several specimens for analysis, her thoughts elsewhere. Once the equipment started humming away, she sat in her lab and faced the murder board. Who else could she add to the suspects list? When and where was Stacy exposed to poison and just what was the poison? Would she find it in the vomit, or did she need a blood test to identify the poison? She didn't have a sample of Stacy's blood and it was likely too late to get one.

Her murderers might include friends, family, co-workers or maybe a serial killer. Really the whole case was getting weirder by the moment. Just because Adam hired her investigative services didn't mean that he couldn't be the murderer either. Her team had researched him thoroughly and Angela and Nathan had interviewed him. Angela hadn't found any inconsistencies in his answers, but Nathan didn't like the man. That's not to say Adam could be capable of his wife's murder, but Nathan said that something was up with the guy.

Maybe she should do additional research on Stacy. Maybe she supported some organization that rubbed people the wrong way. Perhaps figuring out the poison would point her to the killer. Since she now knew that Stacy was poisoned before the start of her presentation that significantly increased the number of poisons that would react in a one to three hour window. She also didn't have to worry about the poison being tasteless in water.

She continued to let her analyzers run for another day and a half. In the end, after sorting through all of the substances in Stacy's vomit, she thought she had her answer. It was a classic for poisoning - arsenic. It was odorless and colorless and had been used throughout the ages to murder political leaders and ordinary citizens. A catholic bishop discovered the substance in the 13th century. Jill thought, 'wow how did people discover things so long ago without today's scientific equipment?'

Continuing to refresh her memory about arsenic, she noted it would be very easy to put a lethal dose in food. Jill was sorting through the stomach contents contained in the vomit and it was her guess that the arsenic was in the blueberry muffin that Stacy consumed around two hours prior to the presentation. As a poison, arsenic was relatively easy to obtain - Jill checked and she could buy it on-line. So that didn't limit the possibilities much. She had a feeling that she needed to return to Dallas to gather more evidence from the crime scene. She wondered if Detective Castillo would be cooperative if she moved back inside his territory.

She looked at the calendar and noted it was the day after Stacy's burial. Not a great day to call, but there probably wouldn't be many good days in Adam's future for a while. She wanted to update him on her findings then get his authorization for additional expenses. She picked up the phone.

"Hello?" said the male voice.

"Hi Adam, it's Jill Quint. Is this an okay time to talk?"

"Hello Jill, this is a fine time to talk. What's up? Are you still in Dallas?"

"No, I'm in my home in California where I have been running tests on samples of the water that Stacy drank as well as a sample from her stomach contents."

There was no need to tell the man that the crime scene

techs had collected samples from two different piles of vomit near the podium where she collapsed.

"What did you find? The police haven't called me with any new information since last week."

"Your wife was not poisoned by something in the glass of water at the podium. It appears it was in some food she consumed prior to the meeting."

"I thought everyone said that there was a bad substance in the water?"

"I think everyone thought that because she passed out so soon after taking a few sips of water. She probably wasn't feeling well and sipped water to see if it would make her feel better given that she was in the middle of delivering a public presentation."

"Why haven't the police called and notified me of that conclusion?"

"I think they'll give you a call within the next couple of hours. They may be waiting on identifying just what did poison your wife."

"Did you identify the poison?"

"Yes Adam, it was arsenic."

"How could she have swallowed a poison and not realized it?"

"It is a tasteless poison, so she didn't knowingly swallow something bad."

After a moment of silence wherein Adam had apparently been thinking he said, "I guess you're done with the case."

Jill was a little surprised at Adam's conclusion and replied, "Not at all Adam! I have simply identified the poison. I don't have any strong clues as to who the murderer is. In fact I would like to return to Dallas to investigate more crime scene angles, but I wanted to check in with you as you're my client and there's an expense to do that."

Again there was silence for a while and then Adam said, "Jill, I think I'll end our contract at this point. Instead I'll just accept the investigation of the Dallas Police Department."

Jill, surprised by Adam's statement said, "Well okay that's your decision to make. I'll make up your final invoice and drop it in the mail to you. Do you have any further questions for me about Stacy's death?"

"Just one. Do you think she suffered?"

Jill hated this question and she was surprised how many families asked it. She thought it was a miserable question and so she usually chose to lie as she did with Adam.

"Our mutual friend, Barb Jordan, said that right up to the end, Stacy was involved in her presentation, then she collapsed and people came to her aid. Her heart stopped inside the convention center, so any suffering that she had would have been very short-lived."

Jill winced over her expression of short-lived, but it seemed to have escaped Adam's attention.

"Thank you, Dr. Quint, for finding the source of the poison that killed my wife. I hope that the Dallas Police Department closes the case soon." After a few polite sentences, they ended their call.

Well, that was a weird conversation, Jill thought as she stretched backward to peer at the murder board. She had just been fired and she wondered at the real reason behind the firing. Was she too expensive? Did Adam not like her as an investigator; did he think he had his answers? Or was he tired of the whole thing and wanting to move beyond his wife's death with young children at home? Jill could think of at least ten reasons for Adam to fire her.

Oh well, her mother had always claimed she couldn't cry

over spilled milk and this sure felt like spilled milk. She would close up the case by e-mailing information to the various parties and preparing the final bill for Adam. She'd have dinner with Nathan tonight and return to working her vineyard in the morning. She sent those e-mails off to the various parties then went inside to change and take Trixie for a run around her neighborhood.

An hour later, midway through her run, her cell phone rang. Trixie was running off leash and Jill called to her before answering the phone. As the dog approached, Jill leaned over, leash latch in hand and simultaneously punched the talk button on the phone, craning it between her head and shoulder.

"Hello."

"Hello Dr. Quint, it's Detective Castillo."

"Oh hi Detective, pardon my heavy breathing; you called me in the middle of a three mile run. Did you have the opportunity to open my e-mail?"

"Yes I did that's why I'm calling. Our medical examiner has just begun to examine the stomach contents from Stacy as well as some blood samples taken from the body before it was returned to Mr. Johnson for burial. She found traces of arsenic in the blood and she'll confirm that it's in the stomach contents today."

"I was hoping she examined blood samples from the victim as I would've expected to find arsenic in the blood as well as the stomach."

"Thanks for keeping me in the loop, Dr. Quint, and I hope you'll continue to do that going forward."

"Actually I won't, as Mr. Johnson terminated my services today. He's satisfied with having your department handle the investigation."

There was silence over the phone lines for longer than Jill

expected as the detective thought about Jill's comment, then he surprised her with a question.

"What steps would you've taken next if you were still on the job?"

"Actually, I prompted the conversation with Adam, by requesting he approve my travel to Dallas. I wanted to look at the crime scene more, talk with the medical examiner and yourself, verify the blueberry muffin as the source of poison and then track it down. I'd also like to interview any cartel members residing in your jails to see if they were aware of anyone in the organization using poison for hits. Why?"

"Just curious. Are you moving on to another case?"

"No, statistically I don't seem to have a case more than once a month, so I'll go back to working my vineyard."

"Thanks Dr. Quint, have a great day."

Jill hung up the phone after she exchanged words to end the call, and thought 'that was a weird call'. Then again she always felt her conversations with the detective were strange as she found him so difficult to read.

She had cooled off from her run while talking with the detective. Now she needed to pick up her pace and begin running, but she'd have to get her breathing under control again. Rats. Twenty minutes later she sighted her front gates and slowed to a walk. She'd shower, change, and then head over to Nathan's for dinner.

Hours later she snuggled with Nathan on his couch. He had seventies music as background noise. Trixie lay at their feet, while Arthur curled up on the sofa's back corner. They were drinking a dessert wine that Nathan had brought back from a meeting with a new vintner who was fast becoming Jill's favorite. She liked hearing Nathan's stories and his advice as she felt that this vintner was about a year and a half ahead of her as far as growing his vineyard. He'd also faced some of the same problems that Jill was facing in regards to geography. She would begin construction on her tasting room in about six months. Her number one worry was how she'd drive car traffic to her tasting room when there were no other wineries in her immediate vicinity.

"Is he holding regular tasting room hours?" Jill asked.

"He's open Friday, Saturday, and Sunday as visitors often travel to the Napa region for long weekends. He said that business is slow but increasing. He had a single visitor his first week-end, five each day on the second weekend. Now he is averaging two customers an hour which is perfect as he can personally serve people and not have to hire additional attendants."

"What's his back-up plan if the tasting room gets slammed?"

"His wife has stepped in to give him bathroom breaks and add a second person an hour at a time."

"I think that is one of the hardest things in the beginning. I may just pay for a second person to be here with me. It might be creepy at times. I'll need to figure out a way to grow my traffic to support that second person. Maybe I'll reach out to a few other newer vineyards to see what they have done with staffing the tasting room. Maybe my imagination is much more vivid than the reality."

"You know, babe, with all the killers that have focused on you in the past two years, I don't think it's your imagination at all. I can help you out for a short time - say the first five weekends you're open, but you'll either have to close your 'second opinion on the cause of death' practice or hire someone from the start for your tasting room."

"That's true. At least I'll have a year to think about this.

How are the sales of the wine glasses you designed for him going?"

"He credits the glasses as being his strongest marketing tool because nearly every visitor has bought one or more glasses and he has seen sales from the internet."

"So are you working on a set of glasses for me?"

"Of course. I'll save my best designs for you. I'm just waiting to hear what wine you're producing in addition to Moscato. I know you would love to operate a tasting room with only that wine, but your tasting room would die very quickly. I did those additional designs for a few varietals you were thinking about, but you need to decide soon."

"I've been stuck on the idea that I should grow what I know, which is sweet or dessert wines. I'm not convinced I have a sufficient palate to taste the best Chardonnay, Riesling, or Pinot Grigio. Those grapes do well in this climate, but I am fearful I will have to hire a wine master to handle the fermentation of the non-Moscato wines, but then it doesn't feel like it is my brand anymore. I don't want to outsource wine master duties."

"I get your dilemma. Why don't I get a selection of three top wines in each of those varietal categories, and then we can do a taste test and discuss what makes them get so many points with wine experts. Then we'll taste a few more wines of each variety and you can give me a guess of how many points they earned. This should prove whether or not you're capable of being the wine master for those other varietals."

"That's a brilliant idea, Nathan, and it will prove whether I have the skill or not. Game on."

Jill had been bothered by her indecision as to which additional wines to grow and now with Nathan's help, she had a game plan going forward. All of a sudden she was tired from the day's highs and lows, so she stood up and pulled Nathan towards his bedroom. It was time to move on to a passionate night and a new day.

Chapter Eleven

Jill returned to her home and vineyard the next morning. She was excited to take on Nathan's challenge on wine tasting. She knew she had the palate for Moscato, but did she have it for any other wine? She would soon find out. She'd checked her email and her three friends and teammates said good riddance to the Stacy Johnson case. Even though they had supported her on taking the case, it was clear they had been uneasy with anything connected to the words 'Mexican drug cartel'. She was just heading outside to work in her vineyard, when her cell phone rang.

"Hello."

"Dr. Quint, it's Detective Castillo."

"Hello detective, what can I do for you this morning?"

"I've a proposition for you."

As with all the detective's words, she spent a few seconds squeezing her brain to guess what he was going to say; giving up, she tuned back-in.

"The Dallas PD is short one detective in the homicide division as well as a supervisor of the special investigative unit. I'm working two homicides, one suicide, and two unexplained deaths that may become homicides. New facts are trickling in on the Stacy Johnson case, but my time is split among several cases. We are under public pressure to solve this crime as it occurred in our convention center, a huge source of tourism to Dallas," the detective paused a moment on the other end of the phone perhaps to gather his thoughts.

"How can I help, Detective?" Jill asked extremely curious to see where this conversation was going.

"I'd hoped that you'd continue to supply me with clues as again you seem to be a few steps ahead of my own crime scene staff. My guys are excellent but like me, their time is divided between several crime scenes that they are processing at the same time. I spoke with my Lieutenant and he agreed to bring you on as a consultant for up to a hundred hours for the Stacy Johnson murder," Castillo said. "That is if you're interested in helping us."

"I'm interested in helping. I've never had my contract terminated before the murder was solved and I'm irked by that."

"Can you send me your resume or biography and a copy of your driver's license? We'll need to do a routine background check on you which personnel is lined up to complete for me today. I'll also send you our standard consultant contract. Are you free to come to Dallas tomorrow?"

"Yes, I'm sure I can arrange a plane ticket and hotel near your building."

"Actually, Dr. Quint, the manager of the hotel you were staying at in Dallas has offered you a room at no charge. She's been quite vocal through the Chamber of Commerce and the Visitors Bureau that we solve this murder yesterday. Groups are asking about the murder when exploring booking the convention center."

"Wow, that's some pressure from outside the department," Jill agreed.

"Yes," came the clipped response.

"Okay, send me the contract and I'll wait to hear that I've

passed your background check before booking my ticket."

"Do you have something in your background Dr. Quint that I should know about?"

"Please call me Jill and nothing in my background should worry you. I just lack faith that your people will move that fast."

"I'll look for your signed contract and I'll see you tomorrow, Jill," and the detective ended the call.

Jill sat back and thought about the call. The Stacy Johnson case was taking some interesting twists and turns. She would have to notify Nathan and her team. She would outsource any relevant research needs to them. She heard the ping of an incoming email, she clicked on it to find two attachments from Detective Castillo; one was their standard background form and the other was a consultant contract. She completed both and sent them back to the detective. She dropped an email to her friends and left Nathan a voicemail. They could talk about the case more at dinner tonight, but she wanted to give him advance notice of her plans.

She entered her lab to check on an organic pest control agent that she'd learned about at the grape growers' convention in Dallas. One of the seminars she attended mentioned Pierce's disease; a bacterium that destroyed grape vines in one to five years after it attacked the plant and was costing grape growers millions of dollars in plant damage. One of the speakers offered a proactive solution to preventing the disease from entering her vineyard plants. She'd been experimenting with his suggestions with live culture of the bacteria and they seemed to be effective. When she returned from Texas, she would study how frequently she needed to spray her plants to keep the bacteria from taking root. She was walking back to her house when Detective Castillo's email arrived. She was approved to work as a consultant for Dallas PD and would she please notify him of her arrival time in Dallas tomorrow.

Jill entered her house and quickly booked a ticket that would have her in Dallas by noon the next day. She was excited to assist the DPD in this murder investigation, though she had to wonder if Castillo wanted her in Dallas so he could arrest Stacy's murderer, once he or she stepped out and took aim at Jill. Oh well, didn't matter, Jill knew she would enjoy the intellectual opportunity to contribute to this case.

She packed her bag for a week, then packed Trixie's food and treats. She would join Nathan for dinner, then leave the dog behind and return to her house to sleep. She had to get up at 3:30 in the morning to make the 6am flight. No sense disrupting Nathan with that early call. She debated taking her autopsy suitcase that she kept loaded and ready, but she couldn't see a reason to take it as there was no autopsy to do. With everything all arranged, she piled the dog in her car and drove to Nathan's house.

She found him in the kitchen staring in concentration at his refrigerator's contents. Arthur moved to a higher perch that would allow him to swat at Trixie if she got close.

Nathan shut the door and turned around saying, "So you're back on the case and heading to Dallas in the morning."

Jill leaned over to hug and kiss him and replied, "The very early morning, 3:30 is my wake-up call."

"That's ugly. Sometimes I don't head to bed until 4am."

"Good thing, I'm a morning person. What's for dinner? You're frowning at your refrigerator."

"I'm frowning because I was in the mood to make one thing, but I'm missing an ingredient, so I have to go with my second choice. You have no idea how hard it is to move your chef's brain from something that was Thai over to something that is Italian."

"Since I have no chef's brain, you would be right about me not understanding your cooking frustrations. We could order in a pepperoni pizza."

"You know Jill since we have been together, I've eaten more pepperoni pizza than in all the decades before you arrived in my life. I'll do a pesto sauce for the fish just to stay away from full fledge marinara sauce."

"Can I help you with dinner?"

"No."

Now Jill realized that Nathan was in a surly mood about something other than what to cook for dinner that night. Usually she was relegated to pouring wine, or making a salad, two things she was normally successful with in the kitchen.

"Are you upset about something else besides the dinner selection?"

"I'm not happy with you taking this job. I just heaved a sigh of relief that you weren't on the case and now you're in harm's way again."

"Hey, I'm more protected in this case than most cases since I'll be working inside police headquarters."

"And when you go back to your hotel at night? Who has your back then?"

"Hotel security? Maybe there is a Nick like person that runs hotel security."

"Maybe?"

"Okay you have a point and I'll talk to hotel security and the detective when I arrive to discuss my personal safety. Are you asking me not to take this case?"

Nathan sighed and didn't say anything for a moment. Finally he asked, "In your gut, who do you think killed the woman?"

It wasn't the question that Jill was anticipating and she thought through what she knew so far about the murder of Stacy Johnson.

"In my gut, I don't have a murder suspect, rather I feel it's not the cartel because I'm stuck on what the kid said to me; it was too much work for the cartel, they'd have killed her in her driveway."

"As much as I hate to admit this, I agree with you and the kid. You know I've been bothered by Adam and isn't he on the detective's most likely to have done it list?"

Jill laughed at Nathan's description then asked, "You've pegged the man for murder since you met him. Why do you feel so strongly?"

"There was something contrived about him and I know Angela says that people behave differently when devastated by grief, but this guy didn't seem that overcome by real grief. I also don't like the fact that he shipped his children off to his parents in the days and weeks around his wife's murder. That seemed more an arrangement to suit Adam than a decision made in the best interests of the children. It was like he wanted the children out of his way - it just seemed like a wrong emotion to me."

"Okay fair enough; that's interesting insight into Adam. So now that we've talked this through are you still uneasy with my traveling to Dallas?"

"Hmmm, better the enemy that you know rather than the unknown? Certainly if the cartel is not involved in this murder case then I have to think that you'll be safe; then again you've had plenty of people after you that were not cartel members," Nathan paused, then added, "I guess I'm talking myself into circles here since I seem to have an equal amount of angst for you whether the cartel is involved or not. Okay travel to Dallas, and I'll take a look at my schedule to see if I can make a long weekend of it and visit you there in a few days."

Jill was pretty happy with the conclusion that Nathan arrived at. She would've turned down this case for him if he had asked, but he didn't which said something about the strength of his feelings regarding this being a non-cartel murder. She walked over to him and gave him a long and thorough kiss.

When she finished, he raised his eyebrows and asked, "What's that for?"

"For being the best guy a girl could have. Have I told you I love you in the last hour?"

"I'm not sure you've told me that at all today."

"Then I've been remiss. Though to be fair I told you 'I love you' when I got up this morning, but you were still sound asleep and missed hearing my words."

He just pulled her close and hugged her, then sighed and stepped away to begin gathering ingredients for dinner. Jill took a deep breath, relieved they had moved beyond the tension of her job.

"The hotel we stayed in is so concerned about the murder that they have offered me a free hotel room for the length of the investigation."

"Wow! The police must be feeling some public pressure. Are you renting a car to go back and forth between your hotel and police HQ?"

"The hotel also offered me a shuttle to use around Dallas."

"Good I was afraid you might walk each day."

"I don't think so; there was one scary block when I did that walk last week in daylight. I wouldn't want to do it at night so if the hotel hadn't volunteered transport, I would have rented a car."

Jill had been chopping vegetables while Nathan deboned a fish in preparation for dinner. Jill had to admire his skill. Despite years spent performing autopsies and cutting through human skin, she could make a complete hack of a fish. Nathan was adding vegetables and a risotto to complete his Italian menu. The food looked and smelled delicious. Their conversation moved on to their upcoming long weekend at Henrik's house in Germany. They had made a friend for life when Jill and crew solved his wife's murder. He'd been such a help on cases since with his facial recognition software that he sold globally.

After another wonderful meal accompanied by the perfectly crisp white wine, they settled in on Nathan's sofa to watch the latest episode of a home remodeling show. He had learned early on that it was impossible to watch any medical or police series on television with Jill as she had a tendency to pick apart the accuracy of such a show. An hour later, Jill knew she needed to head home as her early wake-up call was just hours away. With a hug for Trixie and a longer one with Nathan, she was out the door and home in twenty minutes. She fell asleep quickly which was amazing given her level of excitement to start the job in Dallas.

Chapter Twelve

After an uneventful flight and a check-in at her hotel, Jill presented herself to Detective Castillo's office at noon the next day. He provided her with a consultant badge and an empty office from which to base her investigation.

Castillo had arranged an interview with Dr. Albright, the medical examiner, for Jill and himself. Many of the tests were completed, but some toxicology tests took weeks to get back if they were highly specialized and had to be sent to an outside lab.

Dr. Albright, a woman about Jill's age, appeared friendly and cooperative as she sat to review Stacy Johnson's autopsy file with them.

"In addition to finding the presence of arsenic in the vomit, I also found it in stomach contents, blood, and in most of the victim's organs," noted Dr. Albright.

"Did you conclude that arsenic was ingested via a blueberry muffin?" Jill asked.

"Yes. Her stomach contents consisted of the muffin, coffee, water, and a few vitamin supplements. The blueberries appeared to be marinated in arsenic as there was a high arsenic content in the blueberries. I did a quick search and failed to find any other examples of poisoning in this manner. I was surprised that the arsenic was in the blueberries rather than the cake portion of the muffin. To me, that suggests that the poisoner had to have experimented with marinating the berries in order to assure a fatal dose."

"That's an interesting hypothesis and one I'd agree with. Whoever the poisoner was has to have a chemistry background to be able to test the level of arsenic in the blueberries. I can't believe this was strictly good luck on the first attempt," Jill noted.

Castillo had been following Jill's train of thought and asked, "There was no evidence of chronic poisoning? Is that something you can rule-out in an autopsy?"

"No, there was no evidence and yes that is something I can detect," replied the medical examiner.

"What other testing do you have pending?" Jill asked.

"Toxicology tests. Given that the victim was speaking in public just prior to her death, I didn't look at alcohol or drugs of misuse in her system. However, I did send blood work and liver cells for detection of additional poisons. I wondered if any other poisons have been tried in the past and they didn't work and that caused the murderer to step up her game to a different poison."

"Her?" Castillo questioned.

"Poison has long been the murder weapon of choice for females. Arsenic is used in this country for pest control and the English parliament debated in the 19th century banning the sale of arsenic to females for fear of its use as a poison to kill their husbands."

"Remind me not to make you ladies mad," replied the detective.

The two women just smiled crazily at the detective enjoying his discomfort.

"When do you think you'll get your test results back from the private lab?" Jill asked.

"Actually, I expect them any day now as they're not complicated and the private lab has a contractually required turnaround time for test results. I am not testing anything that is microbial, so there is no need to wait while some grows or doesn't in a Petri dish."

The detective stood up moving to shake hands with the medical examiner and said, "You'll keep us informed?"

"Yes."

Jill and the detective returned to their building discussing the autopsy findings as they drove back to police headquarters. She was now on the hunt for arsenic marinated blueberries. She was meeting with the hotel and convention center security to obtain hours of video tape to watch from her hotel room. She expected it to be mind-numbingly boring, but it was where she would start in the search for the blueberry muffins. Eventually they might have to ask Adam Johnson if his wife brought muffins from home, but for the moment, she was not going to notify him that the police had hired her to work on his wife's murder.

The other angle she was taking was researching the Marsh test. It was developed by a chemist named Marsh in 1836. Jill examined the chemical reaction that measured the amount of arsenic and determined that just about any backyard chemist could set-up the same test and measure the arsenic in the poisoned blueberries. The backyard chemist would need a few chemicals and after a quick internet search determined that those chemicals were easy to obtain.

After the shuttle ride back to her hotel, Jill met with the head of hotel security who pulled the video tapes for her of the relevant locations and time related to the case. The convention center security compiled every piece of footage from every camera inside and out of the convention center for the twenty-four hours before and after Stacy's presentation. Ugh, it was going to be a boring evening. She planned to look at the tapes and eliminate all times that were empty of people. That would reduce the footage she had to watch by hopefully at least fifty percent.

Jill settled in to her nicely outfitted hotel room and connected her laptop to the hotel television - it was always better to view video clips on a larger screen. To keep her mind active, she planned to watch the screen until she felt her concentration slipping, then she would head down to the hotel's fitness gym and get a run in. Once she returned to her room she would wait until she lost concentration again to take her post-workout shower. Later when she needed the next break she would order her dinner through room service. At her final mental lapse in concentration, she would head to bed knowing from past cases the importance of having total attention when viewing video footage. She leaned back and went to work, and by the time she needed the first break, she'd eliminated all of the empty footage which was nearly two thirds.

She entered the gym thinking about the case; maybe she would use a copy of Henrik's facial recognition software to identify the same face in multiple locations and see what that turned up for her. Surely some of the hotel guests on Stacy's floor were also attending the same conference. Had the person who poisoned the blueberries attended the seminar that Stacy was a presenter in to watch his or her evil handiwork? Watch Stacy pause in discomfort, sip water knowing it wouldn't help, then watch her vomit and collapse, watch the conference room attendees come to her aid, the whole time knowing that they wouldn't figure out what poisoned her in time to save her life. Jill shivered at that cold picture in her head.

She purposely shoved that view out of her head and returned to thinking how she could identify where Stacy had gotten the blueberry muffin. She wanted to study the bags that Stacy brought with her into the hotel room. A muffin was easily smashed; and so if it had come from home, Stacy would've probably transported it in a plastic container for protection. She would check Stacy's hotel room inventory from the crime scene report. She should also check to see if someone entered Stacy's room after she left for her speaking engagement and before the police arrived on the scene. She also wanted to check any room service footage. With that thought, she suddenly decided she better not order room service at the hotel in case that was the source of the poisoned muffin. A good sense of paranoia had kept Jill alive on more than one occasion.

There was a restaurant in the lobby and so she would make the trip down to it to fetch food. Until she determined where the muffin had come from, she would avoid room service deliveries. Jill finished off her work-out returning to her room to look at some of the footage she thought about while running on the treadmill. Fortunately she had taken pen and paper with her to the gym to record any brilliant thoughts she had while running. Following her notes, she started with watching Stacy's room and hallway in the twenty-four hours prior to her check-in.

There was a lot of activity in a hallway over a full day when there were fifty rooms serviced by a set of elevators. It was so mind-numbing to watch that Jill almost missed it. Housekeeping entered the room presumably to clean it after the last occupant. Later a supervisor entered the room, clipboard in hand and exited less than five minutes later. Maintenance walked around with a cart. They went in one room with a plunger and changed a lightbulb in another. A few occupants had room service trays brought up to them. Each time the tray arrived on a cart. On one occasion a tray was walked into the room that Stacy would occupy. There was a silver lid on the food so Jill had no idea what was under the lid.

Jill had two concerns; the first being that no other room service order was delivered without a cart and the second problem being that she was working under the premise that the room was unoccupied. She would have to check with hotel security to see if the room was occupied. She picked up the phone and called Rob Gallagher, the hotel's head of security. The man had given her his cell phone, thankfully, as the administrative offices were closed at this time.

"Rob, this is Jill Quint. Can you tell me if the room that Stacy Johnson occupied was vacant the night before her arrival?"

"Give me a few minutes and I'll call you back with that answer."

Jill went back and watched the food delivery a few more times. Then her cell phone rang and it was Rob calling back.

"The room was reserved for a Paul Smith, but he never showed up."

"Did you charge him for the no-show?"

"Yes, and the credit card was rejected, the account closed."

"When was the reservation made?"

"About two weeks before the occupancy date. It took a legitimate credit card to secure the reservation, so that tells you the account was closed sometime after that reservation."

"How was that room selected for him? The story is suspicious but how did he arrange to stay in the exact room slated for Stacy?"

"That's a good question and I don't know the answer to it. I'll have to research it and get back to you. Is this urgent or can it wait until tomorrow morning?"

Jill thought a moment then said, "It can wait until

tomorrow morning. Enjoy your evening, Rob."

"Thanks, I'm coaching a group of six year olds in the fine sport of T-Ball and I can leave if need be, but I'd rather stay."

"Sounds like you have your hands full, good luck with the kids and I'll talk with you tomorrow."

Jill leaned back and thought with some excitement that she might have discovered the origin of the poisoned muffin. The room service attendant could leave it in the room with a note that it was compliments of the hotel for Stacy's breakfast the next day. She would have checked into her room probably viewed the muffin and decided that if she had it for breakfast the next morning she wouldn't have to leave her room until her presentation. That would give her time for another lecture practice.

Then Jill thought about the marinated blueberries. She really needed to try making the recipe herself. Did the arsenic change at all after spending thirty minutes in a 400 degree oven? The melting point of the metallic substance was far higher than 400 degrees, but Jill questions were as much about how the marinated blueberries would fare as about the properties of arsenic. Did the blueberries change color or otherwise decompose due to the arsenic? She would drop Castillo an email with her potential discoveries and request access to an oven. They might have one in the crime scene lab or perhaps she could use the police cafeteria oven to conduct her experiment. She would buy new kitchenware for the experiment then toss it once she had her answers. After composing her email to Castillo, she went back to studying the video.

She tried to formulate specifics about this delivery man. Based on where his head passed under the door frame, she estimated his height at about six foot tall, weight of 190 pounds, thirty five to forty five years old, and no guess on the man's ethnicity. He kept his head turned away from the camera on the way into the room and then he exited a stairwell at the hallway's end, which had no camera inside the actual stairwell. She tried finding the elevator footage of the man and once she did, she found the food tray resting on his shoulder blocking a view of his face. He must have known camera placement before he entered the hotel.

Her cell phone rang and she answered it expecting Nathan. Instead it was Castillo.

"Good work, Jill. This does appear to be a well-planned poisoning. Do you have an answer from the hotel as to whether the room was occupied?"

"Not until the morning. The man with the answers is coaching his child's T-ball team and I thought that was more important at this moment in time."

"I have to agree with you there, it's a question that needs answering but it can wait. You asked about ovens in police headquarters and I honestly don't know what the crime lab or kitchen have at this point. Come prepared to bake."

"Will do. I'm working more on the videos tonight so I'll let you know if I find anything more in the morning."

"One question. Could the man that delivered the room service possibly be Adam Johnson?"

"I don't know. This guy seems of average height and weight as does Adam. I can't identify the race of the man, so as to whether his facial features match his, I don't know yet. I'm going to search other camera angles in the hotel to see if I catch a better picture."

"How about the food cover does that match the hotel's?"

"Good question, let me look again," Jill said and there was a pause in her conversation as she pulled up other footage of other room service deliveries. "Yes it is a match."

"Ok, well I'll see you in the morning."

Jill decided to modify her video viewing plan now that she had found some things to look for. It was much easier to stay attentive when she had something specific to search for. She'd grab a shower now and then head downstairs to order food from the hotel restaurant.

Half an hour later, she found herself back on the sofa with a Chicken Caesar salad sandwich and fries on a plate on her lap. While it would have been great to wash it down with a beer, she was afraid the alcohol content would diminish some of her observation powers so she settled for a fruit flavored ice tea.

She went back and looked at the tape again of the room service delivery and another thing struck her as inconsistent with a normal delivery. The man used a passkey to enter the room. In the past, any room service delivery had begun with an attendant knocking on the door; hotel staff didn't enter an occupied room without an invitation from the client.

She studied all of the cameras for an hour after the delivery and never again saw the man. She grabbed her room key, exited her room, and took the elevator to Stacy's floor. She walked down the corridor looking for cameras as she went. She got to the stairway and entered it. While she didn't think it was a legitimate exit, she took the steps up another twelve floors. She was breathing heavy and her legs were burning by the time she reached the top. She was curious to see if she could get out on the roof; she supposed it was some kind of fire code requirement to have two exits to the stairwell, but maybe not. She pushed the door and it did indeed open and allow her access to the roof. It was rather creepy and dark. Jill had a new fear of heights and it just gave her the willies to be close to the edge of a thirty floor building. First she wanted to be certain she could get back in, so she placed her cellphone between the door and frame to make sure it couldn't lock behind her, then she explored the roof. There were multiple stairways that exited to the roof. She tried the doors and they were all locked.

Jill had her hand on the door and was bending over to retrieve her cellphone, when the door flew open to the roof. She let out a little scream, jumped back, dropping her cellphone in the darkness. She was terrified for a few seconds until she saw the uniform of the hotel security backlit by the stair lights.

She put her hand to her chest and said, "You scared the wits out of me!"

"Ma'am you are only allowed on the roof in an emergency, you'll need to leave now and return indoors."

"No problem, sir. I was just checking the exits up here," Jill replied and then a question occurred to her. "How did you know I was up here?"

"We watched you on the camera enter the roof area."

"I'm doing an investigation that Rob Gallagher is involved with if you need to check me out. Is there a camera on the roof? I couldn't see it in the dark up here."

"Yes, there's a camera and it's positioned to see all four stairwells."

"Do all the doors lock behind you if you come up on the roof?"

"No ma'am we keep one door unlocked at all times per fire code."

"Is it always the same door or do you rotate that?"

"Ma'am I think before I answer any additional questions, I would like to escort you back to your guestroom and contact Mr. Gallagher."

"Ok, I understand. By the way when I spoke with him earlier he was coaching a bunch of six year olds in the sport of

T-ball so he may be hard to reach."

"If you know he's coaching T-ball tonight, you really must be a friend of his so I'll answer your questions on our way back to your room. Yes, we rotate the door that is unlocked each day. Ma'am, do you want to ride the elevator down to your floor?"

"No, lets walk down to the twentieth floor, it's only ten flights. What kind of keys opens those doors and who has those keys? Do you keep footage from the roof?"

"Security has those keys and maintenance and it's just a regular key. As to video footage of the roof, I don't know if we keep it - you'll have to ask Mr. Gallagher."

They continued their walk down the ten flights of stairs, but Jill couldn't think of any other questions to ask this security guard. She'd have more for Rob in the morning. She thanked the guard once she reached her room. Her heart was still racing after her scare up on the roof. She'd give Nathan a call as it was always soothing to talk to him.

"Hey babe, how's Dallas?"

"Just scared myself to death, so I thought I'd call you to calm down."

"What happened? Are you hurt?" Nathan asked going from casual to concern in two sentences.

"I found some suspicious behavior on one of the hotel videos, so I followed a stairway to the roof of the hotel to see if that was a possible exit for my suspect. The roof is high in the sky and dark and I was quite creeped out while up there. Just as I was reaching for my cellphone which I had used to block open the door back inside the hotel, a security guy opened the door from the inside. I'm embarrassed to admit, but I let a little scream out before I saw who it was. My heart is still racing over the surprise."

She could hear Nathan sigh on the other end, and then he

said "Serves you right for being a lone investigator."

"Aren't you the sympathetic friend?"

"Just calling it like I see it."

"Hmmm. How was your day?"

"Not bad, two new clients that I met last week signed contracts for my services."

"I'm amazed you have capacity for additional clients let alone the creativity to do something different for them."

"If I didn't have Ned's assistance, I wouldn't have the capacity. He is handling a lot of the computer layout work that I used to do. Now I just approve the work once he's given it to me in draft. I might someday hire additional help for him on the printing side, but I still have capacity to grow."

Jill settled into her sofa and relaxed over her conversation with Nathan, her nerves calmed.

"So I'm baking muffins at police headquarters tomorrow."

"Honey no offense, but you're not too talented in the kitchen. Are you sure you want to antagonize those cops who will come to your aid the next time you get scared up on the roof?"

"First, you're not supportive of my scary moment, and now you're calling me a really bad cook. That is just plain mean," Jill replied a grin in her voice.

"Okay why are you baking muffins for the police?"

"The medical examiner determined that the blueberries were marinated in arsenic so I'm going to recreate the poison muffins. With my cooking skills I should be really good at this."

She heard Nathan laughing on the other end of the phone and then he said, "You should indeed."

"On my way to police headquarters tomorrow I'm going grocery shopping for a box of Bisquick and some blueberries."

"So where will you get the arsenic? I haven't seen that in

the spice section ever?"

"Ha ha. I'm hoping the police lab will have it. If not, my baking experiment will have to wait a day as I wait for a delivery."

"Why bother trying to recreate the muffins if you already know it's the murder weapon?" Nathan asked.

"I'm trying to understand how easy or hard it is to make this recipe. It will be a part of the picture of the murderer. If it is easy, then my poison muffins add nothing to the case. If it requires any special measurement and handling of the arsenic, then the pool of suspects narrows considerably."

"I hope you'll be picking up bakeware for use in your experiment. I wouldn't want to use a muffin pan after you have been baking with arsenic no matter how many times you wash it."

"Yeah I had those items on my list as well and then I'll see if they can incinerate the bakeware after I'm done using it."

"I'll be able to brag to people now that you poison people with your cooking and be entirely truthful when I say it."

"You know I'd be insulted by our conversation, but I really hate cooking and as long as I keep lowering people's expectations of my culinary skills then I'll escape folks expecting me to cook for them. Do you have any advice on marinating the blueberries?"

"Cooks marinate blueberries all the time for a variety of recipes. Usually they're marinated in an alcoholic drink like a liqueur or rum. There's even blueberry beer. Most recipes have you marinate for a short time - like fifteen minutes. So your experiment should go pretty fast. Where did the woman get the poisoned muffin?"

"That is sort of what my roof top scare was about. I think I may have a suspect placing the muffin in her room prior to check-in and so I was following his potential path through the hotel."

"So has talking to me calmed you down?"

"Yeah, sometimes you need a mundane conversation about baking to put a roof surprise back in perspective. Thanks and I better end this call and get back to staring at my video footage. Love you."

"Glad I could help and love you back babe."

They ended their conversation and Jill returned to the video footage. She had a bunch of security questions for Rob in the morning. She studied the footage of each camera angle for an hour after the unknown man entered the stairwell and saw him nowhere. Where'd he go? Was it possible that he was able to evade roof cameras? The room service guy did enough suspicious things for Jill to believe that it was the blueberry muffin under the silver lid. She looked up at the clock and decided to pack it in.

Chapter Thirteen

The hotel shuttle bus driver had been surprised when Jill asked him to stop at a grocery store on the way to police headquarters. She purchased both the pans and bowls to make the muffins as well as the baking ingredients that she would need. While she was there she also grabbed three dozen donuts for the officers near detective Castillo and those in the crime lab.

When Jill arrived in the homicide unit, Castillo raised an eyebrow at the bags of groceries in one hand and a huge box of donuts in the other.

"Trying to buy your way into the favor of the homicide division, Dr. Quint?"

"Yes and that of the crime scene unit as well. Where can I go to work making poisonous blueberry muffins? Have you found an oven for me? I have everything I need except arsenic and I'm hoping your crime lab has some in stock otherwise my baking experiment will be delayed a day while I find that special ingredient."

"Let me take you up to the crime lab and see if those folks can help you with the oven and the arsenic. Did you learn anything else from the video?"

Jill decided to keep her little scare on the hotel roof last night to herself. For a seasoned detective such as Castillo, he had probably been in lots of dangerous situations.

"Before I came over here this morning, I briefly met with Rob Gallagher who is the head of security for the hotel. He's looking into key card issues and the roof video footage. His answers to my questions will likely provide me with some new avenues to explore. I sent the best image I could find of the room service guy to your e-mail address. I thought you might want to add him to the murder board as a person of interest."

"Already done," Castillo noted. "So besides making poisonous blueberry muffins, what else are you running down today? Have you told Adam Johnson that you're back on his wife's case?"

"For several reasons, I'm delaying notifying Adam that I'm back on the case, but he'll know eventually. Someone needs to ask if his wife brought a blueberry muffin from home to the conference. For now I want to understand what it took to make poisonous blueberry muffins. Then I'm going to call Barb Jordan who was the co-presenter of Stacy's at the conference. She's an old friend of mine dating back ten or fifteen years and I'll feel her out to see if she had a vibe about Stacy. She mentioned they'd had several phone calls to jointly prepare the presentation. So I thought I'd pick her brain to see if I learn anything new. After that I wanted to see if the Dallas police can obtain the DNA of El Chapo. I would like to compare Stacy's DNA to that of El Chapo. I bet the DEA or FBI has a copy of it. And then I'm going on a deep dive into Stacy's background. My team originally did some research on her and she appeared fully formed around age eighteen. I want to determine why her identity is so well hidden before she reached eighteen."

"You want me to obtain El Chapo's DNA? I thought that finding you an oven was going to be my most difficult task today. I see I've greatly underestimated your chutzpah in that you want me to battle a bigger bureaucracy than my own to get one of the most famous criminals in the world's DNA."

"I have a backup plan if you can't get it through your own

channels," Jill offered.

"I'll take you up to the crime lab and leave them to help you make your poison muffins."

While Jill and the detective had been chatting about the case, at least half of the contents of the donut box had disappeared. Jill just shrugged and thought 'it's lighter to carry without all those donuts in it'. Gathering up the box and her groceries she followed Castillo out of the unit and over to the crime lab. He made introductions and then left her to her own devices. As she had guessed, the lab had arsenic and an oven. She got to work marinating the blueberries in a strong arsenic solution, one that was guaranteed to cause death in humans within three hours. Once the blueberries sat in the solution for fifteen minutes she again measured the strength of the arsenic. Ten blueberries equaled a fatal dose. She continued with the baking mix and was soon pouring batter into muffin tins. After thirty minutes in a four hundred degree oven she removed the blueberry muffins. Again she analyzed the arsenic content of the muffin. Looking at the blueberries, she was unable to tell they'd been marinated in a poisonous substance. She wondered at the taste but knew she would be foolhardy to satisfy her curiosity on the flavor. She did her final measurement on the strength of the arsenic and thought that consumption of just half of the muffin would lead to death.

The murderer had either been lucky that their muffin concoction contained a deadly amount of arsenic or he or she was an amateur chemist and re-created the Marsh test to determine the arsenic content in order to make sure the dose was fatal. Given how well designed the muffin delivery to Stacy's hotel room was, Jill tended to believe that the poisoner had tested the muffins ahead of time to know they were deadly.

Jill placed a call to Barb Jordan to get her take on Stacy. The last time they spoke, Jill had asked her questions more from the curiosity point of view rather than an investigator. Now she wanted to see if she could learn anything new about Stacy from Barb.

"Hey Barb, it's Jill Quint. Do you have a moment to talk right now?"

"Yeah, I've got time. I just finished a call with the client of mine in Indiana. What's up? Did you solve the murder of Stacy Johnson?"

"Actually that's why I've called. Her husband terminated my services, but now Dallas PD has hired me and I have a hundred hours to solve the case. How's that for pressure?"

"Frankly I'm surprised you didn't solve the case already," Barb said cheekily. "Why did Adam terminate your contract?"

"I determined that Stacy was poisoned by arsenic in a blueberry muffin that she ate that morning before the conference began. That apparently was enough information for him and he wanted to leave the rest of the case in the hands of the police. Perhaps with the cost of his wife's funeral and possible legal costs associated with settling her death, he decided he couldn't afford my services anymore. Doesn't matter, because I'm still going to find Stacy's killer."

"So where are you now? Geographically I mean - California or Texas?"

"I'm in your time zone in Dallas."

"Blueberry muffins, huh? I remember seeing them at the breakfast buffet before the start of our seminar. I went for the eggs. But that's strange that they served blueberry muffins and no one else got sick."

"That's interesting information about your conference serving blueberry muffins. We believe that Stacy ate a blueberry muffin in her room prior to heading to the conference room where your presentation was supposed to take place."

"Stacy and I probably had four or five phone calls to plan our presentation. I remember her saying in one of the calls that she planned to practice her presentation one more time that morning in her hotel room. So maybe she came down early and got a muffin and went back up to her room but that still doesn't explain why no one else got sick."

"We actually think the muffin was delivered to the room prior to Stacy even checking into the hotel. Perhaps the murderer left a friendly note, something like 'welcome to the quality convention and the hotel staff hopes you enjoy this muffin as you prepare your presentation'. If someone left such a note in my room, I would likely eat the muffin and give silent thanks to their thoughtfulness."

"Certainly that would explain why no one else got sick at the convention."

"So you say you spoke with Stacy about five times to prepare your presentation. Did she share anything of her background with you? Were you aware she was married and had children? What about her education and work experience? What city was she from? Did you learn any personal information about her?"

"Let me think," Barb replied and there was silence on the phone line for a minute while she thought about her interactions with Stacy. "I remember she was married and that she had three children. Her kids and my grandkids were roughly the same age. She named the University of Texas as the school that she got her nursing degree at, but I don't know the schools of that state very well so it didn't stick in my head."

"Was she happy in her job? Did you sense any discontent with being a mother or a wife? What emotions come to mind when you think of Stacy?" Jill asked wishing she'd offloaded these questions to Angela who was so much better at interviewing than she was.

"She was happy in her job and proud of her kids. She mentioned Adam but I don't recall it being favorable or unfavorable. After we've finished with this call, I'll think about the conversations I had with her and see if I can come up with any gut feelings. What's your cell phone number so I can call you back?"

Jill provided her number then ended the call. It was time to circle back to Rob Gallagher and hotel security.

"Rob, it's Jill Quint, is this a good time to chat?"

"I was just about to call you. I took a look at the footage of the room service delivery and you're correct to be suspicious, it's not one of our employees. I was quite disturbed by the ease with which he entered the guest room. I checked our room card key system. When a guest checks out of the hotel, a piece of computer code directs our room key software to deactivate the card key. The last person to stay in that room was a female and her card key was deactivated."

"What if I don't formally check-out? I leave in a rush for the airport and forget to check-out?"

"Our guest services staff begin checking in with guests thirty minutes prior to check-out to see what their plans are and we get a variety of responses - some want an extra hour to check-out, others are in another state and forgot to check-out, and occasionally we wake someone up who forgot to set their alarm. If we get no response then our housekeeping supervisor knocks on the door. If the room has been vacated, then housekeeping checks-out the guest. It's tricky if the room hasn't been vacated and there's personal property in the room."

"I've always left a hotel within two hours of check-out on my prescribed day. What do you do with your last scenario?"

"In legal terms we evict a guest who doesn't or can't pay, or is drunk and disorderly, overstays their original reservation, or is doing something illegal. We then have the right to change the locks once the guest leaves the room. Then we video tape the possessions and our boxing up of them for our own protection later and we store the stuff."

"So back to the room in question, the previous guest left on time and her card-key was deactivated. The room was prepped for the next guest, but that guest didn't show up and had no access to the room."

"That's correct."

"So where did the pass-key come from?"

"It took me a while to figure that out but I have your answer. Earlier in the day, the fake room service guy was also a fake maintenance person. He had a cart just like our staff use and a similar uniform, but that was cover for him using a magnetic card reader. He changed the door pass card reader then simply made a pass card to match that new code. Our housekeeping staff didn't notice as they use a master pass key."

"Were you able to follow him through the hotel to see where he went?"

"No. Just like the room service episode, he left his cart in the hotel elevator lobby room and housekeeping removed it. He walked out of the room and left through the same stairwell. We don't see him leaving the building. We're still looking through all of the footage thinking that perhaps he waited a few hours or maybe tampered with a specific camera, but we haven't seen anything yet. That makes me think that he was a hotel guest who had opportunity to watch our processes."

"That's an interesting notion. If he exited that stairwell, then changed clothes and returned to whatever floor was his, you probably wouldn't see that on camera."

"Yes that's a partial explanation, but the guy had to have hacked into our hotel software to know which room Stacy Johnson was planning on staying in. We are a six-hundred room hotel and he couldn't have just gotten lucky. I checked Mrs. Johnson's reservation and there was nothing in her reservation that required she stay in any particular room number."

"Yes, but he knew which room she was staying in before she checked in," Jill noted. "Does your room reservation system show rooms by the week or something? I guess you're always trying to mix and match the length of a reservation to an unoccupied room."

"Yeah our reservation system lays out the reservation lengths at all times. That's the only way you can book a hotel three months from now and know whether rooms are sold-out."

"Got it. So our suspect has a chemistry background to have developed the process for the deadly blueberry muffin and he has some computer skills in that he could both make a new pass key and enter your registration system to know where Stacy Johnson was staying. Our perpetrator also has a way with disguises as he changed his appearance multiple times."

"That's assuming you're only dealing with one person for this murder," Rob suggested.

"That's an interesting thought. Can you send me the footage for the maintenance guy? Is it possible to be on the hotel's roof at night and escape camera detection? I thought it was pretty dark up there."

"Will do and as the head of security I would say that you're not able to avoid the cameras on the roof, but I'll offer my guys pizza on the night shift if they can walk across the roof and not be seen on the camera. That should be enough incentive for them to be creative."

Jill ended the call with Rob and moved on to the background check of Stacy Johnson. She was going to ask Marie and Angela to also look into Stacy's background with the thought that three friends are better than one. Marie was superior to all of them in this area, but she hadn't found anything when she had searched for background on her last week. Jill would have to give them some new information about Stacy so they had new avenues to look in. Perhaps she would see if Castillo could look into her background to assure them she didn't have a sealed juvenile record or some other legal reason.

She'd been thinking hard about that new angle when an idea came to her. In her email to Marie, Jill asked if she could perform an ancestry search. If they looked at the leaders of the Sinaloa Cartel, could all of their family members be accounted for? If one seemed to disappear then maybe that would be a clue about Stacy. She posed the question to Marie, but knew it would be several hours before she got a response.

In regards to her own search of Stacy's background, Jill was going to try starting at her first year of college and working backward. She would check her high school diploma and college entrance exam score and then look at her college records to see if she graduated with honors or some other special recognition. If you graduated in college with honors for your grades, then there was a good chance that you also did that in high school. Maybe she could look at Texas state high school graduate records.

Jill had another brilliant idea come to her thinking about Stacy's background. What if she did ancestry testing on Stacy's DNA? If her DNA lacked a match for a Mexican or Spanish background that would go a long way to eliminating her as a relative of the bosses of the cartel. She knew there were several companies in the US that did that kind of testing for the average citizen to identify their background, but in the case of a murder investigation, would they be able to turn it around quickly? She picked up the phone to call a few of the agencies to see what turnaround time she could get from them.

An hour later she held a conference call with Castillo and Dr. Albright. They liked her idea of genetic testing and Jill had found a lab in Austin that they could fly the specimen to that afternoon for testing. They would know in the morning if Stacy had DNA of someone from a Mexican family. Castillo was excited to test Stacy's blood since he believed from the beginning that her murder wasn't related to the Cartel.

It was getting late in the afternoon, so she called the shuttle bus for her ride back to the hotel. She had hours more of work, but she was more comfortable working in her hotel room especially since she wanted to get in a run in the middle of that work. She was debating running the two figures through facial recognition software but she thought that both the maintenance and the room service guy were one in the same but each had a different disguise and they had not been caught on camera with a full frontal facial view, so she thought she had an inadequate picture at this time. It was too early in the investigation.

Chapter Fourteen

Settling into her hotel sofa, she was pinged with an email from the medical examiner that the specimen had arrived for DNA testing. She was really anxious to see the result of that test and thinking of doing that test might be her greatest contribution to the case so far, although Castillo was also excited to note the as yet unidentified room service and maintenance guy from the security footage. It gave Jill a feeling that she was earning her consultant's fee.

Now it was about researching Stacy Johnson. She was sitting back staring at the screen thinking about what she'd been told about Stacy's life. She looked over at her phone when she heard the email ping and saw it was from Marie.

Couldn't give it more than thirty minutes tonight, but I did discover something new. Stacy rushed for a sorority on her college campus. Her freshman year sorority book lists her as having a hometown of The Woodlands. You might want to spend some time searching in that city.

Jill looked up the city of The Woodlands and noted that it was a large suburb of Houston. She looked back in her notes from her discussion with Adam and noted that he said she was from a city near the Texas/Mexico border. That description would not describe a Houston suburb. So which piece of information was a lie? What Adam had told her, what Stacy was alleged to have told Adam, or what she put down in her sorority's application? When Jill had been a student in college she'd avoided the Greek houses. It wasn't her kind of socialization. Besides she was one of those students who was also working and between school and work, there wasn't time for a third organization in her life. Her impression of them was they were thorough in checking an applicant's background so Stacy must have some connection or cover related to that city. Maybe she could track Adam's and Stacy's relationship from those college days.

Jill searched the university where the couple attended school and then she backed up. She knew they had bachelor degrees but had one or both also pursued a Master's degree? Was that where they met as graduate rather than undergraduate students? She looked up their profiles on the websites of the companies they worked for and then moved on to LinkedIn. There she learned that Stacy had a Master's degree while Adam had a bachelor's degree. So that meant she was back to the original college she started with; where Stacy was a sorority sister. She started with the national organization of that sorority and then narrowed down to the Houston campus location. She further narrowed the search of names and pictures to eleven to fifteen years ago.

Soon she found younger photos of Stacy Miller which must've been her maiden name before her marriage to Adam. There were many happy times judging by the photos of Stacy. She sent an email to Marie that notified her friend of Stacy's maiden name and moved on to search The Woodlands for the Miller family. She started with the property rolls for that city but there were several hundred Millers. How did she find out if there was a Miller family who had a daughter by the name of Stacy? If that was the case why did she tell her husband that her family was from the cartel? She decided to start with the local newspaper. Usually they published names of graduating high school seniors and if available where they were going to college.

From the various police reports on the case, she knew Stacy's birthdate and so she counted forwards to the likely year she graduated high school. There were about nine public or private high schools that Stacy could've graduated from. Thirty minutes later she found Stacy's name among the many graduates of a large public high school. Jill was beginning to wonder more and more about Stacy having a link to the cartel. It was really beginning to feel like a lie. Again, who was the lie from …. Stacy or Adam? Maybe he made up the entire story to misdirect the murder investigation.

Just to cover all bases she looked for a Stacy Miller in seven other Texas cities that sat on the Rio Grande River which was the border with Mexico. El Paso and McAllen had plenty of people by the last name of Miller but no Stacy Miller. The cartel was rumored to cross the border at El Paso or Laredo, but she could not find a Stacy Miller as a high school graduate of either city. There were sixty-nine Stacy Millers that lived in Texas and she was able to rule out all of them after an hour of research. A boring exercise Jill thought, but someday she would love to explore the Rio Grande. It appeared to be a beautiful river on Google Earth and it served as the defining border between the United States and Mexico.

Jill thought she would take a break, get some exercise, grab her dinner from the hotel restaurant then return to her hotel room. She was 99% sure that the Stacy Miller from The Woodlands, Texas was the same person as Stacy Johnson from Odessa. It sure didn't look like she was related to a cartel member.

While she was running on the treadmill, she got an idea to check the wedding announcements. If Stacy's parents were mentioned in that announcement, then it would surely point to Adam being the source of the fiction about Stacy being related to the cartel. Jill finished up her run, than grabbed a cheeseburger, French fries and an iced tea to take back to her hotel room. She glumly looked at the delicious food in her take-out container. It looked and smelled wonderful and was equal to about three times as many calories as she had just burned off running. How depressing.

Sweaty and thirsty, she sat at the desk in her room eating her cheeseburger with her left hand, while tapping away with her right hand. She alternatively gulped down water or ice tea when she paused with the typing. This case was the first that she resorted to looking at wedding announcements as a source of information. It sounded really lame and a weak link for that idea as wedding announcements in the paper were becoming a thing of the past. Couples were choosing other means via the internet to mark special occasions. However this was ten years ago or more and perhaps couples were still using the newspapers in Texas for engagements and weddings. She spent the rest of the evening searching wedding or engagement announcements in the papers of Houston, The Woodlands, and the college town where Stacy had received her graduate education.

Just as her eyes were drooping shut and her hips were becoming numb from sitting on the sofa, she found it- the wedding announcement of Adam Johnson and Stacy Miller. More importantly, there was mention of Stacy's parents and grandparents. She stood up and stretched and thought that Detective Castillo and she would be having an interesting conversation with Adam Johnson in the morning. There was no doubt about it - he had lied to her about Stacy's background and in a big way. She bet that the DNA sample would come back missing any heritage to the Sinaloa State of Mexico. She updated the detective and her records in separate emails.

Barb Jordan meanwhile had sent her an email with her thoughts about Stacy. In their five conversations, she had looked back at her calendar to determine how many calls they had to prepare the presentation; Barb couldn't remember Stacy mentioning her husband. She'd mentioned her children during almost every call, but nothing about the husband. She'd not thought that odd at the time - it didn't stick in her head that Stacy was having problems with her husband it was just when she thought back to all of their conversations she couldn't remember any mention of the husband.

Okay, the case was growing that there was something off with Adam, but that was a long way away from having any evidence of Adam's involvement in his wife's murder. She'd sleep on this information and see what new angles she thought of in the morning.

Chapter Fifteen

She arrived at police headquarters intending to speak with Castillo. He had done a routine background search on Adam since the spouse was so often involved in a murder. They had asked where Adam was the morning of his wife's murder and it was verified that he was in the office in Odessa. According to Jill's timeframe and the mysterious room service and maintenance guy captured on the video, it wasn't the morning of her murder that they needed Adam's whereabouts - it was the day before. She'd also made plans to call Stacy's parents and interview them about their daughter. She'd been fortunate to find Angela free this morning and she had agreed to handle the call. Since they now knew that Adam had lied about Stacy's background, she was especially curious about the parents' attitude toward Adam. Angela was recording the call and would send her the transcript later that morning.

The DNA test had come back from the Austin lab. There was zero percent of any genetic heritage related to Mexico. Stacy was half United Kingdom and half northern Europe specifically German. It was kind of hard to be related to the Sinaloa cartel with that genetic background. Further proof that Adam had lied.

Detective Castillo had been in a meeting and entered the space that Jill was occupying in the homicide squad.

"Sounds like you've had a productive evening and early morning. Bring me up to speed."

"Last night I was searching through Stacy's college records

and came across her maiden name. That led me to thinking about a wedding announcement from the family. I located that along with the name of Stacy's parents. Someone on my team is interviewing them in fifteen minutes. Also got the DNA results back and Stacy is not related genetically to people that inhabit the Sinaloa state in Mexico or indeed any state of Mexico."

"Next steps?"

"I think you and I need to set up an appointment to interview Adam Johnson. I know Odessa is a five hour drive from here but it's a one hour flight. He's surely up to something suspicious and he and Stacy have three children. If Adam is up to his eyeballs in the murder of his wife, then I think we need to think about the safety of those children somewhere in this equation."

"A guy I went to the police academy with works for the Odessa PD. When I got your e-mail last night, I asked for his assistance in putting the tail on our person of interest. This morning an older woman left the house with three children and dropped them off at school and day care. My contact thinks it's one of the grandparents that's in residence with Adam. He's at work."

"Now would be a good time to fly in for a conversation with Adam with the children safely out of the way in school."

"Let's back up a moment," Castillo suggested. "We know that Adam Johnson has purposely lied to us about Stacy's background. We've an unknown male who likely left a poisonous blueberry muffin for Stacy to consume. Besides a gut feeling, what shred of evidence do we have that Adam's our murderer?"

Jill paused and tried to think of a counter to the direction that Castillo was going but couldn't.

"Good point and one that I've been thinking about this

morning. I checked your original notes on the case and you verified Adam was present in Odessa on the morning of her murder. He simply couldn't have been here to commit the murder that day. Now we need to verify that he was also in Odessa the previous day. Then we need to put the pictures of Adam and the two fake hotel employees through your facial recognition software, to see if a computer thinks they are the same person."

"Do you think they are?"

"No, just having technology verify my opinion."

"So what would you suggest we do to find evidence to link Adam to this murder?"

Castillo had a knack for getting on Jill's nerves. He vacillated between sentences with few words, to a sentence with hidden meanings, to finally asking her endless questions. For once, she'd like him to feed her answers. Okay, to be fair she been hired to do the job he was doing and if Castillo had time to do this himself he would have. After their conversation she was going to head to the cafeteria for a drink. Her brain needed to relax for a few moments and give thanks that the police department had hired her on the case. Each case taught her something new and gave her techniques for resources to use on future cases. But outside of Nathan and her friends, she wouldn't be admitting that wedding announcements were now a new source of information for her.

"As long as Adam is under surveillance, I don't suppose there's a need to rush over there immediately and speak to him. I'll work on framing Adam's background this afternoon. By then I should have some information back from the interview of Stacy's parents as well."

"Jill, I don't disagree that we need to interview Adam at length. I just want to have more holes in his stories and more information about his background so that can be used in the interview. Give me that information."

"You're right of course. When I'm working in the private sector I wouldn't hesitate to pick up the phone and call Adam and ask him about the inconsistencies in his story. But this is your investigation and your rules which are much more confining for the police than they are for a private investigator. I'll see what I can find on Adam since you're keeping him under surveillance. How are your other cases going?"

"I picked up a new suspicious death this morning. It's a five year old, found by the mother when she went to wake her son up to get ready for school. It doesn't get easier and I hate when a potential victim is so young," Castillo said with a sigh.

"I guess the flip side of your coin is I have never been called into an investigation about a child. The police seem to exhaust every resource getting to the bottom of such cases. When I worked for the state crime lab, I'd occasionally perform an autopsy on a child. I always hated them. It seemed that the child died of Sudden Infant Death Syndrome which always devastated loving parents, or I found evidence of repeated child abuse which broke my heart. I don't know if I'd take a case now if the victim was a child."

"Sure you would," Castillo said. "For the same reason we cops investigate a child's death - we all mourn that we weren't around to protect the child and now that it's dead, we owe that child; we owe it the lock-up of its abuser and killer so they can't hurt another one."

"I suppose you're right and the children of Dallas are lucky to have you looking out for them. I'll get to work on Adam and leave you to figure out if the child is a victim and then to find its killer. I'm going to grab a bite to eat then hunker down with my computer here for a while and then in my hotel room. While I thought the cartel was involved with Stacy's murder I thought it was better if I came and went in daylight and I'm sort of sticking to that routine. "

Castillo nodded and they parted ways. He had a heavy load and likely both the child's and Stacy's murder had generated more than the usual media attention. She liked that she was able to lighten his load rather than add to it. She wasn't sure about his decision to wait on interviewing Adam, but she could really see it both ways - interviewing now versus later. As long as they weren't worried about Adam disappearing or harming anyone else, then they could afford to wait and build the case against him.

Jill grabbed an egg salad sandwich and a banana from the cafeteria. She'd really wanted french fries or potato chips to go with that sandwich, but she was doing a lot of sitting in Dallas and knew she couldn't afford the extra calories. Perhaps now that she knew the cartel wasn't involved, she could begin walking back and forth between the hotel and police headquarters during the daylight hours. In fact she would start later this afternoon with the walking route.

Back at her desk, she sent an email to Marie about dropping the search on Stacy and adding if she had time to see what she could find on Adam. Then she opened Angela's email on her interview with Stacy's parents. Angela had also included the transcript of the call, but that was mainly for the police records as Jill trusted Angela's assessment of the Millers. Angela wrote,

That was a sad call. They are clearly deeply grieving for their daughter. They tried to be polite about Adam, but I could tell there wasn't much love there. Other than at the funeral, he hasn't allowed them to spend any time with their grandchildren which I find odd. They said when Stacy was alive they got to spend as much time as they wanted with the kids and even hosted them overnight during school breaks. They didn't understand why he wouldn't let them spend time together. I asked them if Stacy had ever voiced fear of Adam, and they said 'no'. I asked them if Stacy had ever voiced any unusual events in her life - near misses. They said Stacy was driving back from a meeting in San Antonio and was driving through Texas Hill country when a truck tried to run her off the road on one of the hills in that area. She had to do some crazy driving and when she did go off the road after several bumps from the truck, her car didn't roll as it was more a gradual slope. This occurred perhaps three months before her murder at the convention. They couldn't remember any other problems that Stacy was having. They asked me what killed her and I told them arsenic poisoning. Adam told them she'd collapsed and died from a heart attack. I'm sure not liking this Adam character. They seemed like really nice people. The transcript of the call is attached.

So someone had tried to kill Stacy prior to this convention. She'd ask Castillo to find the police report from that crash. She couldn't see how it would be helpful, but you never knew. If Stacy had seen Adam driving the truck that tried to bump her off of the road, she was sure she would have reported that; and he would've been arrested. That suggested he'd had someone else involved in both that attempt and the actual murder. She got up and went over to Castillo's cubicle but he wasn't there and so she approached someone else with the request for the police report. Fortunately, this officer had enjoyed her donut delivery and so was quick to bring up and print the report of Stacy's accident.

She took it back to her desk to study. As the parents had described, someone had tried to run Stacy off highway 305, a small two lane highway between interstate 10 and highway 385 to Odessa. Using Google Earth, Jill took a brief look at highway 305. It looked pretty flat to her and that made it hard to run someone off the road if there wasn't a cliff to go over. She would have to assume there was an edge somewhere on that highway and that whoever had tried to push Stacy off of the highway knew that road well. The police report went on to describe the scratch marks in the back of Stacy's car and the silver paint. Stacy had taken a picture of the retreating truck, but there was no license plate and there were thousands of that make, model, and color in the state. The vehicle was never found.

So what changed in the lives of the Johnsons in the last two months that was so significant that Stacy needed to be dead? Had she discovered something? Was there another woman? Was there an insurance or other financial inheritance that was necessary to Adam? Had she made him so mad or jealous that killing her was the only way? It was time to focus exclusively on Adam.

Chapter Sixteen

Jill reviewed the notes of the original research that they had collected on the Johnsons. She hadn't realized at that time that they had never done a deep dive into Adam Johnson. Their initial research focused on Stacy Johnson and her role in the marriage. Jill began to build her profile of Adam. She soon had his birth date, birthplace, parents, siblings, education, and work history. She moved on to research any legal proceedings. She had his marriage license, driver's license, speeding tickets, car, and property ownership. She saw that he had both a driver's license for automobiles as well as a Class C Commercial Driver's License. Jill looked into the different vehicle classes and determined that Adam could drive what sounded like a hazardous material semi-trailer truck. He had gotten the license about five years ago and had recently renewed it. It sounded like he was driving those kinds of vehicles on a regular basis. He was an engineer working for an oil company so why would he be driving a semi-trailer filled with oil? That didn't make sense to Jill. She wondered if the surveillance on Adam could determine when, where, and why he was driving such a vehicle. She dropped a note to Castillo to alert his team handling the surveillance in Odessa.

Next she went to work on their finances. She'd asked Jo if she had time to look into either Adam Johnson's finances or that of the oil company he worked for in Odessa, as she was so much better at understanding what she was seeing and spotting problems. One other thing she had noted on her legal search was the Johnsons had no bank ownership of any of their property. They had paid cash or paid off all large purchases. For a family of five, even with two incomes, that was fabulous money management. An hour later she was exactly nowhere with nothing appearing to her to be a problem.

Jill leaned back in her chair and stared out the door of the space they had assigned her. Where should she go next? Think Jill, you're a detective. What other information do you have access to? Why is Adam driving semi-trailer trucks? Are they a frugal family, or do they have cash from another source? Who is the fake maintenance and room service guy at the hotel? She thought about chasing down the source of the arsenic, but it was too widely available for that to be useful. Maybe she would circle back to the pictures she had of her fake hotel employees and run them through her own facial recognition software. Henrik Klein, a client that hired them to solve his wife's murder and with whom they had become friends after the case, had provided her top of the line software. He operated an international technology and security firm and several U.S. law enforcement agencies had purchased his software. Jill was likely his only free client. For all she knew, the software used in the Dallas crime lab for facial recognition was Henrik's.

She went back to look for the best frontal picture she had of the two men. There was no perfect mugshot as they'd done an excellent job tilting their heads away from the camera. It would be interesting to see if the software thought the two men were the same. She selected her two best pictures of the maintenance guy and room service guy and entered them into the program. The database contained nearly a billion of the seven billion humans on planet earth. What was poorly documented were children under the age of fourteen which was about 1.8 billion and peoples of the remote and rural areas of the world. In past searches, she'd had a suspect identification in less than five minutes, while other searches had taken as long as an hour and that was with good clear headshots. She made an internal bet with herself that she would end up with a thousand matches over a two hour time period. With her laptop tied up, she went back to contemplating the door frame. Castillo wanted some connection to Adam and so far other than lying to Jill, she hadn't found anything to connect him to his wife's murder.

She wondered if there was any money involved - perhaps a life insurance policy given that she was married with kids. Jill would call her employer to get names of friends who knew Stacy on the job so she could chat with them regarding Stacy's frame of mind. She'd also go back to that wedding announcement and call the bridesmaids to see what they knew about Stacy. That should take care of friends and family and give her just about all she was going to find on Stacy. She was also waiting for Marie and Jo to get back to her with any social media or financial information that they were both searching for. She checked on the progress of the facial recognition search and noted that it was only ten percent done after an hour. It was time to pack it in and return to her hotel and get the run going again. Otherwise at this rate she would be stuck in police headquarters till eight or nine at night.

Since she had proof that Stacy was unrelated to the cartel, she figured it was now safe to walk back and forth to the hotel during daylight hours. The distance was less than a mile. There were a few desolate areas as she left police headquarters and crossed a construction area, then the freeway overpass, followed by the walk-way along the convention center before emerging to her hotel. What could happen in a fifteen minute walk down a four lane road? She felt supremely confident that she could handle anything that presented itself. She hadn't been bothered as she walked by the deserted construction area or over the bridge covering the freeway below. She was nearly home free with just the covered walk-way of the convention center. She could see the edge of the hotel in the distance. The sidewalk edged along one of many convention center parking lots.

Jill got a movement out of the corner of her eye as three men exited a car that was parked two rows in from the sidewalk. Rather than walking towards the convention center they were on a path towards her. Jill had multiple thoughts flow through her head.

Should she run?

Could she outrun them?

They didn't look like runners but one never knew.

Whatever she did, she better not allow one of them to get behind her.

Should she use her laptop bag or purse as a weapon? No, at the most she couldn't take more than one of them out at a time.

A quick glance around showed the odd car moving on Lamar street; should she race out into traffic and get herself killed by a car instead?

Would any cars seeing her struggle, come to her aid?

Maybe she should dial 9-1-1 on her cell, but could she afford the time to look for her cell in her purse and take her eyes off the men to actually hit the three buttons?

She had her orange belt in Tai Chi and was nearly there to qualify for her green belt, but again could she take on three men at once? Further back in her mind she could hear both Nathan and her instructor screaming 'no'.

Crap, they're getting closer…. what to do, what to do?

Then she remembered, Nathan had been paranoid about this case and insisted that as soon as she arrived she head to a store to buy bug spray. Since it was Texas and everyone owned a gun in this state, she thought it was overkill as the person with a gun was likely faster on the draw than her and her bug spray, but she followed his request and had even texted him a picture of the bottle that took up so much of the space in her purse.

She pulled the can out and when they were within ten feet of her she arched the spray at the eyes of the three men. She immediately took two of them down as they struggled with the bug spray in their eyes, the third man was still staring at her calculating whether to risk coming at her or retreat with his buddies to the car.

Speaking in Spanish to his friends he urged one of the blinded men through the parking lot toward the car. Jill now knew she could outrun the men and took off towards her hotel, bug spray in one hand while the other searched for her cell phone. She looked over her shoulder to see if she was being pursued; but the three men had disappeared from view. They could still come after her on foot, but she knew they were slowed by the speed that each man could walk, blinded, to the car.

Breathless from the encounter and her long block sprint she reached the hotel where a doorman was standing outside. He looked alarmed at her wild look, can of bug spray, and something else in another hand.

He cautiously approached, but didn't get too close and said, "May I help you ma'am?"

She stopped, feeling the doorman might at least come to her aid if the three men returned by car; put the bug spray down, and dialed Castillo. She no longer felt the need for a police rescue, so rather than make a bigger public spectacle of herself than she already had, she dialed the detective.

"Castillo."

"Hi, it's Jill and I just fought off three men who were trying to attack me."

"Are you in a safe spot now?"

"Yes, I'm in front of the hotel and there is a doorman standing here."

"I'll be right there."

Her phone call disconnected and she stood looking at the bellman.

"Hi, a detective will be here shortly, and I'm a guest of this hotel."

"May I see your room key?" the doorman asked still not getting close.

Jill reached into the outside pocket of her purse and promptly located the card key with the hotel's name on it.

She saw the doorman relax and approach.

"Are you having a problem with bugs in your hotel room? I'll call housekeeping and they'll handle that for you."

"Oh sorry. I guess it looks bad carrying a can of bug spray into this hotel. I bought it for self-protection because it will hurt your eyes and it has a reach of twenty feet and I just used it on three men who tried to attack me on the other side of the convention center."

"Oh ok ma'am."

Jill had a moment of amusement as the doorman obviously thought she was strange and maybe hallucinating, but she was a customer of the hotel so he was trying to roll with the punches.

Fortunately, she saw Detective Castillo pull up to the entrance in an unmarked police car. While police headquarters was close he must have been walking out to his car to have gotten to the hotel that fast. She noted that the doorman was pleased to have some back-up to deal with a possible crazy woman.

Castillo approached and said, "What happened?"

Jill gave a description of her encounter and showed the detective the can of bug spray. He couldn't help himself and he burst out laughing.

"Bug spray, Dr. Quint?" Jill noted that Castillo added doctor to her title whenever he had emotion to bring into the conversation.

"I made a promise to my boyfriend that I would carry it around for protection. He believes, like you, that I attract the criminal element on these cases. I don't own or know how to shoot a gun, so bug spray is the next best thing. It has a longer range than pepper spray, I can buy it anywhere and it allowed me to take out two of the three men the first time I fired the nozzle."

"After, I'm done taking the report here and we get an APB out on the suspects and their vehicle, I would like to take you to my favorite cop bar so that my fellow brothers and sisters can hear your story. We all need a good laugh; and perhaps their friends and families might benefit from your approach."

"So you all are going to laugh at my expense?" Jill asked amused and outraged at the same time. She was starting to feel stupid.

"No, not at you, we'll be laughing at the stupid criminals. Now give me a description of the car and each suspect."

Jill wasn't carrying her cell phone in her hand when the men approached and thus had not thought to take a picture of the men or their car. She was disappointed with herself for having missed that opportunity. She closed her eyes and pictured the men and their car in her head and then gave Castillo as good a description as she could.

"Did they speak to you or between themselves?" asked the detective.

"They never said anything to me even when they were within ten feet of me. However, after I blinded them they yelled curses, I assume in Spanish as they weren't words I recognized. The guy who could still see led them back to the car speaking to them in Spanish as they stumbled through the parking lot."

"What'd you think they were planning to do with you? Did they have any weapons that you could see? Were they planning on kidnapping you off the street?"

Jill had to think through the scene. It was a good question from the detective. What were the men planning on doing? It was either beat her up or kidnap her as she couldn't recall seeing any weapons in their hands or outlined in their clothing. If they were going to kidnap her, was it to take her elsewhere to kill her or did someone want to talk with her? Either way, it wouldn't have been a favorable outcome for her.

"There were no visible weapons, and although the street wasn't busy, I still think three men would have had a hard time beating up a woman without a car stopping and intervening. So I think the plan was to take me somewhere in their car."

"That'd be my conclusion as well. My guess is that they were planning to take you elsewhere to kill you; they just didn't count on you defending yourself."

The detective finished calling it in and then invited Jill to join him at a cop bar. She took him up on the offer as she'd defer the call to Nathan notifying him of her near misadventure. On one hand she wanted an open relationship with him, but on the other hand she knew it would cause him anxiety that she could do nothing to relieve.

"Do you think they're related to the cartel?"

"Why would you suggest that?" asked Castillo.

"Never mind, dumb suggestion," Jill said with chagrin. "It's because they spoke Spanish which is probably true for half of the people living in this state."

"Bad deduction, Dr. Quint. I speak Spanish and I have no connection to the cartel."

"Yep I know, bad deduction."

"Then again they could be with the cartel. Some of the cartel guys look like average citizens rather than inner city thugs. They're generally not tatted up like our thugs. So in just looking at three men on the street, you wouldn't have an easy way to identify them as cartel members."

"Ok I'll keep that in mind. Not to change the subject, but do you know if the convention center has security cameras aimed at the area I was in?"

"I was just about to call and find out. Why don't we walk back there and see if we can see any cameras while I try to locate someone in their security department."

"Sounds like a plan; let me just run my laptop upstairs to my room and get it going. I was running a facial recognition search with some software I have from a German company. It was going slow, so I decided to pause it and walk back to the hotel in daylight. I think it's going to take hours to run and probably give me 1,000 suspects, but I thought I'd try."

"Ok."

Jill took the elevator up to her room and set her laptop running looking for the mysterious room service and maintenance men. A quick glance in the mirror showed nothing too out of place. She lifted up her arm to smell her armpit and despite the adrenaline rush followed by the short sprint, she smelled okay. She washed her hands thinking she'd have bug spray of her finger tips from the nozzle. She was back downstairs in under five minutes.

Castillo had moved his car out of the doorman's way and she joined him to walk back to the place where Jill encountered the three men. She positioned herself and that of the three men as she remembered and there was still a slight stain where the bug spray had landed on the concrete. She pointed out the parking spot the car had been in. The two of them looked around for security cameras, but the convention center was big and normally a place like this wanted to protect its attendees and had cameras on the rooftop aimed at all exterior places. They would have to wait for the convention center security service to call the detective back.

"So this was the first day you walked back to the hotel?" Castillo asked.

"Yes."

"Rather odd that they were waiting for you as normally you wouldn't come this way; you would have arrived back at the hotel on a shuttle bus."

"Maybe they weren't specifically waiting for me. Perhaps I was the first random woman that walked by."

"Do you believe that?"

"I don't know," Jill replied then grudgingly added, "Every person in a prior case that has tried to make my acquaintance in such a manner has been involved in the case."

"See this is why I hired you. You're like a flower to a bumble bee. The bad guys just can't resist you and stay away. I have a couple of cold cases I'd like your help with when you're finished with Stacy Johnson's case."

"Very funny detective."

"My lieutenant gave me a lot of grief for wanting to use you as a consultant, but she'll probably now be willing to sign off on the cold case idea."

"You know detective I can't figure out if you're joking or not. Regardless, I have a business to operate a life to live in California."

"Too bad, you could be the department's latest technique for crime solving."

"Ha ha, detective. Let's head to that cop bar of yours so some more of your law enforcement buddies can make me the butt of their jokes."

"Okay Dr. Quint, I'll back off. Let's go," Castillo said and directed her back toward the hotel and his car. Ten minutes later they were pulling into the parking lot of the Call Box lounge. Inside there was a mixture of plain clothes and casual clothed cops. No uniforms. Jill guessed they changed out of their uniforms before leaving their stations. It probably wasn't acceptable or necessarily safe to wander around in a cop uniform. Castillo joined a table with two open chairs and quickly introduced her to everyone. There were some other members of the homicide squad as well as vice at the table. Jill soon had a Blue Moon beer in front of her. There were two other women at the table giving her a look she couldn't read. As soon as everyone was settled with drinks in hand, Castillo informed the group of what Jill had been hired for and her altercation with the three suspects that afternoon.

"Jill, describe for them what happened to you on the street."

At first she could see concern in the eyes of the officers at the table. So she decided she would do her best to give them a laugh. When she got to the part about the bug spray and pulled the actual can out of her purse, they all had a laugh at the weapon. Of course, that laughter was tinged with the knowledge that Jill's outcome could have been far worse. The can was passed around and a few jokes were shared about adding it to the tool belt of beat officers. A few minutes later Castillo received a call from the convention center security and after a brief discussion in regards to cameras and the location of Jill's assault, Castillo's caller indicated he could have the information ready for them to view in ten minutes.

They stood and exited the bar heading for Castillo's car. A few minutes later they were back at the convention center heading for the administration offices where security was located. Castillo knocked on the door frame of a room filled with video monitors and made quick introductions of him and Jill.

"Can you show us the camera aimed at the parking lot in question?" Castillo asked.

The security person pointed to a monitor on the top left and Jill and Castillo stared at it to verify in their own minds that it had the location of Jill's assailants under surveillance. They nodded that it was the correct view.

"How long do you record for before you re-record over the footage?" Jill asked.

"One week," replied the security supervisor. "We found that people at conventions, both attendees and exhibitors, will say something happened after the fact - usually at two days after their convention ended. To protect ourselves we found it best to hold on to footage for a week before taping over it."

"Excellent. I want to review Jill's encounter at 3:42pm today and we'll want to back up and view the tape to determine when the car arrived in the lot," requested Castillo.

"I would like to view earlier days to see if the car was there," Jill added.

Castillo and Jill locked eyes transmitting the idea that answers to the timing of the three assailants would tell them a lot about who they were.

The guy running the video playback soon had the episode of Jill confronting the three men. She could see Castillo's shoulders shake with silent laughter as he watched Jill spray them with bug spray and then get walked back to their car while blinded. The operator made a copy of the event for Jill and Castillo. Then they moved on to checking each hour of the playback tape to determine when the three drove into the parking lot.

The answer was scary but enlightening. They arrived in the parking lot about five minutes before Jill passed by the lot. Either they had enormous luck or someone alerted the three to Jill leaving police headquarters. The previous day's tape showed no presence of the men.

Satisfied that they had a copy of all that was relevant, they left the security office. Jill wanted to head back to her hotel room and make that delayed call to Nathan and see how her facial recognition computer search was going. Castillo escorted her to the hotel lobby and told her he would see her the next day. She was also going to try and identify her three suspects as she was sure Castillo planned to do. There was also the problem of who knew she would walk by the convention center at 3:42 that day. She had three sources in her head. The shuttle driver could have relayed the information when Jill cancelled her afternoon pick-up. The police building may have been under surveillance. Someone in the police headquarters notified the thugs when he or she saw Jill pack up to leave.

Once she arrived in her hotel room, she typed a quick email to Castillo asking if his building had security cameras that might answer the question of whether she had been under surveillance. She grabbed a coke from the room refrigerator and sprawled on the hotel couch to call Nathan. California's time zone was two hours earlier than Dallas, so he should be finished with clients for the day. She punched her speed dial button for Nathan on her cell phone and waited for the phone to ring.

"Hey babe, how's it going?"

"Good at the moment. Earlier today I had to fight off three men with the can of bug killer you convinced me to buy and carry in my purse," Jill said, thinking it was best to lead with a confession.

There was silence for a moment and then Nathan asked, "Were you harmed?"

"Not in the least."

"Okay, tell me about it."

Jill thought before beginning with her explanation that this conversation was going to go okay with Nathan.

"I was on the far side of the convention center walking towards the hotel."

"Why were you walking? I thought a shuttle was provided for you."

Okay maybe this conversation wasn't going to go well.

"I had proof this morning that Stacy was not genetically or otherwise related to the Sinaloa Cartel, so I figured it was safe to walk the less than a mile to the hotel."

"Okay, so you walked and were attacked by three men. Explain."

Jill gave him a concise description and then waited for his reaction.

"Sounds like you handled the situation in the best possible way. Did you think about using any Tai Chi moves?"

"Yep, but then I heard you and my instructor yell inside my head to not do that."

"Three against one; yes that was the right decision."

"I have our encounter on tape if you would like to see it."

"Email it to me now," Nathan requested.

147

Jill was soon hitting the send key and then she heard silence on his end. Jill thought he was watching the film clip. So she just waited him out.

"Wow your bug spray was better than a gun. I love how the two blind men were escorted back to their car and I especially like the clear pain they were in with your bug spray in their eyes. The third man believed you were more dangerous with the bug spray than he was. I'm disappointed that the two cars that drove by didn't stop and come to your aid."

"Go ahead and laugh at the video, Castillo and his cop friends have already done that. Yes I know it's not funny that I was attacked, but it is funny that this big ugly can of bug spray was as good a defensive weapon as .357 magnum."

Jill finally heard laughter on the other end of the phone as Nathan said between laughs that, "It was a good thing you're quick on the draw with the can."

Jill laughed in response to his comment and said, "Sounds like a skit from the Roadrunner cartoon with me being the Roadrunner and the three bad guys being Wile E. Coyote. Only in this episode the Roadrunner bought a can of bug spray from Acme Company that actually worked."

"You're going to take the shuttle tomorrow," Nathan demanded.

"Yes, although I have to tell you that the driver is one of my three suspects as to who knew I was walking today and at that time."

"One of three? Who are the other two? How do you know that someone knew you were walking by at that time?"

"We watched the video surveillance of the parking lot and the three suspects pulled in five minutes before I arrived and they weren't in that parking lot at any other time. So the other two suspects are someone doing surveillance on the outside of police headquarters, or someone inside the cop shop who alerted the three men to my walk. My guess is the driver, but Castillo is checking out the other two avenues."

"Can Castillo assign a police officer escort between their building and the hotel?"

"I haven't asked and I think he could, but I would rather stay with the shuttle. I've had a different driver at different times so it might be any of them or someone in the hotel's dispatch area. Regardless, it's a short drive and if the driver tried to take me anywhere but the hotel or the police station, out comes my can of bug repellant."

"You're armed and dangerous," replied Nathan with a grin in his voice. "Seriously, though I'm glad the weapon is working, I don't want you to get overconfident. Keep it in your hand and ready if someone knocks on your hotel room door. Keep it in your hand when riding on the shuttle bus, and check the nozzle twice a day to make sure it's working. What are your next steps?"

"I'm running the fake room service dude, the fake maintenance dude, and the three assailants from this afternoon through Henrik's facial recognition software. Each of these pictures is sufficiently bad that I may get hundreds of matches which I'll then have to figure out a way to eliminate. So it's going to be a lot of boring tedious work spent sitting on the sofa. I'll also make a usual trip to the fitness center here and pick up dinner at the hotel restaurant."

"Is that safe? Are there other people in the fitness area? Could someone poison your food in the restaurant?"

So Nathan wasn't completely relaxed about her situation.

"There have always been at least ten other hotel guests in the fitness area with me. I haven't ordered room service for fear of arsenic; instead I've been picking up meals from the hotel restaurant and so far the chef hasn't poisoned me. There're three restaurants here so I'll dine tonight at a different one than I have dined at the last two nights."

"Sounds like a plan to stay safe and that you're not taking any unnecessary risks other than today's walk to the hotel."

"Yeah, well I learned my lesson there and won't be walking again. The cool thing is I learned just how wonderful a can of bug spray is to disable bad people. I can think of a few other criminals I've come across in the last few years that I would have liked to spray their eyes. In fact I think I should get a few water guns for my home and lab and load them with bug spray. I like shooting people with something other than lead bullets. I like causing these criminals pain but knowing I won't damage them long term."

"Remind me never to make you mad; it seems like I won't be able to see for hours afterward," Nathan replied.

"Ha, as if I would ever spray you! I can take revenge on you simply by cooking for you. You'll be able to see, but your stomach won't be happy."

"Hmmm that's a hard choice, bug spray to the eyes or your cooking."

"You know if I was standing next to you that would have resulted in an arm pinch for that poor remark. How's Trixie and Arthur doing?"

"I nearly fell over laughing yesterday. They slept next to each other somehow without realizing it until they both woke up and realized what they had done. They sprang apart like star-crossed lovers, Arthur hissed and Trixie barked her outrage. I wish I had a camera running to record it."

"I wish I had been there to witness it," Jill said between laughs.

"I also ran into Deputy Davis when I was in town and she

raved about the presentation you did for the kids. When you get back, I think she would like to schedule regular visits to your lab and property. Of all the places she's taken those kids for career or life counseling they responded best to your visit."

"That's really cool. I could tell when I was talking that I lost some of them up front, but others were really interested. I think with a little more time and planning we could do a joint presentation. Your artist skills are so different from my science background that we would cover more of the kids skill sets together. Just think, maybe you could convert some graffiti tagger to a wine label designer," Jill said really warming up to the idea of joint mentorship moments with the kids.

"I'll leave that up to Deputy Davis to figure out," Nathan replied.

"Hey got to get back to work here, I just heard my laptop ping that the first facial recognition search was complete. Love you."

"Love you back babe."

Jill gave a few moments to the thought that her conversation went better than expected with Nathan. She had been afraid that he was going to suggest flying out to provide protection for her. That would have aggravated and dismayed her. She looked over at the can of bug spray and said aloud to it, "Thank you bug spray". It had saved her life today and mellowed Nathan's anxiety.

She sighed, stood up and stretched, then settled back into the couch.

Chapter Seventeen

She looked at the results of the facial recognition search and to her surprise it offered only about fifty names. She thought she would end up with thousands. Perhaps the estimated height eliminated many more faces than she expected.

First she quickly scanned the list to see if Adam Johnson was one of her fifty.

He was not.

Then she looked at the list to see if there were common names shared by both the maintenance guy and the room service guy.

No common names.

Wow, the software had a far more distinguishing eye than she had. She thought there was a 60% chance that they were the same person. So what to do with the nearly fifty names for each fake hotel employee? How to narrow it some more? Maybe if she moved on to additional information about each suspect she would see something to eliminate some of the names, but first she wanted to get another run going on the three men from this afternoon. She would need a better picture of them. She'd refine their pictures to the best of her ability and get that search going, then get a work-out in, followed by grabbing dinner from a different restaurant. Maybe she'd come up with a brilliant idea while running on the treadmill.

An hour later she was back in her room, a sweaty mess, dinner in hand, and with no brilliant ideas. She took a look at the second search for the identity of the three men and saw that it was still running so she went back to the first search. How to narrow down nearly one hundred names? The database included names and faces and additional information from different data sources across the world. Pictures available from passport agencies were different than those used for driver's licenses or military organizations.

Should she narrow it down by country of citizenship? That probably didn't mean anything. Couldn't an Aussie or Brit tamper with Stacy's blueberry muffins as easily as an American? Yes. Other information like height or weight had already been used to narrow the search. Her database didn't give her employer or a travel log, both of which would have given her a thread to follow. She would put the names aside for now and use them when she had suspects.

She decided to swing back to figuring out who knew she was walking back to the hotel today. She dropped an email to Castillo to see if he had any information on building surveillance. This should be an easy question to answer as it was his own department and they had 24/7 security. A ping came back shortly notifying her of his response. She opened it and read that they had reviewed the tapes and failed to see any surveillance conducted on the building. They went a step further and viewed the cameras on the lobby of his building and they noted no specific person picking up a phone shortly after Jill had exited the building this afternoon. Of course in this age of technology, someone could have texted someone her departure and the surveillance video on the lobby would fail to show anyone with a phone to their ear.

So she was back to the shuttle driver or someone else at the hotel that was keeping tabs on her whereabouts. Was this person tracking her movement throughout the hotel? Was it a single person or was more than one hotel employee involved? It was time to reach out to the person from the hotel that had offered to put her up for free. She needed answers from the hotel but she didn't know who to trust. Hopefully the hotel person that had wanted her here could assist her in getting to the bottom of this problem. She asked Castillo for the person's name then put a call into her with her cellphone. Then she disconnected the call before it was answered. She was starting to get really paranoid, but what if her room had listening devices in it. If someone could deliver a poisoned blueberry muffin, then planting spyware in Jill's room was mere child's play. So she exited the room and went outside to the street in front of the hotel. If someone had randomly planted a device on the hotel's exterior and that was pretty far-fetched, then the road noise would hopefully distort her voice.

"Hello," said a female voice.

"Hello, may I speak with Amelia Clark?"

"Speaking."

"Hello Ms. Clark, this is Dr. Jill Quint, the police consultant on the murder investigation of Stacy Johnson. Detective Castillo provided me with your name and number."

"Did you find Mrs. Johnson's killer?"

"Not yet, but I wanted to speak with you about the role of this hotel in Stacy's murder."

"Excuse me! What are you talking about?" exclaimed Amelia.

"Has Rob Gallagher of security spoken with you today?" Jill asked.

"He left a message but we haven't had time to talk yet."

"One or two people, we don't know the answer yet, masqueraded as hotel employees. One of the fake employees was disguised as a maintenance guy and he used technology to create a master key to get into the room that would be assigned to Stacy Johnson. The other fake employee dressed as a room service guy and we believe he delivered a poisoned blueberry muffin to the room before Stacy checked in."

"Oh my god," Amelia said and then when she heard background noise she asked, "Where are you calling from? I thought you were staying at my hotel."

"Part of the reason I'm calling you is you may have some staff problems in the hotel. I'm standing outside on the street for this call as I'm not sure if my room has had any listening devices installed in it. It's rather late at night, so I doubt you're still at the hotel. Can we meet somewhere to chat? I can take a taxi to a location you name."

"Ok, there's a restaurant called the Italian Room located about nine blocks from where you are. We can grab dessert and a drink. Have the doorman get you a cab and I'll return you to the hotel. Let's meet in thirty minutes."

Jill affirmed her agreement with the plan and ended the call. She went back inside to collect some materials to take to her meeting with Amelia. She took her laptop including the film clips of Stacy's room and of her attack that day. Since she had time she also changed from yoga pants and a sweatshirt to jeans, boots and a sweater. Yoga pants were fine when your evening plan was to stay inside your hotel room, but Jill was not one to wear them to do anything other than relax or exercise in. She was down with the doorman awaiting a taxi ten minutes later; laptop bag in one hand and purse containing a can of bug spray in the other.

As they were waiting the few seconds for the taxi to pull up, the doorman asked, "Got your can of bug spray with you, miss?"

"I learned my lesson today, so now I'll never leave the

hotel without it," Jill replied with a smile.

Minutes later her taxi deposited her at the restaurant and she entered to find a woman standing in the entrance.

"Are you Amelia Clark?" Jill asked.

"Yes, you must be Jill," Amelia replied hand extended for a shake.

They soon sat in a booth, dessert menus in hand. When the waiter appeared, they both ordered a glass of wine and Jill's favorite dessert - crème brûlée.

"I like to check out the competition hotel-wise on occasion, and this restaurant is located in one of my many competitors," Amelia said.

"I couldn't appreciate the building's full beauty at night, but what I could see, I loved. Any building that has gargoyles on the exterior is a building that screams for further exploration. On the other hand, this is my second stay at your hotel, and I'm very satisfied as a guest."

"I appreciate your feedback. Has there been any difference in your two stays? Has one stay been a better experience than the other?"

"The first stay was mostly for pleasure and I had friends staying here as well. They were pleased with the hotel. We liked all of the places we could walk to from there. We chose your hotel because I had a convention to attend and yours was the convention hotel. We looked at what we wanted to see as tourists and the location was good. So once the trip became pleasure, we stayed put. The service and the restaurant have been consistent and great for both stays."

"Thanks I'm glad we met your personal and business needs. So despite the good service I have some problem employees."

"You may have problem employees. I'm not sure they're

your employees. I brought three video footage clips, two from your hotel security system and the other from the convention center. This first clip is a man dressed as a maintenance man, but according to Rob Gallagher, he and the room service man, which is the second clip, are not currently employees of the hotel. The third clip is from this afternoon in the parking lot near the convention center. I cancelled my shuttle ride to walk from police headquarters to the hotel and about eight minutes later these men pulled into the parking lot and tried to make my acquaintance," Jill said then she sat quiet while Amelia watched the three clips on her tablet.

She had Jill play them three more times, before leaning back in her chair just as their dessert arrived. They both took a few savory tastes of the dessert then Amelia spoke.

"I don't know all of my employees by face so if Rob says they're not ours then I am sure he's correct. What did each of the men do after the clip? I mean the one guy did something with the room key system but what was the outcome of each of their actions?"

"My guess is the maintenance guy created a master room card based on the technology he used on the room door," Jill explained. "He then passed the room key to the room service person who perhaps delivered a poisoned blueberry muffin to an incoming guest, Stacy Johnson. Of course we can't see what's under the room service dome, but we know that Stacy ate a blueberry muffin in the two to three hours before her presentation. The convention center offered blueberry muffins as well for attendees, but no one else was sick, so we have to think the muffin came from a different source."

"How did these men know which room would be assigned to Stacy?" Amelia said and then followed with, "Oh right they must have hacked into our room reservation system. But then how did they know the room would be empty?"

"Rob said that another guest had prepaid for that specific room for the night before Stacy's arrival, but then never checked-in. So housekeeping knew that and saw no reason to enter the room prior to Stacy's arrival the next day where the blueberry muffin perhaps sat with a note from the convention organizers 'to enjoy the muffin prior to her talk'. I think most people would have thought that it was a nice gesture and done exactly what Stacy had - ate the muffin the next morning prior to her speech."

"So whoever hacked into the reservation system kept the room empty for a night and then assigned Stacy to it," Amelia noted. "That's considerable talent and planning that went into a single murder. Who do the police suspect? And this is why you must fear that your room is vulnerable or bugged and I bet you haven't ordered room service."

Jill liked the way the woman talked pulling multiple conclusions and questions into the conversation quickly. She'd bet she was a good leader of the management team in her hotel.

"Typically in a murder like Stacy's, the spouse is the usual suspect. Stacy's husband has a rock solid alibi for the morning of her death as the police checked that at the outset of the case when they thought she was poisoned by the water. They'll circle back to the husband once we have a clear picture of his role, if any, to your fake hotel employees and my attackers. And you're right, I haven't ordered room service since I arrived, I've been getting take-out from one of your three hotel restaurants. I have become paranoid about the security of my Wi-Fi and conversations inside the hotel room. I'll have that fixed tomorrow by getting my own wireless hotspot and having any conversation related to the case outside of the hotel.

"In regards to my attack this afternoon, I wanted to talk with you about the shuttle driver. The police looked at video inside their building and in the surrounding area and noted no one lurking or surveilling the building. This leads us to conclude that the tip-off to the three men came through your shuttle bus system after I made the call to cancel the ride this afternoon."

"Why did you decide to walk this afternoon?" Amelia asked.

"When I originally came on the case, Stacy's husband stated that Stacy was a long lost relative of the Sinaloa cartel," Jill replied. "I was fearful of walking the mile between the hotel and police headquarters if the cartel was involved as I believe they have infinite resources to kill anyone involved with this investigation. This morning we got DNA evidence back on Stacy that showed she had no ancestral link to the peoples of Mexico or indeed any country of Central or South America. I thought I was then safe to walk. Seems that I was very wrong."

"What did you fight those three men off with? Was it pepper spray?"

Jill laughed and replied, "No it was a can of ordinary bug spray that I purchased at a convenience store on the way here from the airport. Bug spray hurts the eyes and has a longer range than most pepper spray canisters. So that means I can attack from a little farther away and I don't blind myself. I know you all own guns here, but I felt pretty powerful with my can of bug spray so much that I actually debated for a few seconds chasing down the men and going after the third guy so that the police would have time to apprehend them, but I decided I had been lucky and I should run for the hotel so that's what I did."

Amelia laughed with her and then quieted with, "So you think someone in my shuttle service offered you up to these men. I believe that I've contracted for that service with a transport driver service that services many hotels and car rental companies in this city. I'll have Rob follow-up with them as he manages the contract."

"In the past when I needed your shuttle, I called from my room or from police headquarters to your front desk. They in turn arranged for the shuttle, and would give me an estimated time of arrival. So the leak as to my whereabouts could also be coming from your front desk."

"Yeah it could, but did you wonder why there were three men in a car so close that they could be in position to harm you so quickly. If you hadn't cancelled the shuttle, was my driver going to drive you somewhere to make the acquaintance of the three men?"

Jill shuttered at that thought, and kudos to Amelia for thinking a step beyond where Jill had stopped.

"Amelia that is a very good observation. Were you a private detective in another life?"

She laughed and responded, "No I just like the world to make sense and the response time on the three men is a gap in my reasoning."

Jill then thought of another alternative and said, "I suppose they could have planned to run the shuttle off the road and harm both the driver and me if I had taken a ride this afternoon. By the way, I hope it doesn't harm your business, but a cop is going to serve as my driver to and from police headquarters. If it looks bad for your hotel clients, we could arrange a pickup in the loading dock area or I could walk through the convention center and out one of their doors."

"Don't worry about it, I think the average hotel client will see you voluntarily get into the car and not wearing handcuffs and wonder what kind of a VIP you are. You'll help my image and if anyone looks distressed, my doormen will have a few suggestions about who you really are."

"Sounds like a plan. Thanks for meeting with me on such short notice."

"No problem; I want to help. The Convention and Visitor's Bureau and by extension my hotel have already had one client cancel their convention and two others are waiting in the wings for cancellation if this case is not solved within the month. In my case that means I'm losing nine hundred hotel day stays if all three cancel. That's a lot of revenue so I want to help as much as possible."

Shortly they were waiting for Amelia's car from the valet and ten minutes later Jill was dropped off at the hotel. Upon entering her room, she wondered if anyone had been there in her absence. She looked around the room and saw nothing out of place. She'd taken her laptop with her to meet with Amelia so she was not worried that someone had accessed it. If there were cameras or listening devices planted in the room, so be it. She would have her phone conversations outside this room. She would admit she was creeped out by someone watching her undress so she decided to either turn the lights out before changing clothes or the closet was big enough to go inside. Perhaps she would alternate her methods between those two choices or she could check to see if there was a shower in the spa she could use as a guest. Showering in the dark sounded like a prescription for falling, but it was kind of fun thinking of ways to outsmart any listening or viewing bugs placed in her room.

Chapter Eighteen

After an uneventful night, Jill arranged for her police escort and arrived safe and sound to police headquarters. She was thinking about the sophistication of this case. There were different skill sets by the various players in this case so far. There was more than one person involved; it seemed likely there were at least five men and perhaps a sixth one behind the scenes directing the actions of the men. She didn't have a motive for Stacy's murder yet. Although she'd caught Adam in some whole-scale lies about Stacy, as Castillo would say, that wasn't enough to convict him. Then there was the situation with the three men attacking her yesterday. Besides the police and hotel, who knew that she was on the case?

She'd wanted to speak with the officers conducting surveillance on Adam. She was curious as to what his movements were. Maybe she would even begin surveillance herself on Adam if the Odessa police were unable to keep a constant watch on his movements. It seemed as though there was nothing more to investigate in Dallas. She could just wait for another attack to come her way, but the first one hadn't yielded any answers, and the next time the outcome of the encounter could be death. She decided to talk about relocating to Odessa with Castillo.

"Castillo."

"Hi it's Jill. I wanted to talk the case over with you. Do you have a few minutes?"

"Yes, go ahead."

"To be frank, I've run out of clues to unearth in Dallas. I think I should get a hotel in Odessa or Midland to get closer to Adam. I haven't been able to explain a few things in this case like an undocumented individual as part of your crime scene team, but even if I figure it out, it won't solve the crime. So if I get closer to Adam, I might end up with more clues to follow. "

"So he's your suspect?" asked Castillo.

"It's my gut feeling. He told outrageous lies when he hired me and someone doesn't do that unless they have a lot to hide. Besides I'm bothered by the semi-truck driver's license. It's my experience in the past that an inconsistent fact like that is the tip of the iceberg that I need to find under the surface. I think I can do that better if I relocate there. Perhaps I could make the acquaintance of the officers that are tailing him for my own protection and to have a deep conversation about what they have seen so far."

After a moment's pause Castillo said, "Frankly, I agree with you, but let me check with my lieutenant. I'll give you a call later this morning.

Jill sat back in her chair and prepared to go through her email. Then she felt a surge of excitement when she saw an email from Jo. She opened and read it, and her surge became a shiver as she grasped the importance of Jo's comments. Jo's email read,

I reviewed the financials of the company that Adam Johnson works for and something strange is going on. I've never read the Security and Exchange Commission filings for an oil or gas company, so perhaps I've got this wrong. According to reports in Adam's company's filings, their operating costs are stable, their oil reserves are dropping (which I would suspect if you're continuously drawing oil or gas from the earth) and their revenues are climbing. It's like a cash infusion was pouring into the company because the oil price per barrel had dropped over the past two years. I looked at the management report and there is no explanation of a new technology that would have cut the cost of production by that percentage. I then pulled a few other SEC filings for oil companies and didn't see the same trend. Maybe an owner or board member is infusing cash from a personal account.

That's all I can gather for you on the company. Glad to hear you're no longer being pursued by the cartel. That, my friend, was making me nervous.

So what could Adam's company be doing to infuse cash like Jo mentioned? If she went to Odessa and watched the company perform, it's not like she had the expertise to see a brilliant stroke of management decision making. She knew next to nothing about it as an industry. Maybe she should look at the officers of the company and the management team to see what their backgrounds were.

Castillo got back to her and indicated she had the department's support to travel to Odessa as long as she made no attempt to contact Adam. He also provided her with the name of his contact in Odessa. He ended with a request for at least twice daily emails of any discoveries she made. She looked up at the clock and decided she wouldn't wait till tomorrow to travel she'd get a rental car and check out of the hotel and hit the road with the plan to arrive in Odessa by early evening. Midland and Odessa were similar sized cities of around 125,000 people about twenty miles apart. She wanted to reduce her chance of being accidentally seen by Adam, so she would get a motel in Midland and drive a white Ford F-150 truck that would look like a hundred other vehicles on the road. They said everything was bigger in Texas and this included cars. She liked the fact she had this big truck frame around her - it felt like she was in a tank rolling down the highway. She'd hit a department store on her way out of Dallas to purchase a disguise that she planned to put on once she reached her destination. Fortunately, Halloween was coming up and she had a wide choice of items to cover up her appearance.

She purchased a Katy Perry wig of shoulder length black hair as well as a few hats. She also bought a few plaid shirts, in style at the moment; but something Jill never wore. A new can of bug spray and sunglasses and she was ready to travel. She put the wig on trying to grasp how long she could tolerate it being on her head. She was hot in five minutes, but then she imagined her ski helmet and just pretended that the wig was just like that helmet. That helped and she soon forgot she was wearing it and startled herself in the rear view mirror when she caught sight of the black hair framing her face. It was a good thing she had trimmed her long hair just prior to coming to Texas, she wasn't sure what she would have done with a long blond ponytail sticking out the back of the wig.

It was a pretty boring drive, a four lane highway shared with flat landscape and lots of semi-trucks. The drive seemed to be changing from prairie to desert. She made a stop for gas and a bathroom break but otherwise keep the cruise control on at seventy-six miles per hour. Her niece had received a very expensive speeding ticket while moving to Texas and Jill didn't want to add any more family money to the Texas State Troopers.

Arriving in Midland, she checked into a moderate hotel. She had searched for a hotel with a good fitness center and found a hotel that offered her daily entrance to a fitness chain for fifteen dollars. She thought it terrible that she would have to spend fifteen dollars to run on a treadmill, but for her own safety, she needed to work out somewhere with a crowd. If she hadn't found this alternative she would've located a high school track or decided to be a couch potato for her stay in Midland. Since she was going to be doing a lot of sitting and surveillance, she wanted an outlet for stretching her legs. The fitness center they'd lined her up with had lockers, so she could walk in wearing her wig and leave it in the locker, run and lift weights, shower, then exit looking like Katy Perry's aunt. Her hotel room had a small kitchenette and she grabbed a few groceries so she could limit extraneous visits to restaurants for food. Of course there were always drive-through fast food restaurants, but when confronted with the smell of French fries and hamburgers, she was usually incapable of ordering a healthy alternative like a salad.

On her way west to Midland she'd had a phone conversation with the officers involved in the surveillance of Adam. They would meet her at the police department which was next to the Municipal court building on business route 20 the same highway that had brought her from Dallas to Midland and Midland to Odessa. It was hard to get lost in this state of Texas. Just before five in the afternoon, she found herself in the lobby of the police department awaiting the arrival of the officers.

Two men in plain clothes approached and introduced themselves as Detective Robert Guerrero and Officer David Rogers.

"Hi, I'm Jill Quint, a forensic pathologist by training but hired by the Dallas PD to help with this homicide."

"That's a little unusual, I can't recall ever hearing about a doctor being hired as a murder consultant," Guerrero commented.

"I've been consulting to families for murder investigations

for the past five years. I also have a team behind me that does some special investigations like reviewing financial records or social media data searches."

"At Detective Castillo's request we have been surveilling Adam Johnson at regular intervals," Guerrero began. "We don't have the resources to watch him all day and night or even for eight straight hours so our observations are spotty at best. He seems to have hired a nanny for his three children and either he or she are moving them around in the morning and I haven't observed when they come home in the afternoon or evening."

"Why do you say nanny?" Jill asked. "Could it be a girlfriend?"

"She is an older woman and I see nothing lover like in their interactions."

"Okay."

"He either goes straight to work or drops his kids off at school and then goes to work," Rogers said. "We have only surveilled him for a little more than two days and so far there hasn't been much variation. He seems to come home in the evening by five each day and one of his kids is playing soccer in the evening. There has been no suspicious behavior or people around Adam Johnson. What makes you and Castillo so sure he's involved in his wife's murder?"

"I can't speak for Castillo, but in my case it's because he's told a few enormous lies. I happened to be in Dallas for a convention; I live in California. Adam hired me to look into his wife's murder. The moment I clarified that she'd died from arsenic poisoning, he ended my services saying he had faith in the police getting to the bottom of Stacy's murder. It's the first time my services have been terminated before the end of the case, but it was Adam's decision. No harm, no foul and I was grateful on some level to exit a case that allegedly involved the

Sinaloa cartel."

"Sinaloa cartel?" Guerrero exclaimed. "What do they have to do with this case?"

"When Adam hired me, he was convinced that the cartel killed his wife. When they had married after college, she told him she was related to the leaders of the cartel, but she had escaped, changed her name and had surgery to hide her identity. With some investigation we discovered holes in this story. Then I located their wedding announcement from a Houston newspaper more than a decade ago and we verified that her DNA excluded any heritage from the peoples of Central or South America, or Mexico. So that was a whopper of a lie for Adam to have told."

"So you're basing your suspicion of murder on a few large lies?" Guerrero asked one skeptical eyebrow raised nearly to his hairline. "They sure must do things differently in California."

"I've never found in my twenty year career in the justice system, a spouse telling such strange lies at the time of death. Yes, different people react differently to death. He's also making every move possible to keep Stacy's parents apart from their grandchildren," Jill raised a hand and added, "It's weak but it's my gut feeling that something big is going on with Adam. Even members of my team couldn't place it but thought there was something that Adam was covering up. I've never had my gut screaming so loudly despite not a shred of court ready evidence that Adam is guilty. Detective Castillo may have something more, but I think he thought Adam was the murderer long before I did based on his experience and gut feeling. So I'm here to observe Adam and understand some inconsistencies in his background. The oil company that he works for has some strangely successful financials and Adam has a Texas license to drive semi-trucks. What do those two facts have to do with this case?"

The two men looked unconvinced, but they thought it would be interesting to watch her work. Then Rogers reached out a hand with a card in it and said, "Here are my contact details feel free to call me at any time." and Guerrero did likewise. Jill ended with the story of the three men approaching her at the convention center. She showed them her new can of bug spray.

Guerrero observed that it was easier to just carry a gun, but Jill could call him day or night if she found herself in a tight situation and Rogers seconded the remark.

She was just about to leave the station when she paused and asked, "Do you have cameras on the roads here?"

"On some roads, yes," replied Rogers. "Why?"

"I would like to find footage of Adam Johnson driving a truck to satisfy my curiosity on that question. Where can I get a copy of the footage for the past week?"

"We can request that footage from the state and have it probably by tomorrow morning if we mention it may be linked to solving a homicide," Rogers said. "I'll take care of that for you and let you know when the information arrives."

"Since you know the city well, if you can think of any other cameras near Adam's oil company that you would have access to the footage, let me know," Jill said and then they shook hands and ended the conversation. As Jill left the police building, she glanced over at the municipal courts. She wondered if she would have access to Stacy Johnson's will, had it been filed in the courts? After a quick search, she determined that Adam, as surviving spouse would not have to file their will in order to probate their joint holdings. He would also need nothing more than the death certificate to gain access to any life insurance money.

Jill decided she would do a few hours of surveillance of Adam tonight then head back to Midland. As she was driving down his street, he was piling two of the kids into the car. She circled around the block to prepare to follow them. A short time later she observed him pulling into a park where one of the kids in a sports uniform ran out on the field. Adam took the younger child over to a different group that he seemed to be the coach of and they practiced soccer moves. Thinking that this was it for the night, she started the truck's engine and headed back to Midland. She was a one woman show and she'd have to be careful in how she spent her surveillance time. Since there was something unusual with Adam's employer, she thought she would be better served following him to work and watching his company, so she promised herself to be in place at seven the next morning and see where the day took her. Castillo could avoid interviewing Adam for perhaps two more days at the most, and then it would appear to be bad detecting if Adam wasn't sought out for a second interview.

Jill arrived back at the hotel and made herself a large salad from the supplies she had purchased earlier. It was time to summarize where she was with the case. She felt like she had loose ends that she had lost tract of. She had the murder weapon, but no identification of the two men that might be the murderers. The hotel had not provided any information as to how someone might know which hotel room Stacy was assigned or how a man got himself assigned to that same room in advance of her stay and who so conveniently hadn't shown up the night before Stacy's stay. She had over one hundred facial matches for her two suspects and she hadn't figured out how to narrow it down. She had nothing on the three men that accosted her near the convention center. She didn't know how they'd been informed that she would be walking at that time. She didn't know why Adam had a special driver's license that allowed him to operate large tanker-trailers.

If Adam was the murderer, what was his motive? Was he angry at something Stacy had done? Was there a financial gain for him with Stacy's death? Sure there might have been a life insurance policy, but then he'd also lost Stacy's salary. Was Adam into the power or thrill of killing? What was the cause of his alienation of Stacy's parents? He seemed like a loving father but wasn't it a bit premature to return to his coaching duties in under two weeks since his wife's death? Maybe he was trying to give his kids a sense of normalcy; since she wasn't a parent, she could only speculate what she would have done, but she thought she would at least take a few weeks off from normal activities.

Jill decided she needed to work the motive angle. If he killed Stacy and banned her parents from seeing the grandkids that suggested to her - anger. What did Adam have to be angry about? Was Stacy cheating on him, did they fight over finances? Given that they had no debt that Jill had discovered, there probably wasn't a shortage of cash. Did they fight over their parenting of the kids? Jill tried to think about things that couples fought over and there were a multitude of reasons, but after ten plus years of marriage and three children, some of the reasons should have gone away. She doubted it was ideology; they couldn't have stayed together as long as they had if they were fighting over religion or politics or some other ideology mindset.

She revisited the police report to track Stacy's movements. She had taken a flight from Odessa to Dallas the day before her presentation. She'd checked into the hotel about four in the afternoon and had met with Barb Jordan at 4:30 to go over their presentation the following day. Stacy then went out to dinner with other staff from her company attending the conference. Her co-workers said the dinner broke up at about 7:30 and they all returned to their hotel rooms. Dallas Police obtained Stacy's cell phone records for the twenty-four hours prior to her murder and noted that she called home and that was her only call until the next morning. She called home again before the conference started the morning of her death and that was it. She'd not received any texts and the police had a subpoena for Stacy's private email, but had not worked through the legal issues of gaining access to her work emails. There had been no threatening communication from any source the police had access to.

Jill thought about the room again and questioned if the fake room service dude had circled back to Stacy's room after she left it but prior to her death to remove any evidence of the muffin? She dropped off an email to Rob Gallagher to get a copy of the tape of Stacy's room after she left it the morning of her death. She couldn't recall if she had looked at the hallway videos for any time after Stacy's death.

At this point, as in all of her cases, Jill always felt like pulling her hair out. There was no action going on, she had small extraneous questions unanswered, and not at all a clear path to follow. It happened in every case - that moment in time when she questioned whether she would be able to solve who Stacy's murderer was. Usually, if she had the patience to wait long enough, something happened, to direct her further in an investigation. She'd shut down her mind and computer and do something completely different that would give her brain a break from the investigation. She looked up movie times at the local theatres and settled on the latest James Bond movie. She'd been planning to see it with Nathan, but she knew she enjoyed that movie series far more than he did. There was a showing in thirty minutes, so she gathered her purse, hopped in the truck, set the GPS for the movie theatre and bought a ticket fifteen minutes later. Buttered popcorn in one hand and a soda in the other, she sat comfortably by herself in the theatre prepared to be maximally entertained for the next ninety minutes.

It was late by the time she returned to her hotel room, refreshed but with no plan for the next day other than to watch Adam Johnson drive to work, and then park her truck near the entrance to the business and wait for something to happen. She knew she would also receive the highway video footage sometime and she hoped that had something useful on it. She was soon asleep after replaying her favorite James Bond on skis chase scene from the movie.

Chapter Nineteen

Guerrero and Rogers had given her an approximate time that Adam seemed to be leaving for work. Jill parked the truck on the first street that Adam turned on after leaving the street on which his home was located. In a previous case, a suspect had surprised her by coming upon her surveying his house. The cops in that town had told her she was lousy at surveillance, so in her spare time between cases she had read a few books on surveillance and now applied those techniques.

A few minutes later she saw Adam's car drive by. She let two additional cars pass her before pulling out and following him. He appeared to be taking the path to work. She'd checked it out and knew what his most direct route to work was. She'd also studied where she could park to observe his employer, looking for answers as to where their profits were coming from. Adam's company seemed divided into two functions - a corporate brick office building and a dusty truck depot with petroleum trucks seeming to come and go with regularity. She did a little research and determined that as a petrochemical engineer, Adam would be designing ways to extract oil or gas from the ground. His company seemed to own oil wells, retrieve oil out of the ground and transport the oil from the rig to somewhere else. Jill would have to follow a transport rig to see where they went but she bet it was to a refinery or to the oil rig. Maybe in the afternoon she'd follow a few trucks. If she was lucky Adam with his semi-truck license would be driving an oil tanker. Were they such a small company that the Chief

Operating Officer found himself driving rigs?

Jill had a pair of small high power binoculars so she could look at every face entering and leaving the company. She didn't know what she was looking for other than the fake hotel maintenance or room service men or perhaps one of the three men that had accosted her near the convention center. Luck was with her when two hours after she arrived, she found Adam in the driver's seat of an oil tanker pulling out of the company's yard. Okay she would follow at a discrete distance and see how he contributed to his company's profits. Perhaps he had an engineering task at the oil rig and as long as he was driving out to the rig he may as well take an empty tanker with him.

Jill dropped behind the tanker truck and tried to stay as far back as possible. After following the truck for some twenty minutes mostly accompanied by other vehicle traffic, she saw him pull up to an oil rig with the truck. She continued driving past the rig wondering where she could hide and watch what he was doing. According to her satellite map there weren't any mountains or hills nearby. There seemed to be some ramshackle houses that perhaps she could draw cover from. She turned into the driveway of the first house and it appeared deserted or perhaps the occupant was off at work. Taking her purse and binoculars, she walked around the back of the building to check out her view of Adam. She was dressed in khaki colored clothing as that seemed to be the color of the landscape and perhaps the best way to fit in.

She saw Adam examining the machinery, writing a few numbers down, and then flipping a few valves to write some more things down. Then he finished, moving everything back to its original position. He walked over to the oil tanker truck, climbed in, and was soon driving back down the highway from where they came. Jill quickly returned to her truck and waited a suitable amount of time before following in the tanker's wake. She discovered that she'd waited too long to tail the tanker-truck and now it was gone from sight. Darn. What to do now?

She thought about going back to the rig to look at what Adam had been fiddling with. However if there were security cameras on the rig, she might be caught on camera. Since she didn't know much about the petroleum industry, she decided she would learn little looking at the rig. With no better ideas in mind she returned to stake-out Adam's employer again. She presumed he returned to the tanker yard a few minutes before her, but maybe he went somewhere else. It just made no sense to her that you would use a tanker truck to make engineering calls on your oil rigs. It was bulky to drive and a gas hog, but then when you owned a company that pulled oil from the earth, maybe gasoline was free. She wished she done a better job following him.

Watching the front entrance she heard her phone ring and looked down to see Castillo calling.

"Hello Detective."

"What are you doing at the moment?"

"Watching the front entrance of Adam Johnson's employer."

"Why?"

"Something fishy is going on here, I just don't know what it is and I'm not sure if it's related to Stacy's murder."

"Are you pursuing a hunch?"

"Yeah. I'm trying to sort through the lies in Adam Johnson's life."

"What'd he do today?"

"He drove an oil tanker truck to check on an oil well about twenty-five minutes outside of town."

"I'm not sure I understand what you just said Dr. Quint.

Our suspect drove an oil tanker to an oil well but didn't fill it up. Is that correct?"

"Yes. Why wouldn't he just use his own car to drive out to an oil rig?"

"If this is a clue, it's about as strange a clue as I've come across," Castillo said disbelief in his voice.

"I lost track of the tanker truck, but given that he didn't refill it at the rig I assumed he drove back to his company's headquarters. So I thought I would sit here and wait for him to leave with the tanker for the next visit to a rig. Do you have any news for me? Were you able to identify the three men that accosted me at the convention center?"

"Sorry no new clues for you and due to the camera angle, our pictures of the three men are all partial to full side views of their faces."

Jill was watching an oil tanker approaching her target company and, using the binoculars, identified the driver as Adam Johnson.

"Hey this is odd, Adam has just returned with the tanker truck and it appears to be empty as it's bouncing up and down which it wasn't doing earlier. So he must've visited a refinery and dumped a tankful of crude oil."

"You're making an assumption that it was filled with crude oil," Castillo noted.

"I think that's a reasonable assumption considering it's pulling out of the yard of a company that manages oil rigs."

"Let's verify that the tankers are filled with oil as opposed to any other substance."

"Detective, I'm not following you; what else would you put in a tanker truck? If it was carrying milk, it would need to visit a dairy."

"Perhaps it's carrying grape juice for Texas grape growers

to make wine with."

"The sign outside the yard where these tanker trucks are pulling into does not include the word winery in it. It has words like oil and gas pumping and exploration. As a vineyard owner, I would never want to see my grape juice arrive in an oil tanker truck. I don't care how many times you wash out or sterilize the interior of the tank, I know that it would affect the taste of the grapes. So from a grape grower's standpoint, I am absolutely sure that tanker truck is not carrying grape juice."

She heard Castillo chuckle on the other end of the phone. She realized she sounded really prissy about how grape juice was transported, but she didn't care; she was passionate about making great tasting wine.

"Since you're running with gut feelings at the moment, all I can tell you is to go check out the contents of the next tanker truck that you see Adam drive away with. I do agree with you that it's odd that someone in management would be driving a tanker truck to oil rigs to perform measurements."

They ended their conversation shortly and Jill resumed her surveillance of the oil tanker yard. She used her phone to look up the specifications of the model of oil tanker that Castillo wanted her to look into and judge its contents. She read about the valves on the underbelly of the tank and learned how to open one of those valves to spill the contents. The problem was that oil was a hazardous material and she had no idea how much would gush out with the slightest turn of the valves. Maybe she could sneak into the yard across the street and check the tanker out there. If the owners discovered a spill, they would have the materials on-site to deal with it. She supposed she could also open the valve when she followed Adam to another oil rig. She thought back to the time that Adam was away from the truck today and there was sufficient time for her to open the valve and shut it again. She could take a container with her so she had something to dump it in. She wasn't clear on which valve was the right valve to open so she would just move down and open and shut each valve. She thought about quitting when the first valve gave her oil, but really she should sample each liquid to determine its contents.

Three hours later, Jill saw Adam leave the yard in another tanker truck. This time she was going to be sure not to lose him. She wished she had the opportunity and the equipment to put a GPS tracking device on the truck, but she didn't carry those kinds of gadgets with her on a case. She gave it some thought and debated if she should take off her smart watch and wrap it around some piece of the truck so she could follow it without being too close. She decided that was a risk worth taking. Everything on her smart watch was backed up on her iPhone, so she did a hard reset on the smart watch so that if anyone found it on the truck they wouldn't be able to tell who it belonged to, but she hoped to retrieve it once her surveillance was finished. She would have to crawl somewhere under the truck where the watch wouldn't be visible. Hopefully, it wouldn't be too scratched up after this trip.

Plan in place in her head, she followed the tanker truck to an oil rig located north of Odessa. Luck was with her when she discovered that the rig was parked close to several houses. She pulled in the driveway of one house, keeping watch in case someone came out of the house, as well as Adam's motions regarding the oil rig. She took the watch off her wrist and found the perfect place to attach it to the truck. She scuttled back to her car and returned the way they came, looking for a good spot from which to observe the truck's movement. Jill couldn't help but pat herself on the back for being so creative in her tracking of Adam and his tanker.

She parked at the first convenience store parking lot she could find upon leaving the location of the oil rig. If Adam happened to look over at her truck, all he would see was a woman wearing a baseball cap with black hair underneath; from the back he would not be able to view her face. He could memorize her license plates and so she'd have to think about switching them around depending on her surveillance going forward.

She tested her iPhone connection to the watch and let him get a mile ahead of her. She noted that the tanker truck had stopped and figured he must be at a refinery unloading his crude oil which was the form it came out of the ground in. When she arrived at the tanker's location, she was puzzled that she couldn't see the tanker parked in front of any of the series of warehouse type buildings. This didn't look like a refinery, but maybe they did things differently in Texas. The refineries that she had seen in California were full of pipes and always had a flame burning somewhere. This just looked like a warehouse industrial area. The truck stayed in its location for about an hour and then according to her phone it was on the move again. She parked her truck down the street from the warehouse entrance and the opposite way that Adam would take to return to his place of employment.

Now what should she do? Should she try to figure out why the tanker was parked inside one of the warehouse buildings? Should she get behind Adam and see if he stopped anywhere else that was either interesting or would provide her with the opportunity to sample what was in the tanker or to retrieve her smart watch? She decided she could come back later to the warehouse area. She might ask Guerrero or Rogers if they knew what was in the warehouse area; it was better now to follow the truck, if for no other reason than to get her watch back.

Again she hung back out of sight of the tanker as it drove through town, taking the path back to Adam's employer. She decided to get close to it so she could tell if it was weighted down or not. Her unscientific measure of weight was how it handled the bumps. The weighted down tanker seemed to sink then roll out of road hazards. The empty tanker bounced like a skipping stone, in and out of the divots. This truck was bouncing, so it must have unloaded its weight at the warehouse. She backed off again expecting it to return to the yard; but to her enormous luck Adam visited another oil rig with good enough coverage in the surrounding area for Jill to run over and retrieve her watch. She then returned to her truck and returned to her viewing spot in a parking lot near Adam's employer. She'd settled in with binoculars in hand when a tanker truck approached the yard. She noted Adam's face and the license plate of the tanker truck which was different from the one he drove that morning. No surprise there, as something had to have filled the truck up and that something was not located in the truck yard across the street.

So tanker trucks were arriving at the yard fully loaded with petroleum, and then exiting the yard, being driven around Odessa to oil rigs only to be unloaded in a warehouse not connected to an oil refinery. What a strange picture. She picked up her phone and dialed Detective Guerrero.

"Hello."

"Hi, Detective. It's Jill Quint from the Adam Johnson case."

"Yes I remember your name."

"I've been watching Adam's employer for most of the day and something unexplained is going on. I wondered if you might help me."

"Sure, how can I help?"

"There are a series of warehouse type structures over on

Almond Lane. Do you know what business that is and what they keep in the warehouses?"

"I don't offhand, but give me thirty minutes and I can look it up in the city records. Do the warehouses appear to belong to a single business or are there several at that location? Do you have a street number?"

"The warehouses are not all uniform on the outside so I would guess more than one company is in there. There is no sign at the entrance and the address is 971 Almond Lane. I didn't see any building numbers or letters that might constitute an address within that address."

"Okay. Should I call you back at this number?"

"Yes."

They ended the call and Jill went back to writing down license plates of the tankers that entered and exited the oil company yard. She didn't see Adam behind the wheel again that day other than his drive home. She decided to call it a day and head back to Midland. On her way she called Nathan as much to cleanse her brain of oil tanker thoughts as to relax. He wasn't happy to hear about her smart watch surveillance, but she could also tell he didn't have a better idea. Like her, he was comforted by the thought of her driving around in a big pick-up truck. He'd thought he might visit her that weekend, but since she was working in Odessa there didn't seem much reason to fly four hours each way only to sit beside her in a truck watching her do surveillance. He thought that they would likely get on each other's nerves. She'd agreed with his line of thinking and they moved on to chat about other things.

As she reached Midland, she pulled into the gym's parking lot. She opened a locker and waited until the room was empty to remove her wig and place it inside. A few minutes later she was out on a treadmill undoing the damage of hours of surveillance duty sitting on her butt. They had a stretching cage that she used to contort her body a number of ways, loosening up her muscles and joints. Her mind felt much better after her workout and she could summarize for herself what she wanted to look at that night. Putting her Katy Perry wig back on, she was out of the gym and back at the hotel room in under ten minutes. Before going to the shower, she took another look at her email.

Detective Guerrero left her a voicemail with the property ownership of the warehouse area where the tanker had been that afternoon. He indicated that only one company owned that piece of property, but he didn't know if they had sub-leased parts of it to another business. Both the business license and property ownership records indicated the warehouse was owned by the BDC Company. Their mailing address was listed as the warehouse address and the primary business contact was Mary Garcia with an El Paso telephone number. Ok, she had some new contacts to search for later. Guerrero ended with the comment that he asked a few officers if they had ever been in those warehouses and the answer was 'no' and there were no crime reports filed on that address. She sent the BDC Company to Jo and Mary Garcia of El Paso to Marie to see if they could find her information. She didn't know their schedules that night to know if they had any time to work for her so she would do the same searches. Oftentimes if Jo and Marie spent twenty minutes in a search in their respective areas while she spent two hours doing the same thing, they got better results, so she would have to wait and see.

After a shower, she sat down with a sandwich, fruit, and a glass of wine to begin her search. The detective hadn't told her what the business license was for, but she noted on the city's website that there was a license relating to gas pumping and she would have bet that if that was the license he would have mentioned it. BDC seemed to be a subsidiary of a subsidiary. She hadn't yet found any names attached to the company. Worse still was looking for Mary Garcia of El Paso - there were sixty of them in every age group. The telephone number was disconnected. What had seemed promising an hour ago was fading. She paused on chasing that thread and looked at the tedious footage that the Odessa PD had obtained for her on the traffic cams.

She was able to locate several pictures of Adam driving different tanker trucks. She studied the license plates and determined that as many as thirty different tanker trucks entered the yard of Adam's employer, but Adam restricted himself to just four tanker trucks that he drove. Jill studied the four trucks to see if she could detect a different engine or weight about the tankers, but she couldn't detect anything that different about the tankers. Overall she saw perhaps three or four different models turning into the yard. The four trucks that Adam drove all were the same model but there were additional trucks of that same model that he didn't drive. How strange? Furthermore, he was somewhat predictable as to when he would take the trucks out. It was on a Monday, Wednesday, and Friday schedule, once in the morning around ten and then again around three. What was in those tanker trucks that Adam drove? What did it have to do with his wife's death?

She thought she'd have to do another day of surveillance to figure out this odd behavior. She'd read more on the petroleum industry and see if different oils were extracted from the earth and transported differently. Maybe some of it was natural gas. Could those oil tankers carry natural gas? Did you have to keep the two products completely separate from a safety perspective? She wrote Castillo a summary of what she was seeing and then copied Guerrero just in case he ever needed back-up or additional information from the local police.

She then gave up the search for a while and tuned into a cable television show devoted to watching a buyer examine houses for purchase, buying and then moving in. She made it a game to try and guess which one they would pick. She was only about fifty percent correct with her guesses. That show was followed by another show in a similar vein in some international location. Understanding property values around the United States and in the rest of the world was always good entertainment. She had one part of her brain tuned to the show and the rest of her brain focused on the trucks.

National Geographic had a nice website on petroleum. It was amazing that all the oil in the ground and the sea came from long dead fossils. Jill hadn't given thought to the number of dead dinosaurs that it would take to make the oil quantity that the earth seemed to have. Wow. Okay time to move on to more relevant facts to Stacy Johnson's murder. It was easy to get distracted by amazing but irrelevant pieces of knowledge. So beyond the dinosaurs it seemed that there were different types of petroleum related to where in the world the oil field was and it was primarily differentiated by sulfur. The oil of North America was distinctly different from that of the North Sea and the Arab desert region. Those main three types were easily separated by sulfur and color, but beyond those three major locations, minerals in the ground always played a role in what was contained in the oil. So there was no reason to think that Adam's company was extracting different types of oil when they were in the region of West Texas Intermediate crude; she supposed that the oil wells themselves could be comprised of enough different chemicals that it made sense to transport them by specific tankers and maybe Adam was pitching in when his company had a shortage of drivers. She pulled her Department of Motor Vehicles report and looked at when he had gotten the special trailer truck license and it was five years ago. That was a long time to have a labor shortage; but maybe it was seasonal shortage based on oil production fluctuations. She reviewed the literature on that idea and tossed it. Oil was oil and it came out of the ground at the same rate.

She couldn't figure out the answer as to why Adam regularly drove just a few trucks of his company's fleet. So she decided to move on to the question of what was in the warehouse that he drove the truck to. She'd made the assumption that he drove the truck to the same location and vowed to verify that the next day as well as follow another driver to see where they ended up. She knew there was a massive pipeline that moved crude oil to a tiny city in Oklahoma which was where the price of oil futures was set by the New York Mercantile exchange. Jill had never studied oil futures but knew that one of the airlines had made a considerable profit based on where the price was headed. She speculated that Adam's company extracted oil and then transported it either to a refinery in Big Spring Texas or to a storage or pipeline facility. She decided now she was just spinning her wheels with all of her speculation. She had to spend the day tomorrow following the trucks. Jill decided to sleep on it and start again the next day. She pulled out a book from one of her many favorite mystery authors and was ready to sleep after about ten pages.

Chapter Twenty

Jill was in position the next day to start following all trucks leaving the yard at an early hour. The first truck left about thirty minutes later and Jill followed it for forty miles. She was about to give up when it pulled off to an oil rig. The driver hooked a hose up to the rig and connected it to the tanker. It took about an hour to fill it and then the tanker drove back to Odessa, stopping at a pipeline company to unload.

Okay then that was new information. She followed two more trucks that fortunately were not that far out of town and they went through the same routine as the first driver she followed. So why were Adam's trucks different? It was time to sneak into the warehouse that he drove to. She thought back to the security around the area and couldn't recall any. Perhaps if she went after dark she could take a look at what was in the warehouse. Perhaps they had a hidden pipe line that ran inside the building and he was stealing crude oil from his employer. She bet herself she would find a hidden oil pipeline in the building.

She called Castillo to let him know about the situation and her plan to check out the warehouse.

"Jill, are you nuts? You want to go into an alleged vacant building under cover of dark to see what is inside because you think Adam is stealing crude oil? That doesn't make sense; you told me your friend had noted record profits from this company. How could they have record profits if someone is stealing two tankers full of crude oil three times a week?"

"That detective, is a real good question; I had forgotten that Jo said that somehow the company was making a lot more than its competitors even though the price of crude oil has dropped so much. Okay I'll have to re-think my thinking on this case. It can't be crude oil in the tanker. That's why I need to get into the warehouse to see what is in there."

"You have no back-up. Don't go in alone to a vacant building, that's law enforcement 101."

"When I was there earlier it seemed like an industrial area and I'll bet at night that no one will notice my snooping."

"And if they do? Your bug spray must nearly be empty and it only has a range of twenty feet" Castillo added sarcastically.

"Castillo, I am as big a chicken as the next person. If I see any signs of people being on the scene, I'll cancel my operation and go home to the hotel."

"How about calling Rogers and Guerrero for back-up?"

"Castillo, you know the cops can't sanction my entering private property with no cause."

"Yeah, but at least they could call the coroner sooner to take away your dead body."

"Ouch. Okay, I'll call and let them know that if I don't call them back in a certain amount of time to send the coroner for me."

"Jill, I'll call them and then call you back. Don't move from your hotel room until you hear from me."

She wasn't used to listening to orders, but she was a chicken and she likely thought that the least little noise would scare her off. She didn't like surprises and wasn't someone who went looking for trouble. She'd wait for Castillo to call back.

She looked at her closet and noted an array of black clothes and she had the black wig, so her hands and face were left to be covered up. Unknown to Nathan, she kept a black ski mask and gloves in a side compartment of her luggage. Unless she had a good reason to confess, she'd not tell him about her nighttime surveillance. There were no circumstances that she could imagine that conversation going well, so best not to detail it for him. She grabbed the mask and gloves now. She couldn't hide her white pick-up truck but she would remove the license plates so if someone did drive by, there would be no distinguishing marks about the vehicle.

Her cell phone rang and she answered, "This is Jill."

"Castillo, and Guerrero is also listening in on the phone. None of us are happy with your idea, but we don't have another way to understand what is going on in that warehouse. Whatever the activity is, it's likely breaking some law. Guerrero is going to provide you with night vision goggles, a vest, and helmet from their special tactics supplies. Rob will be at your hotel in about thirty minutes and he'll go with you onto the property."

"Awesome, thanks for your help detectives," Jill said cheerfully. This was far better than she expected. She'd get help and protection and her uncourageous soul would have the detective there to calm it down. The call ended after she gave the detective her hotel's address in Midland.

After twenty minutes had passed, she gathered her hat and gloves and stuffed her cell in a pocket along with a twenty dollar bill and went down to her hotel's lobby to await the arrival of the detective.

A few minutes later a large, dark vehicle pulled up to the entrance and Jill saw Guerrero inside; she approached the car and got in.

"Thanks for your help tonight and for the protective gear. I might have to think about getting my own vest for when I am on one of these cases."

"Just a vest? Not a gun or are you happy with a can of bug spray?"

"Go ahead and make fun of me, but it works and I don't like guns."

"Lady, you're in the wrong state. Guns are a part of every Texan's DNA."

"Yeah I know about the DNA thing; my friends in Wisconsin feel the same way about guns. I guess I loathe and detest them from seeing all the damage they inflict on the human body."

"I have a different perspective when I see the damage they do. Usually I am pleased that they're dead and I'm not because I had better aim."

"Wouldn't it be easier if they didn't have guns to begin with?"

"How do you propose to remove all guns from every American Citizen?" Guerrero asked. "We're talking millions. Beside the gun manufacturers, the entire hunting industry would put a bulls-eye on your back. The horse is so long out of the barn on this issue that you can't see it or hear it. When has banning something worked for America? Did prohibition work in the 1920s? Are we winning the war on drugs or marijuana? If Americans didn't overthrow the government on that idea and let a new law pass that banned the average citizen from owning a gun, don't you think the gangs and the cartels would soon control the gun trade and now you've just made them richer?"

"Yeah, I've thought of all those arguments too, and I've not intellectually figured out a way around them, but I'm not quite ready to let go of my fantasy of getting rid of guns in America."

"All right, well until you figure that out, I'll be backing you up with a gun tonight."

The car arrived at the warehouse location. Guerrero drove

past it once, assessing the layout and lighting, looking for a good place to hide their car and enter the business premises of the BDC Company. There appeared to be no cars parked inside the yard. There were no street lights in the area as it wasn't a main street or residential area. Jill thought that there appeared to be not another human being within ten miles of this place.

They parked the car on the second trip around the rather large block that fronted the company. To call it a block implied that there was a neighborhood or park of some sort but in this case it meant a series of country roads that with four right turns returned them to the warehouse location. They hadn't passed a single car during those four turns. The land was flat and hardscrabble. There was an abandoned oil rig less than a mile further down the road. They parked the vehicle behind the rig and walked back to the warehouse.

Guerrero used the night vision goggles to make sure they were alone. He then studied the property and building for cameras. Jill asked to use them and was impressed with what they brought into focus. She'd buy a set of her own in the future. There were many cameras on the end of the buildings and it seemed impossible to sneak in without being caught on a camera. Jill slapped herself in the helmet for thinking that she could have done this on her own without Guerrero's special equipment. Her idiocy was going to get her harmed or hurt in the future and she vowed to listen to the next law enforcement person who told her to do something in a particular way. She had a feeling this was going to be like sugar. She had signs in her office and kitchen that said 'no sugar', but she ignored them every single day.

"I see fixed cameras everywhere; they may or may not be plugged in," Guerrero reported. "Our best tactic might be to try and cut the power to this location for a few minutes while we take a look around."

"How do you do that?"

"See that fuse box over there," Guerrero said pointing to a grey box on the end of the first building. "I'll shut down the main. We may be caught on tape, but that assumes someone is watching on the other end or reviewing tapes in the future and that may or may not be the case. There is nothing identifying about you or me other than our height and perhaps sex. Try to keep your head turned to the ground as we move forward. Whatever you do, don't look up directly at any of the cameras."

"You're really good at this. Is this standard police training or did you come from some other agency?"

"I was a Navy seal and participated in a few covert operations around the world."

Jill guessed that was likely an understatement as the detective seemed to move with an ease and professionalism that spoke of extensive training. Castillo had probably known that when he lined her up with Guerrero.

Minutes later he'd thrown the main circuit. Jill couldn't tell the difference as it had been dark and quiet before they cut the power and it was still dark and quiet. Guerrero studied the other building looking for additional fuse boxes and saw one on each building. Hopefully they'd taken the cameras out by shutting off the power of the main building first, but they had no way of knowing how the security system was wired.

They saw a headlight in the distance and soon it appeared that a pick-up truck was approaching. They tensed, backs to the building with some cover from the front entrance. They both sighed when the truck continued past with no break in speed. Guerrero watched it for a minute longer just to make sure their car parked behind the oil rig did not claim the attention of the driver, but they could see it speeding along in the distance, no brake lights apparent.

They turned back to the work at hand and Guerrero asked, "Which of these buildings did your tanker truck enter?"

"Third one on the left," Jill said pointing to a large building.

Guerrero waved her on and they quickly moved to the building in question, staying in the deepest shadows along the way. The building had a garage door like those found in fire stations to accommodate large trucks like an oil tanker-truck. There was also a human-sized door on the left side of the large garage door. Guerrero pulled out a set of lock picks and proceeded to have them inside in a short time.

Jill stood there astounded. The cavernous room was completely empty. It looked like the large building had been picked up and placed on this piece of real-estate but the owner hadn't decided what the future use of the building was. There weren't even tire tracks to verify that the tanker-truck had been there.

"Are you sure you got the right building?"

"I thought so," Jill replied. "Did you see garage doors large enough for a tanker truck on any of the other buildings? Wait a minute! This is a completely dumb moment for me. I have a picture of the tanker entering the building." Jill said as she searched for the picture on her phone.

Guerrero leaned over and looked at Jill's picture. Yes, they definitely had the correct building.

"Let search the other buildings to see what's in them. BDC Company owns all of the buildings, correct?"

"That's correct," replied Jill as they walked towards the next building. A while later they had opened all of the buildings and found them in the same condition - clean, with no indication whatsoever of what the buildings were used for. Each of the buildings were so clean that it was hard to imagine the purpose of these warehouses, no shelves, equipment, or stains.

"I think we have seen all there is to see here," Guerrero said. "About all we could do is get some sniffer dogs in here, but they're limited to fruit and drugs. Perhaps my office can check with county tax folks to see if this business is paying sales taxes. Let's get out of here."

They were moving towards the front gate, still staying in the shadows when they saw more headlights in the distance. This time it appeared to be two cars and this time they did slow down as though to drive into the BDC lot.

Guerrero said in her ear, "This looks like trouble; let's take cover around these front gate posts. It's dark enough and they're big enough to provide us cover until the cars leave or their attention is diverted. If we need to make a run for it, can you jog?"

"I run three to four miles several times a week so I can jog all the way back to the car. I may be a little winded with the weight of this helmet and the vest."

They watched from their hiding place as the seven men spread out and entered all of the buildings with keys. Apparently they were owners or employees of BDC. They were talking in Spanish and at some distance from them.

Jill asked, "Do you speak Spanish?"

"Yes, but I'm only catching about a quarter of their words; they're too far away."

"Are those guns in their hands?"

"Yes."

Jill would've smacked herself a third time on the helmet but she wanted to stay quiet. How could she be so stupid to have thought she could've handled this on her own? Seven men with guns? What the heck was going on here? She was in way over her head.

They stayed down, knees drawn up, backs pressed to the stone pillar providing them a place to hide and waited out the men. They didn't have long to wait; after a full check of the property except the front gate pillars, they piled into the two cars and left and all was quiet.

When they could no longer see their lights, Guerrero said, "Even though it appears that they're gone, let's jog back to the car and we'll get the hell out of here as soon as possible."

With that they stood up and started jogging back to the car. Guerrero held a flashlight lighting their path, otherwise it would have been too dark to see the road. Jill was winded by the time they reached the car. Whether it was from the additional weight or the scare she didn't know. Later she would think about the risks she was taking; maybe Guerrero might be the person to discuss this with as he seemed to have a very wise head on his shoulders.

"Thanks for taking the lead on this nighttime surveillance effort with me. I admit, I was way over my head thinking it was safe or wise to do this on my own. I have had a sub-par performance each time I've tried surveillance. How did you learn to do what you did back there? Was it the Navy or your law enforcement training?"

"It was my SEAL training and then the use of that training on operations. You drill so much in the military that it becomes second nature. Within law enforcement, we drill entering a building in which dangerous people are hiding, but it's possible depending on your career as a cop to go through that career and never be faced with the need for some sort of covert action. If you want to learn the skills yourself there are a couple of military contractors that can train you for a price. You could hone your skills a little playing paintball."

"Paintball?"

"Yeah, depends on the course, but you need to be able to sneak around on a paintball course so as not to get hit by paint. Try it sometime."

"I will. That sounds intriguing. My boyfriend, Nathan is a Master Black Belt at hapkido and I'm sure he would enjoy reminding me how I need to absorb more self-defense and a sense of self-protection skill. He'd probably have me covered in paint in under ten minutes, but if I could learn to last longer on the course with him, that would help me with operations like tonight. Thanks Detective, for your help and advice."

"What's your plan for tomorrow?"

"More surveillance, I guess" Jill said. "I want to see if they go back to those buildings again with tanker-trucks."

"How does that help you solve Stacy Johnson's murder?"

"Wow, you really know how to cut to the heart of my decision making."

"Why are you so focused on Adam driving these trucks to this building?"

Jill thought for a moment. It was really clarifying to talk to Detective Guerrero.

"Because past experience has taught me to look for pieces of any picture that don't fit and that is what this tanker-truck is. Stacy had the marriage and the three children with her college sweetheart. That sweetheart is a petrochemical engineer driving just four trucks of his company's fleet. So here is what doesn't make sense - we have a highly educated engineer who is driving a truck six times a week to this warehouse where there is no refinery or pipeline located. The truck looks visibly lighter when it leaves this building so something is happening here that I need to witness to understand."

"I'd advise against doing that tomorrow," Guerrero said.

"I'm sure the seven men with guns from tonight will be in this area."

"Yeah, I agree with you. Is there a police reason you could invade their property while the truck was there?"

"You could call me on your cell phone when you see the truck pull in and report suspicious activity. That would give me a reason to get pretty far onto the property. I wouldn't have probable cause to search the property, but if I can walk into the warehouse because no one stops me, I will."

"Will you have a partner with you?" Jill asked.

"Yes, you never walk into a suspicious activity call without a partner."

"Good. I'll do as you suggest. Now I just need to decide how to track Adam and his truck. I assume he'll go to a particular pump station to check it and from there swing over to this warehouse. I think I'll rent a different color truck and get a different wig so if he does notice me following him he won't connect it to today's journey."

"Good idea and maybe I can help you on the tail. When you see it leave the yard, follow him, and call me. I'll pick up the tail for a while, and then you can reappear and take over."

"Thanks, Detective, for your help with this case. I realize it's not your homicide investigation and I appreciate the time you're giving it."

"This is my town and something is going on in those warehouses. I don't like seven men showing up with guns to investigate a security system breach. I don't believe they were on my side of the law," said Guerrero.

"Okay, I'll be in position around 9:30 and I'll text you to confirm."

They had been talking on the drive back to Jill's hotel and the detective pulled up next to the portico. Jill exited the car and entered the hotel lobby and was shortly back in her room. It was closing in on midnight which was way beyond her usual bedtime. She still had a partial adrenaline feeling from their encounter with the seven men. She'd tell Nathan much later and perhaps never about her experience tonight. She was asleep soon after her head hit the pillow.

Chapter Twenty-One

Jill awoke refreshed and ready to tackle Adam and his trucks this morning. She arranged a second rental car and hit a Halloween store in town to pick-up a new costume. She decided on a Donald Trump mask as she liked the idea of looking like a male rather than a female if Adam caught a glimpse of her in his rear view mirror. With a baseball cap over the mask, and a loose jacket covering her curves, she looked like a male driver. She wondered if she would explode from heat between the mask, hat, and jacket. Even though it was sixty degrees outside, she had the air conditioning on inside the car trying to cool off.

She arrived at her surveillance spot thirty minutes before she expected Adam to leave his company's yard. She put her iPhone on her dashboard so she could read the phone and catch movement coming from the yard at the same time. She had an email from Jo about the BDC Company.

"I expected the company to be owned by a famous celebrity. I chased the company through at least six other companies before I lost track of it when the parent company became Romero Enterprises of Mexico City. Then I had to do a quick search to understand how businesses are owned and operated in Mexico. Nearly 90% are family owned so finding the connection between companies and their leadership structure is like doing an ancestry search. It was one of the more intriguing searches I've done for you. I could give you the labyrinth that I traveled, but I'll cut to the chase and tell you what is at the end of the tunnel. BDC is connected to the family that operates the Precursor Chemical Cartel which does exactly what it sounds like - it moves chemicals that are used in the production of drugs and especially methamphetamines. I did the lightest of searches on this cartel and from my five minutes devoted to them, they

are worse than the Sinaloa Cartel. Quit this case and GO HOME."

Wow, that was the strongest advice that Jill had ever seen Jo provide. Worse than the Sinaloa Cartel? She didn't think you could get worse, but she guessed there were all levels of sickos in these cartels and their personalities were reflective of their leadership.

She was musing over Jo's email when she caught a truck movement out of the corner of her eye and noted that Adam was on the move. She made sure her mask and cap were on straight and put the car in gear to follow him, texting Guerrero as she went.

As in the previous trips, the tanker drove to a pumping oil rig and after some notations, moved on. Guerrero had taken over for her about four miles into their journey and then they switched back again. Jill had stopped a little less than a thousand feet away. She'd used her binoculars to verify Adam's actions at the oil rig, then she turned around her car and parked in a convenience store lot waiting for his tanker truck to drive by on its way to the warehouse location. Fifteen minutes later, the tanker truck went sailing by. She let it get further down the road before picking up the tail.

They were in a busy part of Odessa and so she could hang back and not worry about the driver seeing her or her losing track of the truck. She was most surprised when the truck continued beyond the turnoff for the warehouse. She sped up until just three cars separated the distance for fear of losing him as she called Guerrero.

"He missed the turn-off for the BDC warehouse. Can you look up that company and see if they own any other properties in town? I got an email from one of my teammates who is a financial whiz and she tracked the company through Texas and into Mexico. It's a subsidiary of a subsidiary and so on until the company shows up as related to someone in the Precursor Chemical Cartel. Have you heard of them?" Jill asked.

"No. Did you make that name up?"

""No, the Mexican Government did. Apparently their focus is moving around the chemicals used in the manufacture of heroin, cocaine and methamphetamines."

"I haven't heard about that cartel, but I guess it makes sense from a manufacturing perspective. While we were talking, I looked up BDC Company in the county tax records and there're additional properties owned by that company. Looking at the addresses, they're all within two miles of the interstate, evenly spread around the city. Since you're traveling west, there're two properties that could be his destination. The first property is off of State Highway 338."

"Adam's truck is coming upon that exit and he's not signaling that he plans to exit the freeway. Now we're past that exit ramp, so what's the next property he might be visiting?"

"Okay the other property is in the direction that you're going. It'll be two off ramps from where you're presently located. That will take you a few miles outside the city, and less than a mile off the interstate. I'll warn you that that area is flat and with few houses so it will be hard to hide your car if you follow too closely."

"If I stay on the interstate and sail past that exit, how far do I have to go before I can turn around? Trucks have to slow down so much getting off an Interstate, I fear it will be very hard to stay well back in a car."

"The next exit is four miles away. You could speed up and pass the tanker truck, take the second exit make a U-turn and get back on the freeway to come back east and get off at the exit I suspect Adam is taking. That exit will provide your car some cover."

"My binoculars are good for a thousand feet, but I assume this property is a little more distant than a thousand feet. How about if I go back under the interstate and travel perhaps a quarter-mile before I pull off and pull out the binoculars. Do you think I'll be able to see the property that you're speaking about?"

"Yes. The odd thing about this property is I don't believe there are any buildings on it. So not sure what he's doing."

"I'll call you back when I'm in position," Jill said.

"Call me back regardless in six minutes."

"Okay," and they disconnected the call.

Jill was trying to watch in her rearview mirror for the tanker truck, but there was just enough of a rise that she occasionally lost sight of the traffic behind her. She saw her exit up ahead, got off, made a turn under the interstate, and got back on going the direction she'd come from. Another three minutes and she was back to the designated off-ramp which she took. Watching her odometer she traveled about a quarter of a mile and pulled off the road. Picking up her binoculars from the seat beside her, she looked ahead for the tanker truck. It had just made a turn into an oil rig off the road that she was on. She observed Adam connecting the tanker truck to something on the oil rig. That was a first, she hadn't seen him connect the truck to anything in the previous couple of trips.

She noted that the rig was not moving. All of the other oil rigs that he pulled up to had that circular pumping motion going, indicating that they were pulling crude oil out of the earth. She noted that but didn't take any pictures as she was sure her camera did not have enough zoom on it to catch the truck in the distance. She made a U-turn and returned to the freeway ramp that would take her back to Odessa. She put her car in reverse and backed up as far as she could and still stay hidden from the main traffic of the interstate as well as from the tanker truck when it eventually went back to Odessa.

Jill updated Guerrero a few times as she waited another thirty minutes or so before she saw the tanker truck enter the interstate to travel back to Odessa. She was torn whether to follow the tanker or to go look at the oil rig. She had plenty of daylight hours ahead of her so she could come back and look at the oil rig later. It was more important to see where the tanker truck drove.

She relayed the information to Guerrero in a text. It soon became apparent that Adam was heading back to his employer's truck yard. The story kept getting stranger and stranger she thought. She could've sworn that the tanker truck was full when it approached the oil rig and empty upon its return to the petrochemical company yard. Why would you unload a tanker truck into an oil rig? It should have been the reverse. Why wasn't the oil rig moving? Was there a public database that told her which oil wells were producing and which ones had been abandoned for a lack of production?

Jill acknowledged that there were several strange and probably illegal actions on the part of Adam Johnson, but was that information getting her anywhere with Stacy's homicide investigation or was she on a wild goose chase? She really didn't know. She called Castillo and checked in with him.

"Detective Castillo."

"It's Jill. I wanted to update you on where I am with this investigation including a connection to a different Mexican cartel than the Sinaloa cartel."

Jill went on to explain the developments over the last twenty-four hours including the trip to the oil well.

"I think we need to get a sample from these tanker trucks

to understand what's inside them. I'll give Guerrero a call and see if he has any tactics we could use to examine the truck. Maybe we could have a state trooper pull it over for a traffic violation and get a sample at that time. I agree with you, Jill, that you're not making fast progress with this case, but what you may be uncovering is a motive. If Adam was transporting an illegal substance and his wife found out about it and she's worked in the healthcare field, then as a couple, they may have had some kind of moral compass crisis within their marriage. Then we have our motive."

"Is there something I'm not investigating, that you think I should?" Jill asked.

"Based on what you described I think something illegal is going on here. If you don't catch Stacy's murderer, I think you will catch someone else who's committing some kind of crime based on whatever is in that tanker truck. If it's cocaine or if it's ephedrine which is used to make methamphetamines, then we'll solve the crime for the Odessa Police Department. My gut tells me you're on the verge of something big and you just need to hang in there and wait for it."

"Okay, I'll keep trucking along as they say." Jill said and they ended their call.

Jill looked at her watch and assumed she had several hours before Adam went out on another trip. She could grab a bite to eat then go visit the oil well to see if she could figure out what they put in it, if indeed something was put in a well there. Guerrero was also working his end trying to figure out if he had found all the properties owned by BDC Company and looking at a couple of state databases to see if anyone was required to report oil production at each well and whether it was active or closed. She'd asked him some of the same questions she'd asked Castillo and got the same answers.

She brought with her a compact test kit that allowed her to perform a few tests on site. However, if she was dealing with liquid cocaine, if there was such a thing, or ephedrine, then she couldn't test for it. She did have some test tubes that she could fill with whatever she could pull out of the oil pump. While she ate her lunch, she studied a diagram of the model of oil rig she thought she'd seen this morning. She needed to know where to extract samples from without having oil under pressure explode all over her. She had an idea of what to do when she reached the rig. She cleaned up after her lunch, hit the restroom and planned to drive out to the oil rig.

Having performed her fair share of surveillance in her short private detecting career, she was attentive to who was around her. If she could spy on people, then they could do likewise and it never paid to put down your guard. She hadn't noticed anyone following her which was a good sign. She exited the Interstate and stopped at the point she had that morning and used her binoculars to scan the terrain in front of her. She saw nothing - no movement, no cars, no people, and no cows. Why had they built an off ramp at this location? Maybe all the activity was on the south side of the Interstate rather than this north side. With five minutes of study and no activity she felt safe to proceed to the oil rig. Like this morning, it wasn't in motion. She pulled to the side of the road again as she got closer to check for cameras on the rig. She'd no desire to encounter the seven men with guns from last night. There was no camera that she could spot on the rig. There were utility poles in the area and she studied those as well, but couldn't see all sides of the pole from her single vantage point. She drove down the road beyond the oil rig and again studied it and the utility poles for any surveillance cameras. It looked like the coast was clear and she could visit the rig without discovery. Before she put the car in gear, Jill again studied the diagram of how the rig worked and where she might sample the oil. She had a final thought that she should leave her car well beyond the oil rig and walk back to it to avoid someone seeing her car from the interstate. It helped that her subcompact car was sort of that same desolate dirt color of the landscape around the road. She took her purse containing car keys, cell phone, test tubes, pipette and tubing, and bug spray and set off down the road in a jog. Better to be quick and get the heck out of this area.

She approached the oil rig and pulled out her camera to study where Adam had connected the truck's hose. It appeared to be connected to a tank which made sense. What did an oil rig do with the oil that comes out of the ground; it must be stored somewhere. She opened the cap on the storage container and used a paper napkin to wipe the edges. She then stuck a small-bore plastic tubing into the storage tank and used the pipette to suck the tubing to get the flow of whatever was in the tank going. She soon had her sample for her test tube. She put her stuff in separate plastic bags then screwed on the cap and took off on a jog to her car. She checked her watch and it had taken a total of seven minutes to jog to the rig, get her samples and jog back. She was in her car and moving forward to the interstate overpass. As she was under the overpass, she noted in her rearview mirror, one of the cars that appeared at the warehouse the previous night. She remembered the car as it was a 1970's gas guzzling large car. She gunned it onto the interstate ramp watching in her mirror to see if the car followed her. It must not have seen her as it continued toward the rig with apparently all eyes trained on activity at the oil rig. Jill heaved a sigh of relief and headed back to the Odessa Police Department. She would dump the specimens with the detective, return to Midland and return this car, then get back in her pickup truck and come back to watch Adam's afternoon run.

Jill completed everything in her plan and slid into her surveillance spot with just a few minutes to spare. She hoped that Adam hadn't changed his schedule and left early. Guerrero was again going to join her in surveillance as they had received the Odessa Crime Lab results on the substance in the test tube that she had collected. It was indeed methylamine in a solution of methanol, ethanol, water, and tetrahydrofuran. This was a major chemical precursor to methamphetamine and there was no legitimate reason for that chemical to be stored next to a dead oil rig. After they followed Adam's second tanker-truck drive, Jill and Guerrero would be meeting with the Narcotics unit.

Around his usual time, Adam pulled out in one of the four trucks. Guerrero provided her with a list of all the oil wells and Adam's employer had around one hundred. If they were unable to track Adam, they simply had too many oil wells to guess where else the truck might be. Guerrero was joining her tail shortly and then she could fall back for a while. Adam made it easy for them this time, picking an oil rig that was close to a residential tract. It was easy to track him this time and the oil well he visited was in motion pumping.

After spending five minutes of reading the gauges and writing down measurements, Adam got back in the truck and was on the move. She studied how the truck moved on the road and thought the tanker full. So either Adam was going to do something different, or he would visit another oil well or warehouse to dump his load. Jill and Guerrero were in communication trying to anticipate where the tanker truck was going. They had their list of BDC company property locations which was much smaller when compared to the number of oil wells owned by Adam's employer. It soon became clear he was heading for one of those properties and Jill, following at a safe distance, caught a glimpse of the truck entering a warehouse.

They had enough information to hint at a large drug manufacturing operation. It was time to return to police headquarters and bring more people in to discuss next steps. They had arranged for Castillo to join them by phone and they sat down with a number of fellow officers from Guerrero's department as well as Chief Swanson. He'd asked Jill to begin the conversation with Castillo filling in where necessary concerning the murder of Adam's wife. Jill included the research done by Jo about Adam's employer, and the pattern of truck and chemical movements occurring in the city.

"We need some more resources to understand this complete case," Guerrero said. "It appears we have cartel activity in our city and if I'm honest it's probably more than one of the cartels operating here. The required chemicals to make methamphetamines are being distributed and stored through the BDC Company and some oil wells. I think our next steps are to get inside and search all of the buildings of the BDC Company as well as any non-pumping oil rigs owned by Adam's employer."

"What's the name of the company that Adam Johnson works for?" asked another cop.

"Vernon Oil Company," replied Jill.

"What do we know about the company besides its strange financials?"

"They've been around for about fifteen years and they own perhaps a hundred oil wells in this state," Jill said. "They operate their own transportation and deliver their tankers of crude oil to a processor in town. They employ about thirty people who are either sourcing, drilling, or maintaining their present oil wells or they drive the trucks that move the crude oil from the wells to the processing point. Vernon Oil was started by two men and it's privately owned. Adam Johnson was hired to work there out of college; he's one of their longest serving employees. By training, he's a petrochemical engineer and he's had a semi-truck driver's license for several years."

"So what do you think is really going on here?" asked someone in the room, of Detective Guerrero.

"We have a petrochemical engineer who is making regular, perhaps even scheduled, deliveries of the chemicals used to make methamphetamines. We have at least one nonoperational oil well owned by Vernon Oil that is storing one of those chemicals. We have several properties owned by the BDC Company which according to Jill's expert eventually traces back to the family operating the Precursor Chemical Cartel in Mexico. In the middle of all this, is the death of Stacy Johnson which was quite sophisticated and generally not associated with a hit from a cartel. Furthermore, an attempt was made on Jill's life in Dallas and we don't know who those men were or why they have not followed her here to Odessa and really what their role was in the case."

Castillo asked, "Detective, what do you think are the next steps? I really need to question Adam Johnson in regards to his wife's murder. I've been sitting back waiting to see what information could be collected on him. Stacy's poisoning by blueberry muffin seems to be the sort of murder a petrochemical engineer might try. I'm sensitive though to the size of the drug distribution center that you may be close to uncovering there in Odessa."

"It would be helpful if you could hold off a day or so, on interviewing Adam Johnson. I'm no narcotics expert, but for the safety of my fellow officers, I think we may need to bring in the bigger guns of the DEA."

"The agency has an office in El Paso and I would guess that methamphetamine chemicals are crossing the border between Juarez and El Paso. I'm going to step out of the conference room and see if I can get them to come to Odessa," and the narcotics detective left the room.

"While he's lining up help with the DEA, I think we can do a little more detecting on our own here," Guerrero suggested. "Normally we would want to pursue a search warrant to sample the non-pumping oil wells of Vernon Oil and investigate the buildings of the BDC Company. I'm afraid if we tip our hand we could lose the opportunity to shut down this operation and the people involved. I also don't think we even know the scope of the operation without a little more investigation."

There was silence in the room as they thought about the scope of the narcotics operation and the risks both from a legal and physical safety perspective to some undercover work. The narcotics detective stepped back in.

"The DEA is highly interested in joining our operation and they're taking one of their border surveillance planes to get here within two hours. They're aware of this cartel and would love to be involved in an operation that puts a dent into their transportation network."

"Looks like it's going to be a long night for all of us, let's all take five to let our families know we may not be home for dinner," said the Chief and the room quickly emptied leaving Jill and Castillo on the phone.

"Detective, are you going to join the party here?" Jill asked.

"Sent an email to my lieutenant to see if I can make the 6pm flight to Midland."

"Let me know if you're coming and I'll fetch you at the airport."

"I think you can probably plan on it. I'd be surprised if the lieutenant denies it as it's good for the department on several levels."

"Okay, I'll keep you posted on what's happening here and see you at the airport later."

She disconnected the call and sat there for the moment. She knew she was going to be barred from joining them on the actual operation which was fine by her. She didn't need to be shot at to feel like a valued member of their team. She could contribute by doing computer searches on stuff like how were the chemicals arriving in Odessa. She had plenty of views of Adam leaving Vernon Oil but none of the tanker-trucks driving into the Vernon yard. Maybe she could go back to the footage she had requested of Guerrero that first day and see if she could spot the trucks driving into town.

Ten minutes later, after using the license plates as a marker, she found numerous views of the same four trucks traveling up the interstate. They all came from the same direction at nearly the same time. She guessed that the cartel was good at the logistics of transportation. She then checked the license plates on a few of the trucks that Adam didn't drive and found that they individually came from a variety of directions towards the Vernon Oil yard. She contacted Guerrero and asked if he could obtain the footage of trucks crossing the border in El Paso as she was searching for the four trucks that Adam drove. He thought he could and within the hour she had footage of the traffic on Interstate 20 from about a month ago. Using software on her laptop, she set her facial recognition to look for the four license plates of the trucks that Adam drove.

The footage was for a period of a week and she observed the four trucks crossing the border checkpoint traveling in both directions several times during that week. Likely the border guards stopped the tankers at the border and looked for oil. Either the tanker was specially engineered to hold oil and something else, or they had bought off the border crossing guards. She thought it was likely the former. In order to build their legal case and understand the size of this operation, she asked Guerrero to see if they could obtain tapes from a year ago or even four years ago. He passed on her request to his contact but did not expect a reply until the next morning.

The Chief had an arrival time of the DEA agents and scheduled a meeting to accommodate that arrival time. He gave thought of others to invite and decided to keep the group limited as one never knew where the cartel had informants including inside the State of Texas. With everyone kicking back over the next two or more hours, Jill decided to give Nathan a call and update him on the situation. He would be pleased to know that the 'real' cops would be doing any hidden surveillance.

Chapter Twenty-Two

"Hey babe, how's Odessa Texas," asked Nathan.

"Interesting at the moment," Jill said as she gave Nathan a review of the day's developments.

"I'm very glad you're not going out with the police to investigate the oil wells and buildings. If this is the tip of the iceberg of a cartel transportation business, it's going to get violent at some point."

"Yeah, I agree," Jill said and then went on to tell him about the previous night's caper.

"Why didn't you tell me about that this morning?" Nathan asked.

"It was too early in the day for you to worry about me."

"When you're on a case, I have a baseline level of worry about you every day, but in this case I might have actually felt better knowing there was a cop with you and you were wearing body armor."

"Have I told you how much I love you today? I really appreciate your support for my job."

"Love you too, Jill and this case worries me. You know these narco guys carry automatic weapons. They don't have to have precision to kill you rather they do sweep arcs with the gun which makes it very hard to survive; it's rather like a firing squad. Your bug spray will lose against the might of their guns."

"Actually I agree with you and I'm content to stay behind the cops. Even Jo said to quit the case. I don't think any of us are underestimating the fire power of this group."

"When do you think you'll be home?" Nathan asked.

"I really don't know," Jill replied. "I don't have proof of the murder, yet. The DEA and Odessa police may break open a huge narcotics transportation and manufacturing scheme for which Adam will surely go to jail, but I've got nothing that ties him to his wife's murder. It's been very frustrating. Perhaps if they have enough to arrest Adam today and get a search warrant for his house, we'll find the arsenic used in the blueberry muffins, but even that may be hard to prove. If Adam is thought to be in jail for a long time, the Dallas PD may decide that's enough for them and fire me as a consultant. Arsenic is not used at all in the petroleum industry and is really only used in the manufacturing of semi-conductors. So if some of the compound is found in his house, he would have no reason to own it. It's circumstantial evidence but people have been convicted with much less."

"Trixie is beginning to miss you. I took her for a run yesterday and she wasn't happy that I run at a faster pace than you. She didn't have sufficient time to sniff all the animal scents that she wanted."

"I can imagine," Jill said with a laugh. "You run the mile nearly three minutes faster than I and as a breed known for running along with horses, she has the speed. She just can't multi-task like she does with me."

Jill looked up as people came into the conference room and said, "Got to go, love you."

Jill viewed the new faces that filed into the conference room. She waited for introductions and had her thoughts confirmed that these were the DEA agents. She looked at her watch and noted that Castillo's plane arrived in half an hour at the Midland airport. Jill knew she didn't want to leave this conference room and go pick him up so she texted him suggesting that she was needed here and for him to get a rental car or taxi.

Guerrero had been given the lead on this group from the Odessa group and so he began the meeting by calling for introductions and an explanation of why they were in the room. When Jill's turn came she could see surprise on several faces when she mentioned the murder and her role with Dallas PD.

"Dr. Quint, do you think there is a connection between the murder and this chemical transportation network?" asked Agent Black of the DEA.

She provided a lengthier explanation of Adam's lies about Stacy's relationship to the Sinaloa cartel and her encounter with the men in the parking lot in Dallas. Then she answered the agent's question.

"Yes, I think there is a relationship between the two events. I think that Stacy somehow found out about Adam's role in the transportation. Maybe she saw his truck license and asked, or maybe she was driving around town and saw Adam driving the truck. She had a life insurance policy through her employer and getting that money was probably icing on the cake. Adam seems to have a central role in this transportation process and this has to be generating income for him."

Jill continued, "One of my team members researched Vernon Oil and said the company had strange financials. It was gaining more cash for its shipments than other oil companies. So Adam can't be the only one that knows those tankers are filled with something other than oil. My team has been unable to locate how Adam is personally profiting from his role and he must. Why would he risk it all if not to have a financial benefit? So perhaps he has a separate identity and bank account in Mexico and payments are deposited there."

She finished her explanation and noted a text from Castillo

that he'd landed and rented a car and would be at Odessa PD in about twenty-five minutes.

"And you have been unable to identify the men who posed as hotel employees nor the three in the parking lot in Dallas?" questioned Agent Black.

"I have what I consider to be the best facial and object recognition software in the world, and because we don't have full frontal facial pictures of the men, I've been given over one-hundred matches. If these are cartel minions, and they haven't touched the justice system in Mexico, then it is possible that they are not in any worldwide databases and my list of matches."

"Did you try to pare down those one hundred matches?"

"No, would you like the list?"

"Yes, we have a separate database that collects pictures of cartel men that we have captured on cameras placed in areas that we know they hang-out like bars and stripper clubs," replied Agent Black. "So this picture collection of ours is not on any known database worldwide."

"It would be helpful on many levels if you could identify these men." Jill said. "I just sent it to you, so you should see it in your in-box."

"Thank you, Dr. Quint. I've a much smaller database as you can imagine and it excludes men's names often given the circumstance in which it is collected, but we do have the men identified by cartel affiliation. Detective Guerrero, tell me about the operation you were planning on running tonight."

"We have all of the properties of the BDC Company that we'd like to explore. Jill and I did one warehouse last night and found a perfectly clean and empty warehouse where a tanker truck had sat for an hour earlier in the day. There were cameras on the building dismantled by cutting the power, but the camera caught our image before that happened. We had seven armed thugs show up to take us on. So I would expect the other properties to be similarly wired if they're used for the same purpose. I also worry that we're tipping our hand to this group if we activate additional cameras."

"We also have the tank storage next to the non-pumping oil rig," Guerrero continued. "I'm guessing there are more storage tanks out there among the one-hundred plus wells Vernon Oil owns. I would really like to get a full inventory of the sites this group is using. We'll also have evidence in the four tanker trucks that Adam Johnson drives. We called the DEA into this operation because we need more manpower to get a full view of the evidence of the cartel operation. The last thing I want to see happen is for us to shut down a single warehouse, arrest Adam and the seven thugs, but allow the rest of the cartel's operation to stay untouched; so I would like to have a discussion of how we achieve our goal of getting the entire operation closed and as many people arrested and sent to prison for as long a time as possible."

Castillo walked into the room and more introductions occurred as he was quickly briefed on the discussion. The DEA agent asked Castillo what the role of the Dallas PD was.

"All I have so far is a gut feeling that Adam Johnson orchestrated his wife's death. As it occurred while she was speaking at a convention, visitors and the business community want to see this case solved. If you guys convict Adam for narcotics trafficking, that's great but it would be far better if we can get him on both charges. I'm happy to add my manpower to whatever operation you decide on, but that's the extent of the involvement of the Dallas PD in your case. You're chasing a narcotics kingpin, I'm chasing a murderer and I think they're one in the same person."

"You probably need to include to some degree, the Mexico side of the operation," Jill suggested. "I bet those four tanker trucks have some kind of document that shows that they are coming from a Mexican oil company. Crude oil is legitimately moved across the Mexican border to American refineries. According to the schedule I have seen on tape, a truck will cross the border early morning tomorrow. It would be helpful to get a copy of the documents the truck shows to the border guards. Can you place an agent at the crossing to do that?"

"Dr. Quint, for having no background on the narcotics trade, you're doing a great job thinking about the full scope of this operation; that's a great suggestion."

"For me, this is still a murder investigation and I'm used to thinking about all the threads of evidence I should follow, often not knowing which one will bear relevant new information."

Another DEA agent in the room spoke up, "We have a match on your three suspects from Dallas to the Precursor Chemical Cartel. Do you want their names?"

"Yes," Jill said. "I want to look them up in my database to see if they were one of the more than one-hundred suggestions."

"Marco Aurelio Lopez Franco, Edgar Flores Lopez, and Jacobo Montellano Minero."

Jill went to work searching for them in her database and found them. She sent the names to Marie to see what she could find on them. At this point, their only relevance was in finding out how they knew when Jill was walking from police headquarters to her hotel.

"How are you going to identify everyone connected to this operation?" Jill asked. "Is it all the employees of Vernon Oil? How about the drivers crossing the border - how do you collect everyone in one sweep? How about the guys that attacked me?

Where are they now? I know I sound like I'm having a panic attack on capturing this group, but as I said earlier to someone in this room, we are only seeing the tip of the iceberg with my one tank filled with methylamine. There's a bunch of logistics in play here that need to be identified."

"Dr. Quint, this is not our first rodeo as they say in Texas," replied Agent Black. "I know we need to gather more names and better understand the scope of the operation so we snuff it out completely. Let's keep the discussion going and see if we have any more brilliant ideas like your suggestion of the border crossings."

"Sorry Agent Black, I like speedy resolutions to my investigations and I'm lacking the patience with this case. Just ignore my outbursts."

The agent smiled at her and moved on, but Jill still felt like she was six inches tall in this room of giant law enforcement personnel. She'd have to learn not to think out loud with this group. Jill tuned back in to see Agent Black defining an operation on the whiteboard. He started with the scope they were aware of and then added tangents of information they needed to collect. He also added legal actions they would take at the appropriate time and projected outcomes. The discussion went on for several hours as the group fleshed out the plan.

It was getting late and Jill still had the twenty minute drive back to Midland. Her two points of interest in solving the crime were the interview of Adam Johnson and the search of his home. They might be able to match any arsenic found in Adam's home to that which was in Stacy's blueberry muffin. Agent Black was laying out a plan to investigate the oil wells owned by Vernon Oil. When he assigned another agent to map out the wells then stop and get a sample at each, Jill remembered to add something to the discussion.

"By the way guys, I forgot to mention that when I sampled the non-moving oil rig this morning, I escaped a second round of the seven thugs. I passed just out of their view to get back on the Interstate as they exited and headed towards the oil well. So they must have some kind of security that I set off."

Half of the room was giving her a look of awe for almost coming in to contact with the seven thugs while the other half was giving her a frustrated look for her leaving out such a key point.

So she added, "Just saying you'll want to be careful that the entire operation doesn't get suspicious and disappear to set up this activity in another town. I would think they would already be on edge between our entry into the warehouse last night and my setting off security at the oil rig this afternoon. Also I have facial and object recognition software on my laptop that is very good. If you want to feed me a satellite view of the oil wells, I bet I could have them identified in about ten minutes."

As this would result in a much quicker answer than driving to each well, an agent made arrangements to get Jill the footage and she was forgiven her earlier lapse. She wanted to talk to Castillo about the murder without the rest of the room listening so she texted him.

If the three thugs from the convention center are from the cartel and Adam is doing deliveries for the cartel, then I would assume he knows I'm working with you.

It was a long text but she'd never mastered texting shorthand. He texted back.

I think that's a safe assumption. So what?

Good question on Castillo's part; so what did she care if he knew she was on the case? She thought about that one for a while.

I guess I can dump my current wig and move my hotel from Midland to Odessa.

Jill began looking up hotels in Odessa when the text arrived.

He may not know that you've been in Odessa for two days. He may think you're still in Dallas.

She thought about Castillo's response then replied.

No way could he think that when I haven't used the shuttle for a few days or been spotted near the hotel.

The cartel guys had her under surveillance when she was in Dallas to know when she exited the police building.

True

Okay the master of the short response was back. Maybe she'd stay in Midland since she had the small kitchen and the gym worked out and she might not find the same in Odessa. Besides she didn't need to be close to the action as she wouldn't be participating. Jill sat back to think about the murder investigation and what more she could do. Then she noted the ping from the DEA agent with the satellite footage. She ran it through her software and quickly had the locations of the non-working oil wells. There were forty of them. Either this was the largest storage cache of drug making chemicals in the history of America, or not all of the non-working oil rigs were being used for that purpose.

Jill tuned back in to the discussion about how to organize the surveillance of the non-working oil rigs and an idea came to mind.

"We know that there are four trucks that are crossing the US-Mexico border and those same four trucks are driven by Adam Johnson. If we looked at road cameras, I bet we could see if those four trucks are visiting a non-working oil rig and from that we would have our answer. It wouldn't tell what was being stored there, but it would tell you that it was likely not oil."

"Dr. Quint, you're redeeming yourself with these excellent ideas," said a grinning Agent Black. "I assume that software program of yours would be able to process that information quickly. I would like to see your software in action on this search. Where did you get it?"

"Almost two years ago, I solved a murder in Belgium. The man who created this software sells it worldwide and was the husband of the victim, so I first used it to solve his wife's murder. I'd be happy to demo it for you and give you his contact information if you want to pursue a purchase."

"Depends on his price, but as you've used it in this room, you've cut hours off of our investigation and that can mean we've a bigger net to catch more thugs if we move quicker. Do you have any ideas on the warehouse?"

"Same approach, let's first make sure those four trucks visit all of the locations. Once we have confirmation we need to use some kind of camera blocker - it's being watched somewhere because the thugs showed up about twelve to fifteen minutes after I got there and I guess my face is on their recording and now that I think about it, it may have given the whole game away if they identify me. Perhaps we should spread out immediately among the warehouses and oil rigs to see if they're dismantling something. The chemicals that they are transporting and storing must have a street value. Is that something to walk away from or do they try to move out their inventory elsewhere?"

Jill comments caused the room to go quiet. With her few sentences the timing of the operation had changed from days to minutes.

"That's an interesting observation," Castillo said. "Jill, these men react to you this morning, but you still observed Adam pull out in a tanker this afternoon, visit a pumping oil rig, then drive to a BDC property. If you're a key member of this narcotics operation and you think the cops have a fix on you, is that how you would spend your afternoon? I would change the plates on the tanker trucks and move whatever I could to another city in the Permian Basin. I wouldn't waste twenty minutes taking meter readings at a pumping oil rig with a full tanker-truck; I would get the hell out of here."

"That's a good observation Detective Castillo. Maybe they don't have video; perhaps it's just a motion detector that you're setting off. We need to send manpower to the BDC Properties to see if we have any action going on," replied Detective Guerrero. "We've some patrol units that could survey two of the properties. Who else wants to take a road trip?"

Jill, Castillo, and two DEA agents volunteered. A short few minutes later they left the room with directions to the BDC properties. Twenty minutes later they'd all reported back that no activity could be viewed from the street. Another twenty minutes and everyone was back in the conference room. From what Jill could see, they had moved up the operation substantially, bringing in DEA agents from around the state so they could make an early morning raid on Vernon Oil, Adam Johnson, and the BDC Company. It looked like Jill and Castillo would finally have the opportunity to interview Adam regarding his wife's murder.

While she was out visiting the BDC company site, one of the agents had gotten several weeks of satellite images of the BDC Company locations and six of the seven had been visited by one of the four tanker-trucks. With some forty plus non-working oil rigs, they would have a lot of locations to cover. Furthermore, they didn't know who or where all of the thugs related to this drug cartel operation resided and they didn't want to alert them ahead of time. They would work through the night to try and gain that information before dawn.

Chapter Twenty-Three

Jill tried to think of how she could help this operation given her skill set and a few thoughts came to her. With a little help from the Odessa Crime Lab, she could set up test kits for the officers and agents involved in the raid. She had a list of chemicals used in the manufacture of illicit drugs as well as cocaine and heroin. She guessed that if they could rig the tanker truck to move methylamine, then they could rig it to move cocaine powder. She thought she could create a kit for them to test the contents of tanks and buildings.

She tuned back into the discussion and listened for an opportunity to break in. She found her moment fifteen minutes later.

"Agent Black, with a few supplies from the Odessa Crime Lab, I believe I can make kits for officers and agents on the raid to know what substance they're faced with. Also, I might make a good decoy to at least bring the seven thugs out of hiding as the official start to this raid."

"Okay to your first suggestion and explain more about your thoughts as a decoy."

"I don't know how you're going to bring these thugs out of hiding and arrest and identify them other than by getting them to pile into their cars and come investigate someone threatening their oil-rig or warehouse. They have become complacent to some degree as they have chased me down twice in the same cars. I'm thinking I could purposely trip one of the storage locations and you folks can protect me from them;

I've tripped their security system twice so my face may be a familiar sight. In fact, we might want to try this before dawn as that generated a larger response than my mid-day raid. While you guys discuss that, I'm going to head over to the crime lab and see about making test kits for this operation," and Jill got up and left the room with Guerrero.

"That was a bold offer from you," Guerrero said.

"Not really, if I have all you guys protecting me and if the DEA put a helicopter in the air, all the better. It's just that we've no information on who these men are and where they're dispatched from. Being an identified face of a DEA computer system isn't good enough justice for me. Where is their command center with security devices monitoring the suspect rigs and warehouses? They can arrest Adam and the drivers and they can shut down the storage and transportation, but that doesn't get the men or infrastructure behind this chemical cartel. If you want to avoid having them set up shop in the next county over, you need to get more than Adam and the drivers."

The detective pushed open the door to the crime lab and introduced Jill to the staff member inside. Jill explained her desire to create some fifty test kits for anyone to use at the sites to identify the substances. The lab already had test strips to identify heroin, cocaine, and methamphetamines. Jill was making kits for the precursor chemicals. She'd excelled in chemistry in college and so knew how to make the right combination of chemicals so that substances would change colors if certain chemicals were present. An hour later, she had field kits with instructions ready to go for everyone on the raid. She boxed stuff up and returned to the conference room.

She watched the folks eye her with a combination of awe and bewilderment like she had invented something miraculous. She demonstrated her products and Agent Black responded,

"When this case is over Dr. Quint, can we talk about you being employed by the DEA? You have so many odd and useful skills."

"No thanks, I don't like guns so I would never pass your test to be an agent," Jill replied smiling. "You can always call me for advice on a case even if you haven't hired me as a consultant."

Castillo spoke up and added, "Dallas PD hired her because if you look at her past high profile cases, her very presence seems to bring out the criminals as we witnessed in Dallas and now you have seen here in Odessa."

There were a lot of smiles at Jill during this exchange. The group went back to their planning as the room was expanding with ever arriving additional DEA agents. While she'd been in the crime lab making up kits, they agreed to start the operation by having Jill break into one of the warehouses. The group discussed whether to go with someone else as the decoy, but in case she was captured on video, it was better that her face alert the thugs. That action would allow them to capture some of the henchmen in addition to the drivers and Adam. They monitored the border to know there were two trucks on their way here and as they stopped at the border, a DEA agent had placed a GPS tracker on the trucks. They were expected to roll into the Vernon Oil yard just as the agents wrapped up their operation elsewhere.

Jill got a ping from Marie then signaling an email. Glancing at the time, it was close to eleven in the evening. Marie got up around five to get a work-out in before work, so she tried to fall asleep between nine and ten. It started with,

Couldn't fall sleep, so I got up to research your three men, wanted to make sure you're fully briefed on them and can I say that they may be about as bad a criminal you've ever come in contact with? They're wanted in Mexico on charges of rape, murder, decapitation, and child abuse. They seem to have no redeeming qualities as human beings if they are such...

This is what I was able to find on a possible location of them. I collected some pictures I found referencing them. They aren't in the pictures but there is mention that they were with these groups of people. Perhaps if you could find these locations around Odessa, it might tell you where they are staying...

One more thing, I did a little more research into Adam Johnson - looking at a circle of acquaintances around him from college onward - I've been working on this off and on for a few days. Poor guy seems to be the grim reaper. He's lost a college roommate, two co-workers, a neighbor, and he was even friends with Stacy's first boyfriend who all died young. I'll forward you the cause of death for these people when I locate them. Can I say these are red flags and don't hire this man!

Jill smiled at Marie's human resources attitude towards the facts she uncovered with one of her searches for Jill. She pulled up the five pictures that Marie had attached after quickly sending her a thank-you email and again broke into the conversation concerning the operation.

"A member of my team who performs background searches collected some interesting information tonight. First, these five pictures are referenced to the three suspects that the DEA identified earlier. They may or may not be a part of the gang of seven that appeared at the warehouse. It was too dark to identify them. If you know where these locations are in Odessa, you might be able to round them up," Jill said while connecting her laptop to the screen. The DEA agents weren't that familiar with Odessa, but the Odessa police department recognized three of the pictures immediately.

This discovery became another tangent to deal with for this operation. She could see everyone energized by this new facet to account for, so she delivered the second piece of information which probably most interested Castillo.

"Secondly, my teammate noted that Adam Johnson is somewhat of a grim reaper. By analyzing his social media comments, she was able to put together a picture of him attending the funerals or otherwise mourning the deaths of a college roommate, a neighbor, Stacy Johnson's previous boyfriend, and two co-workers. Poor guy seems to have lost a lot of people close to him. When you get a search warrant for his home, I'd like to be there. Perhaps someone here or in the Dallas PD could research the cause of death of these persons in case we find any connection to them in his house."

Detectives Castillo and Guerrero were both interested in that piece of information as they would be leading the search of Adam's residence likely with a DEA agent. Castillo took the names from Jill and used his own laptop to tap the records on those deaths.

The Odessa Police Department, with a little discussion among its officers, was able to locate the two addresses in the five pictures. They were different angles of the same street. When Jill acted as decoy, the task force would have groups in place to take the men down as they left their streets. Another team would search the houses for evidence and look for the location for the camera security room for all locations in play by this cartel. If they had the security camera locations, they might learn of additional chemical storage facilities.

"Has your team understood the relationship of Vernon Oil's leadership to this illicit operation and the profits it's generating?" asked Agent Black.

"No with so many other suspects to try and run down, we hadn't focused on that question. Let me see what we can find."

Jill dropped a text to Marie,

I hate to be rude, but I hope you're still sleepless in

Wisconsin. What can you find on the Executives of Vernon Oil? Text me back if you're awake to do this search.

When she got a text asking her the names and titles, Jill gave a silent thanks to having friends that would give up sleep to help her. Knowing the path that Marie took, Jill decided she would again look at the financials of the company. It was Jo's area of expertise, but it was closing in on midnight and she wouldn't wake her friend up. It was going to be a long night and she would have liked to get some sleep, but she didn't want to miss out on the action even though she would only be in the background. She really thought the case would end once Adam was arrested as she believed him to be Stacy Johnson's murderer which was the job she had been hired for.

She searched out some coffee and then sat back down to work on her assignment. Listed on the Vernon Oil website and in the records of the State of Texas were the corporate officers' names. Jill was convinced that if there was anyone inside the company beyond Adam who knew of the chemical transportation, it had to be the CFO, so she focused on him first looking for any comments related to his company out-performing other oil companies. She found nothing; the guy was not shouting his good fortune from the mountaintops. She really didn't want to do the same work as Marie so she backed off completely from people and instead focused on the company. Could she find a connection between Vernon Oil and BDC and the chemical cartel?

That new hypothesis gave her a surge of excitement. Like other cases that she'd been on, sometimes she took down an individual and other times, there was a bad company that needed dissolving along with the perpetrators. This was one of those cases.

She'd researched Vernon Oil previously and nothing was

startling as she reviewed her notes, other than the profits mentioned by Jo. Had the company tried to merge or expand in its history? The two founders had started with five wells on their own lands and merged and then over the past twenty years bought additional land or mineral rights to over one-hundred rigs. They managed to survive the fluctuations in oil prices that weaker companies closed over. As Jo noted they were surviving the current drop in oil barrel prices and actually thriving. This was something none of their competitors, large or small had managed. She began looking for their public documents; and there were not many. She copied down any name mentioned in any report or tax statement. They all, but one, checked out on the surface as being what they said they were - an owner of a drilling company, the CEO of a refinery.

The one that didn't pan out was the owner of their transportation system. It changed about five years ago and their costs increased. On one hand, why change contracts if the first one was cheaper and on the other hand it was expensive to drive a chemical truck across the border from Mexico northeast to Odessa. The new company was PC Transport and so she did a further search on them after looking at the clock and noting it was one in the morning or so. Yikes, it was only the thrill of taking down a potential murderer and a definite drug cartel operation that kept the adrenaline flowing through her veins.

Jill looked up as she heard one of the DEA agents monitoring the moving trucks and the two streets in the background, say something.

"Agent Black, I believe we have a problem."

There was instant silence and Jill felt her lingering tiredness evaporate with that single sentence.

"Yes?" asked the agent, his tone suggesting he proceed in his description of the problem.

"The trucks have exited Interstate 10 prior to the Interstates 10 and 20 connection and have reentered the freeway heading back toward El Paso and the border. We are also seeing activity at the two residences that we are monitoring. We don't have eyes on the oil rigs or BDC warehouse locations, and there is no increased activity at Adam Johnson's house."

"Well folks it looks like we need to put our plan into action now rather than waiting for just before dawn. Johnson may have escaped from his house before we began surveilling it."

"Why don't I assign an officer to Detective Castillo and Dr. Quint and the three of them can monitor the Johnson house," suggested Guerrero looking at the two of them who both nodded their assent.

"Good idea," replied Agent Black. "The rest of us will be split among the other residences, the oil rigs and the warehouses. We're going to be thin on resources, but I want two agents or officers dispersed to each location."

Agent Black continued directing the distribution of resources as Jill and Castillo left the room. A patrol officer met them outside the conference room. Having stopped in a room for body armor, they filed outside to Castillo's rental car which was deemed the best vehicle for surveillance.

On the drive to Adam's street Castillo said, "Let's set some ground rules. We'll all silence our cellphones and we'll keep them with us at all times. Pete and I are armed and Jill, you're not nor are you trained in this kind of operation."

Jill took the moment to pull her can of bug spray out of her purse to remind the detective that she was indeed 'armed'.

"Jill, he may have an automatic weapon that will spray you with bullets before you ever find the can in your purse, so consider yourself unarmed."

"You're right but I have already done surveillance on Adam's house and I think I can help with a plan on what to do. There is only one way out of his street, so I would suggest we park on the next block. There's a hedge that separates his house from the next and I think we could take cover on the ground to observe." She paused a minute to show them the pictures she had taken on her first day of surveillance. "The other side has a large tree between his driveway and his neighbor's front yard. He could go over the fence in his backyard, but he needs transportation to do that. He's a devoted father, so I can't imagine that he'd tangle his children up in this op. So if he's had advance notice he would move those kids to friends or grandparents hopefully. Just know there could be three kids under the age of ten inside."

"Thanks for the pictures," Castillo said. "Pete can take the hedge for cover and I'll stay behind the tree. Jill, you stay in this car and notify us if there is action on the street. Pete and I will use night visions goggles when necessary. Jill I believe the light is too bright where you'll be so they won't work for you. Let's program our cells and communicate with texts and phone calls. Let's do a roll call every fifteen minutes."

"What if someone does approach the street, do I stop and pick you guys up or chase after them myself?" Jill asked.

There was silence for a moment then Castillo said, "I guess it depends on the speed of their departure and the sighting of any guns. Unless Adam looks ready to shoot, follow his mode of transportation rather than taking your eyes off of him and coming to get us."

Okay, Jill was happy with that response. It indicated that rather than wasting time trying to protect her, they wanted her to chase down the bad guy. She would do what she could to live up to their expectations that she carry her own weight. With phones programed for group texts and phone calls, Castillo and Pete crept down the street to get in position. Jill was hoping she wouldn't embarrass herself and fall asleep. If she felt herself nodding off, she'd call Nathan and he'd keep her awake. Soon they split apart and manned their posts. Jill parked on a street that had the odd car traveling down it and so she was ducking down whenever she thought an auto's lights would hit where she was sitting in the front seat. A car came about every ten minutes and the roll call every fifteen and so far, she felt alert.

Jill wondered what was going on in the rest of the op. They had known they wouldn't get updates as Agent Black wanted outside communication limited during the op. It had been ninety minutes since they left the station, so the tankers should have been stopped and confiscated on the Interstate by now. Then she caught a movement in her peripheral vision.

Chapter Twenty-Four

It was one of those moments in time when half of your brain is screaming 'oh my god, what did I just see', and the other half of your brain is screaming 'do something', but your body is paralyzed because what you saw has yet to register. The panic of the moment stayed with Jill for another sixty seconds, then everything came into focus. She grabbed her binoculars and focused on the dark shape emerging from the side of a house.

It was Adam Johnson in all black clothing and hat, but she caught his face in the shifting light of an approaching car.

Keeping her eyes on Adam, she grabbed her cellphone and dialed her two partners. When she heard their phones answered, she said in a low voice, "Adam has just emerged from a front yard of a house on the street I'm on. There is a car approaching that may be his ride."

She ducked down as the car passed, and saw the red brake lights in her driver side window. She peeked up over the dashboard setting her binoculars on the surface. She again verified it was Adam. He got in and the car took off.

With her first words Castillo and Pete had grabbed their backpacks and ran for the end of the street where Jill's car was parked. They reached the car as Jill saw the lights of the car almost getting out of her line of vision.

She stomped on the gas, throwing the binoculars to Pete who was in the seat beside her. She could hear both men breathing heavy from their sprint. Pete sighted the car nearly a mile up the road and Jill raced to follow.

Castillo suggested, "Jill, why don't you pull over and we'll switch drivers. You probably haven't been trained in chase procedures."

Jill said over the loud noise of the adrenaline rushing in her head, "And lose Adam and the car he's in? Are you nuts? In prior cases, I've been chased by a Black Op helicopter and had a massive SUV try to push me off a cliff on a mountain road in Colorado. I'll do fine on these flat roads, just buckle up and hold on" and Jill punched the gas even more. The hell with coming to a stop and switching drivers, what was the man thinking?

Suddenly the car they were pursuing disappeared in front of them. Jill gaped and then it clicked what had happened.

"They shut their headlights off; grab the night vision goggles and direct me. Do you think I should shut our light off?"

"Both men yelled "no" at the same time. It was bad enough being driven by a female non-officer, but the thought of leaving her without headlights was more than the men could handle. Jill just grinned at the two men.

"They have to know we're tailing them, let's not make it harder on ourselves," Castillo said.

"Can you watch the car for Jill?" Pete said. "I need to update my department on our whereabouts and the movement of Adam."

They listened to him call the command post and report their chase in-progress. Resources were spread so thin, that no one as yet could be dispatched to assist them. There were simply too many oil wells and BDC properties to cover. If they'd had more time to plan the op, then more resources would have arrived to help but this was one of those cases where the criminals set the timetable.

Jill had gained ground on the car carrying Adam according to Castillo. She couldn't see it ahead of her as she was focused on driving fast and staying on the road.

Then she saw brake lights in the distance and knew the car had turned left and said to Castillo, "I can see the car turned left; can you make sure that I pick the correct street to turn left on?"

"Yes," Castillo said.

"Turn at this upcoming street," Castillo said.

Castillo re-sighted the vehicle ahead; they were in a residential area and Jill was grateful that it was the middle of the night so she didn't have to worry about hitting children playing in the street.

"I wish I'd grabbed emergency lights before we went out tonight," Pete lamented. "It would have made it safer for the community. I think they're going to try and lose you, Jill, in this maze of streets; there are a bunch of short blocks coming up so you need to get closer or we'll lose them."

Jill concentrated on being as fast a driver as she could. She blocked everything out except looking for anything that might get in her path and following the directions issued by Castillo. In the very back of her head was the worry that this was his rental car and she better not wreck it. She pulled within half a block of their suspects' car and did a lot of screeching around corners to stay there. The occasional house light popped on as the sound was unusual for this neighborhood at this hour of the night.

Castillo was intently watching the occupants of the car and he yelled "swerve left" and she did. Seconds later there was a massive flash of light and noise. If Castillo shouted any more instructions, she couldn't hear. Pete and Castillo had instinctively known that a flash bang was thrown at the car and had time to cover their ears and close their eyes. Jill hadn't had the luxury and fortunately she was on the other side of the car which helped minimize the effects for her. She felt a little nauseous, but otherwise she kept the car speeding along.

Pete began writing notes for Jill to read in very large print and held up to view while steering the car.

Flash bang grenade. Hearing will return in about fifteen minutes.

She'd thank him later for legible writing.

Good evasive action with car!

Castillo leaned forward to say something and Pete didn't have time to put it in writing for her. Instead he gestured wildly to swerve left again and she did. This time the flash bang couldn't affect her hearing as she was already deaf from the last one. She managed to speed up even more and the bang went off farther behind the car.

The two cars had been making a series of turns through the neighborhood and then they were back out on a four lane major thoroughfare. Jill began to close in on the car, when it suddenly braked hard as guns came blazing out the left side windows at them. When Jill saw the guns, she slouched low and put the pedal to the metal flooring the car to nearly ninety miles per hour. She thought she felt a bullet ping off the helmet she was wearing as a part of her body armor. Then she felt Pete's hand on her arm and he gestured to slow. She looked at him in disbelief then glanced in her rearview mirror to see the other car had stopped by running up over the curb and crashing into an ATM machine in the front of a bank.

She slowed and turned around, heading back toward the crash site. Pete wrote her another note.

Castillo threw a flashbang into their car.

Jill quickly glanced at Castillo and mouthed, WOW! Then slowed as she approached the crash site. Her nausea had receded and she wondered if she was hearing the bank alarms going off or was it the ringing in her ears? She still couldn't hear what her companions were saying, she just saw their lips moving.

Pete put out his hand gesturing for her to do a hard stop and she brought the car to a screeching halt assuming he meant her to stop on the dime. She'd taken tread off the tires with her driving and it had been an adrenaline-filled lifetime passing in front of her eyes. She thought she had comported herself well as a race car driver managing not to get them killed or hurt. Her ears were still ringing although she couldn't tell if that was from the flashbang or if there was a bank alarm now that they were nearly on top of the noise.

Pete wrote her a final note.

Stay in the car with the doors locked.

Jill was torn on following this direction. The two men exited the car, guns in hand and ran across the street approaching the car in a shooter stance, guns aimed at the occupants. She could see a patrol car coming from a mile down the road. Pete must have called it in. She wanted to hear what they found but all she could hear was a hum as though she was underwater in a pool. The patrol car soon pulled up and then down the road she could see an ambulance.

The sight of the ambulance jarred her out of her hearing deprived stupor. She was a physician, she had a duty to attend the men in the other car even though they'd tried to kill her about five minutes ago. Castillo and Pete and the two additional officers were checking the men over in the car. She walked over to them, pad of paper in hand and wrote,

"I'm a doctor, let me see the men."

On one hand she felt foolish writing a note to the two of them and on the other hand, she wasn't sure they could hear over the noise of a bank alarm which was starting to sound shriller to her.

She did a rapid assessment of the car and noted the men were not wearing seatbelts - probably no surprise there. Didn't seatbelts get in the way when you were trying to throw flashbangs or aim a gun? Then she noticed and wrote a few words.

"Adam's not in the car."

Castillo and Pete had only seen his picture and as the men inside the car were covered in blood, they hadn't immediately recognized that he wasn't in the car.

They spread out around the bank, and noted the back door was ajar and an alarm could be heard ringing from it. Behind the bank was a residential community similar to the one that they had sped through earlier.

After a quick consultation, they split up and did a quick search of the first six house yards on both sides of the street. No backyard gates were ajar. The lights were on in the first two houses probably due to the noise of the car crash. They knocked on the door and yelled, "Police".

Frightened occupants opened the door in each case and indicated that no-one had entered the premises. Given the darkness, and lack of police resources to do a full scale search, it was all they could do for the time.

Returning to the front of the bank, an additional ambulance had pulled up. They had extricated the front seat and back seat passengers, who were conscious and cuffed to the gurney. The driver would need the jaws-of-life to extricate him. Jill was holding pressure on something that was bleeding. The paramedics indicated they thought all three men would survive and Castillo took one man and Pete the other to see if they could get anything out of them, but since the flashbang had gone off inside their car, they were both momentarily blinded and deaf.

The ambulance doors closed and, with an officer inside, the ambulance left for the local hospital. A fire truck arrived and they began wrenching parts of the car away from the driver. Twenty minutes later, the unconscious driver, was loaded into another ambulance and was gone.

All of a sudden, Jill couldn't hear the bank alarm anymore.

She asked Pete, "Did you get the bank alarm shut off?"

He looked at her puzzled, "What bank alarm? Banks have silent alarms to protect employees when a bank is robbed. If alarms go off, a robber will think about taking hostages. Did you mean the back door alarm?"

Jill laughed because she heard about eighty percent of what Pete said.

"My hearing must be coming back because I just heard most of what you said. The ringing in my ears was so bad, I thought I was hearing an audible alarm when we pulled up to the bank."

"That's a flashbang grenade for you," Castillo said. "Adam Johnson got away. Pete's talking to the command post about next steps. Glad you can hear again; that was the scariest car chase once your hearing was gone, but you did really well and managed to read notes while chasing that car. That was excellent driving; I couldn't have done better myself."

"Wow! I think that's my first compliment from you Detective."

Pete walked up to them to brief them on the op.

"They've captured the tanker-trucks close to El Paso. In addition, they picked up several men here at the various BDC warehouses and the two residences that were under surveillance. They haven't seen any activity yet on the non-working oil rigs. We discussed doing an aerial search for Adam, but we'd just alarm the neighborhood and it would likely be fruitless by now. There haven't been any gunshots from the cartel members elsewhere in the city. They're waiting to hear from us on next steps."

"At a minimum, I think we should pile into the car and head over to Adam's house," Castillo said. "We should have probable cause for a search warrant that we could execute right now with a judge's approval."

"The command post indicated we have a search warrant, so we'll head over there now," Pete said as they walked towards Castillo's car. He put his hand out to Jill for the car keys which she gladly placed in his hand. It was approaching four in the morning and she had enough of an adrenaline rush to keep her awake until she hit the sack tonight.

They pulled up to Adam's house and Jill's hearing had fully returned. She was really vulnerable to someone sneaking up on her and she was glad she could hear crickets in the bushes. There were no lights on anywhere that they could see from the outside. With body armor in place and guns pointed down, but ready, they approached the front door and rang the doorbell. Jill followed in their wake, purse over her shoulder and bug spray in her hand. After three more pushes of the doorbell which they could hear ring inside the house, there was still no answer.

Castillo said to Jill, "Three children under the age of ten potentially inside?"

"Yes."

Pete tried the doorknob finding it locked and said to them, "I can probably pick this lock; give me a moment."

Three minutes later they were inside with the lights on. Castillo said to Pete, "You do the search of the upper floor and

I'll have Jill follow me down here. Call down to me if you need help or if you come up empty."

A short, but fast heart beat time elapsed and their search turned up an empty house. Each time Castillo edged his way inside a room and opened closed closet doors, her heart jumped into her mouth and she held her breath. She felt like the world's biggest chicken; on one hand she wanted to run out to the car and tell them to call her when they knew the coast was clear and on the other hand she wanted to climb into one of the closets and stay there until it was safe. It was a good thing that being a cop was not her occupation; she would have flunked out of the police academy out of imaginary fright.

Castillo, Pete and Jill met in the central hallway and discussed how they would split up the search. Pete would take the upstairs again, and Castillo the lower level, but leave the kitchen to Jill. There also might be sheds on the property and they would search the exterior later, probably about the time daylight arrived.

With children in the house, Jill had to think that Adam would have hidden his arsenic well out of view and reach of the kids and Stacy. At the same time, he had to have made the blueberry muffins somewhere. Jill carried with her a test kit for arsenic - she had potassium iodide liquid, powdered zinc compound and then mercury test strips. The arsenic could be grey, yellow or black in appearance and in a solid state on quartz rock or in liquid or powder form. She had a lot of ways to look for the substance. On the other hand, Adam could have taken whatever he used with him or discarded it after he made the muffins. It was available for sale online and easily replaced.

Jill had a bet with herself that she would find it as a piece of quartz somewhere in the house on a high shelf as a decorative item. She was coming to know Adam and he seemed to cover up his lies with the thinnest of veils. She'd warned Castillo and Pete to look for the rock formed version as well. Standing in the kitchen she looked at the mahogany cabinets and started opening doors. There was also a laundry room off the kitchen and a pantry inside. She did a sweeping view of all the cabinets and surfaces looking for arsenic. Nothing.

Crap, now she had to search through every nook and cranny of the kitchen and this room was her least favorite room in any house. She heaved a huge sigh and hunkered down to dig in. She was making lots of noise shifting pots and pans and glassware, dragging a chair around to see the tallest surfaces. She was on top of the chair peering into a tall cabinet when she felt cool air from somewhere. Glancing over her shoulder, she startled and let out a gasp.

Chapter Twenty-Five

She looked into the eyes of Adam Johnson and then to the gun he was holding aimed at her. She froze then said, "Adam, what are you doing here?"

What an incredibly stupid question, Jill thought; it's the man's house. What she meant to say was why had he come here while the police were searching his residence.

"It's my house; why wouldn't I be here," Adam replied. "What are you doing in my house?"

Part of Jill's brain was telling her to step off the chair so she didn't break something when he shot her and she dropped to the ground. Another part of her brain was saying try the Lotus kick from her Tai Chi training. She could make a sweep of her foot and knock the gun out of his hand. She thought about that for a few milliseconds and decided that while she would have better balance on the floor, the height advantage of staying on the chair while executing the kick, and then making a run for the door was her better option. She just needed him to take a step closer.

"We're executing a search warrant and no one answered your front door. Why don't I call the two officers here with me in the house and you can chat with them?"

"Why don't you shut up and climb down from that chair?" Ok thought Jill, here goes.

She leaned back on her left foot, moved her arms like Bruce Lee and executed a Lotus kick that her instructor would have been proud of. She heard the gun clatter to the floor, as she overbalanced and went flying off the chair. She slammed into the kitchen cabinets hard, grunted, then was up and running for the door to the living room. A bullet hit the door frame inches from her head and she rounded the corner yelling,

"Castillo! Pete! Help, Adam is in the house!"

She kept running even though she didn't hear any more shots. Castillo and Pete had both rushed to her. After quickly reassuring them that she was fine, they ran out the back door to see if they could catch Adam. Jill grabbed her can of bug spray ready to take aim if the wrong person came back through any of the kitchen doors. The two men returned in about twenty minutes and had had no sighting of Adam as they searched the neighborhood.

"We didn't find him," Castillo said. "Tell me what happened."

Pointing to the chair, Jill said, "I was standing on the chair searching the top shelf of the cabinets when I felt a cool breeze in the room. I looked over my shoulder and saw that Adam Johnson had entered the kitchen through the back door and was holding a gun on me. I debated what to do and decided to stay on the chair and try a Lotus kick to knock the gun out of his hand. When he took a step closer, I executed a perfect kick, but my momentum carried me off the chair and into those cabinets. The moment I could, I ran for the door and he fired the gun at me and you can see where the bullet grazed the molding. I kept going and yelled for you guys."

"Did he say anything to you?" Castillo asked. "Did he recognize you?"

"I asked him what he was doing here and he replied by asking me what was I doing in his kitchen and yes, he recognized me. Guess I don't need any disguises anymore as he knows I'm working with the police. By the way, he had cuts on his face and hands which I presume are from the broken glass when the car hit the bank."

"What should our next steps be?" Pete asked Castillo. "Should we continue our search? Maybe we should check in with the command post, give them our update and see what else is going on in this op."

"Good idea," Castillo agreed.

On speaker phone, the three of them checked in with the command post. There was good news there. The two tanker trucks and their drivers were in the custody of the Texas Rangers. The other tanker trucks were found at the BDC warehouses and were also confiscated along with the men in the location of those warehouses and the two addresses. Overall, they had a total of twenty probable cartel men in custody. Law enforcement had spread out among the non-working oil wells and identified ten storage sites for precursor chemicals. Other non-working wells were still under investigation. The command post would be sending resources to support the three of them and it sounded like they were the only three living an exciting life chasing Adam Johnson. With more resources if they had any other sightings, they could chase after him through backyards and hopefully capture him next time.

Jill had a couple of outstanding items that she wanted to review now that she was no longer worried about dying at the hands of Adam. Then she thought of something else to add.

Jill relayed to the command post, "Besides Adam, there has to be at least one other person on the loose. He couldn't have got back to his house as fast as he did unless he had a ride. We were a good ten minutes away by car and so he would have almost needed the speed of an Olympic marathoner to get from the bank crash site to his home in about the hour he had."

"Good point, Jill. Maybe the command post can work on finding his getaway car."

As they concluded their call, they heard the doorbell ring indicating additional resources were arriving. Jill wanted to get back to her laptop and check on a few things but first she showed the new arrivals a picture of what arsenic looked like in its various forms so they could continue the search of the kitchen without her.

She looked outside to see if the sky was lightening up like it did as dawn approached and she thought in another half an hour they would have the assistance of the light of dawn to explore the backyard.

She returned to her phone curious to see if Marie had found anything. She also wanted to complete the search of which oil rigs were visited by the tanker-trucks. There was an email from Marie and Jill opened it with that inner sense that this was it, there was some secret contained in the message. Likely if her hair wasn't so tired from the hair-raising night it would have stood on end and tingled for her. Now it just sagged like her own energy levels.

Jill opened and read the email, then she smiled at the phone.

Castillo caught the look and said, "What did you find? You're looking very satisfied."

"I didn't find anything. It's my brilliant teammate, Marie. It would appear that Vernon Oil's CEO is either a puppet or dumber than a box of rocks. Adam and the CFO are the crooks and the CFO is likely the mastermind. Oh, by the way, Adam reports to him."

"Who's the CFO and what did you find?" Castillo asked.

"I'll explain but as time is of the essence, can you trust me on this and ask the command post to round him up? The name is Brian Campos and there's a picture of him on the Vernon Oil website."

As Jill requested, Castillo asked the command post to locate Brian Campos under the category of wanted for questioning for the movement of chemicals used to make illicit drugs. Then Pete and Castillo sat down to listen to her explanation.

"From the beginning, I thought the CFO had to be crooked. How could he fail to notice that his oil profits were so much higher than any other company and that was with not all of his oil wells working? I figured that Adam couldn't launder the money without internal help and the CFO again was the most likely person as he or his department would see the invoices. Follow my line of thinking so far?"

The two men nodded.

"So BDC stands for Benito Del Rio Campos; he owns those warehouses and he is then owned by a company that's owned by a company that tiers into Sinaloa. The CFO is the nephew of Benito, who manages the Sinaloa cartel's transportation network for all products. Benito is also the owner of PC transport, the trucking firm that moves the oil tanker-trucks. We appear to have a large cartel relationship underlining the leadership of the company. Vernon Oil exists to sell a little oil and a lot of chemicals."

"How do you know that Vernon's CEO isn't involved?" Castillo asked.

"We don't know that for sure, but in looking at everything he is ever quoted as saying as well as his employment background, my expert in human resources teammate's analysis is that the man doesn't have a clue how he became so lucky as to get a higher per barrel oil price than anyone else. He appears to be mostly a silent partner, more interested in his cattle ranch that's located in King County, which is some distance from here. He's quoted as having ceded day to day operations to Adam and Brian. Among the other employees of Vernon Oil, only the truck drivers could have known that there was something in the tanker other than oil."

"Okay, so we're on the hunt for these two men to wrap up the operation and then perhaps we'll get our answers to whom and why Stacy Johnson was killed," replied Castillo.

"I recommend we look for the Johnson children as that might tell us where Adam is or speak with his parents in Houston," Pete suggested. "Hopefully the kids are there and if they are, it would make sense to me that he needs to cross the border with his children to run from American authorities. If I ever committed a crime and believed I could outrun authorities, I would grab my children and take them with me."

Jill and Castillo looked at him in surprise and he said, "Hypothetically speaking. Just trying to get inside Adam's head."

"Does he have access to a plane or a pilot's license?" Jill asked.

"I'll check," said Castillo as he began punching buttons on his computer tablet.

"Can we search Mexican property records?" Jill said. "If I was involved in a drug smuggling ring, I would know that the gig wouldn't last forever and that I should make plans for an escape. I wonder if there was something in this house that he needed? It was quite a risk to come back here after the car chase."

"Good point, but we observed him leaving this house in a rush to get into the car," Pete said. "What would he have forgotten to take with him? Was he carrying a backpack or some kind of bag?"

Jill sat for a moment, thinking, and then said, "It was too dark to see so I don't know if he was carrying anything."

"How about a few minutes ago, was he carrying anything?"

Again Jill had to think about her thirty second interaction with Adam. She'd turned around and there she was gazing into the eyes of a suspected killer holding a gun pointed at her face. He had nothing in his hands and she couldn't recall seeing a shoulder strap of any kind holding a bag and then she said, "No."

"So he ran out of here earlier without having the time to grab something that he wanted and unless the item was in the kitchen, he still didn't have it when he left after firing his gun at you, Jill," Castillo said. "It says something about him that he was so willing to try and kill you."

Jill shuddered; she couldn't recall being that close to someone holding a gun pointed at her face. Maybe she was too tired to be as scared as she should be. She looked around the kitchen to see if she remembered anything missing that Adam might have taken with him. She paused then went back to the shelf she'd been reviewing. Was something missing?

She looked over at the coffee pot and thought about getting some caffeine, but she was in the house of a suspected murderer and even if they weren't executing a warrant, there might be arsenic in the coffee tin. Lost in thought, she didn't hear the conversation going on around her. Then it clicked. When she started the search, she had opened all the cupboard doors and taken a few pictures with her cellphone in order to capture all that was in the kitchen in case it was important. She opened the pictures and compared them to what she was looking at now and something was missing.

"Guys, there was what looked like an ugly cookie jar on the shelf I was working on and it's now missing; here, look at this photo."

Castillo, Pete, and two of the other officers searching the kitchen gathered around her. They looked from her phone to the shelf and back several times and then around the kitchen just to make sure it hadn't been moved. Sure enough, it wasn't anywhere. Adam must have taken it after firing a shot at her.

"Maybe Adam fired the gun at me to get me out of the kitchen and not to kill me," Jill said.

"You think that hitting the door frame, an inch from your head was a random scare you off shot? Newsflash Jill, the man was trying to kill you." Castillo said. "If he'd hit the bottom of the doorframe, then he would have been trying to scare you; top of the frame is a kill shot gone wild."

"Destroy my optimistic attitude why don't you?" Jill replied with a tired grin. "Adam's eyes did have an empty look about them. So what are our next steps?"

"Find Brian Campos and Adam Johnson," replied Castillo.

"I've got that," Jill said. "How?"

"I think our best bet is turning all the resources of the command post on them," replied Pete. "With the help of the DEA and the Texas Rangers, we have a lot of extra personnel to search for Adam. Now that daylight is here, it will be much harder for him to hide. How would you suggest we find them?"

"I don't have any brilliant ideas; rather I'm panicked that since we're so close to the border the two of them may already be in Mexico by now and if they are, we'll never capture them."

"Our relationship has changed with the Mexican police. They are not likely to help these two and will do what they can to assist us in finding them," Castillo said. "So all is not lost."

Castillo paused for a moment, then added, "I wonder if there's a way to use you as bait to get him to surface for us?"

"Gee thanks, Detective." Jill said with clear annoyance.

"Hey, I told you from the beginning that you seemed to have a track record of being an attractive target for the criminals," Castillo said. "How do we use that to our advantage?"

The two men pondered that question for a moment, while

in the background other officers were still searching the house for evidence. Jill had no experience with Castillo's question and she was partially brain-dead from the long sleepless night. If they didn't come up with a suggestion soon, she'd fall asleep on them.

"How about if we call a press conference today? Announce the arrests and breakup of the chemical precursor pipeline, put Jill on stage to talk about the connection to the arsenic murder in Dallas and provide her with some words to incite Adam to come out of hiding?" Pete suggested.

"Let's head back to the command post and talk that idea over with others; I like it," Castillo agreed.

Jill sighed then added, "Maybe we could say something about the missing ugly cookie jar. That ought to irk Adam that he didn't get away with stealing something under our noses."

Piling into Castillo's car, the three of them headed back to the command post. The morning sun seemed unusually bright to Jill's tired eyes. They arrived in the parking lot as traffic was picking up all around the city for the morning commute. On her way into the conference room, she asked Pete in desperation "Is there some bad police coffee somewhere in this building?"

He smiled and asked, "Cream? Sugar?" and turned toward Castillo silently asking the same.

Pete pointed the way toward the conference room, as he went in a different direction for coffee returning a short while later with a large black for Castillo, and a large with cream and sugar for Jill. She never used real sugar in coffee because of the calories, but desperate times called for desperate measures.

As they entered the room, Agent Black gave Jill a tired smile and said, "I heard you've had some hair-raising adventures overnight. The rest of us just quietly arrested the bad guys and confiscated their equipment."

"It's my new method for staying awake during an all-nighter," Jill replied. "You ought to try having a criminal hold a gun aimed at you while you're standing on a kitchen chair for excitement. It was like drinking a gallon of coffee."

"How did you avoid harm?" Guerrero asked.

"I've been training in Tai Chi - I've got a green belt. Before I took this case, I'd been working on the Lotus kick which was a perfect action to knock the gun out of Adam Johnson's hand with my foot. The trouble was that I hadn't practiced it while standing on a kitchen chair. When I executed the kick, I knocked the gun out of his hand, but my weight followed my foot and I went flying off the chair and into the kitchen cabinets, bounced off those and ran like hell out of the kitchen. I wish my instructor could have seen my kick; I did him proud."

"You're very brave," Agent Black said in a quiet voice that carried across the hushed room.

"It wasn't a hard decision when you come face-to-face with Adam Johnson's empty eyes. My first thought when I looked over my shoulder and saw him was I'd better get down off the chair, so I didn't break anything when he shot me and I fell off the chair. I had no doubt he would pull the trigger - there was no hint of nervousness or hesitation in his face. Then I decided that allowing him to shoot me was stupid, so I shifted my weight and came up with a better scenario in my head."

"That was excellent judgement and decision making. I don't know if any of the specially trained men and women in this conference room could have done better than you," Agent Black stated.

Jill's tiredness was seeping away to be replaced by embarrassment. If the agent had one more word of praise, Jill was sure that because she was so tired and therefore her emotions were close to the surface, she'd do a full body blush.

She tried to change the topic of conversation.

"Has anyone seen Adam Johnson since he left his house?"

Chapter Twenty-Six

Adam returned to the SUV after his encounter with Jill Quint inside his own house. He was enraged she was in his house, enraged that he hadn't been able to gather everything that he wanted, and most of all enraged that his gunshot missed. He had to sprint over several fences to return to the car. His three kids were in the back seat and were silent or asleep. They'd been through a lot in the last couple of weeks - the death of their mother, and now this upheaval yesterday. At least he had the presence of mind to hire a Mexican citizen as their nanny before he killed Stacy. The children had her for a comforting presence and she wouldn't mind relocating south of the border.

"Did you get all that you needed?" Brian asked in a soft voice.

"No, that bitch, Jill Quint, was in my house along with at least one other agent. I tried killing her but my aim was off and she ran yelling to a cop so all I had time for was this ugly cookie jar."

"What's so important about it?"

"It has the arsenic metal that I used to poison Stacy, and it has a fake passport and Mexican ID. I wanted to grab some of the kids' stuff, computers, cash I had stashed under the house and a few other personal belongings. Maybe once the heat dies down I can go back and get those things."

"You know that the U.S. government is going to hunt you down the rest of your life? I have my family to protect me in

Mexico, but other than doing work for the cartel, we have no family allegiance to you. Just saying."

"Yeah, I know," Adam sighed. "This transportation scheme was going so well for so many years, but I've been preparing for this day. I bought the property in Culiacán, saved a lot of cash and the kids and I can be happy there. We just need to get there. How soon will we be at the ranch?"

"Another forty-five minutes at least. As you know, there's a runway behind a private house owned on paper by an aunt of mine. I kept my larger plane at the Midland airport, but I'm sure we can't get near your plane or mine or that airport. The trouble with this back up plane is it seats four adults. Who do you want me to take? By the way two of your kids equal the weight of one adult so maybe they could share a seat."

The implied question was did he and the three kids go and then wait in Mexico for Brian to fly back with the nanny, Sofia, or did Adam give up his plane seat to her? Since he was wanted by the police, and she was not, it made sense to leave her behind.

"It'll take you nine hours to fly us straight there," Adam suggested. "We could land in Juarez and charter a different and faster plane to get to Culiacán. I have a second identification with me, although I am not sure I have a pilot's license in that name. Let me look."

"I didn't use my real name to file the registration for this plane so I'm sure I could use it in Juarez. The problem is that I'm not rated for anything more than a single engine. I could get us refueled in Juarez, but not switched to a faster plane. I've a few hours of instruction in bigger engine planes but I'm not certified. Added to that is some of the mountain peaks are nearly 9,000 feet so I wouldn't recommend a straight route to Culiacán."

"We're talking about flying my kids, so I agree with you that it would be a bad decision to fly them all the way to Culiacán in a small plane. I don't have fake passports for them and I don't want to find out that there's a notice at the airport to take them into custody. The kids and I could rent a car and take a few days to reach home. Once you fetch Sofia, you could bring her back to Juarez and put her on a commercial plane to Culiacán."

'That's a possibility," Brian mused. "I could then fly on by myself the long way to Culiacán. By going back to pick up Sofia and then taking a longer route with the plane, I should get home about the time you will with your kids."

"Sounds like a plan, let's proceed that way. Sofia will be comfortable for a few hours until you return for her."

They drove up to a ranch with a series of outbuildings. They'd both been there before and knew which outbuilding housed the plane. There was a landing strip at the side of the house that would allow them to depart as soon as the pre-flight check was performed. While Brian went through the flight check, Adam made sure that Sofia was comfortable in the house for the few hours she would have to wait for Brian to return.

The kids were buckled into the back seats of the plane and a car seat containing the third child was strapped to the floor. They were soon in the air. They had been in the air for about an hour on a direct course for Juarez and they could see off in the distance, a faint line ahead that was hopefully the Rio Grande River; the border between the United States and Mexico. The population density was also changing suggesting they would be heading for El Paso and Juarez just across the river. They had GPS and knew how far away the border was, but there was no cellular service yet and thus they had missed the text from Sofia that someone was approaching the house of the ranch. Adam hadn't told her that he was wanted by American police - the less she knew the better; so she was surprised to see both plain cars and cars with emergency lights on top.

Chapter Twenty- Seven

"That's the million dollar question," replied Agent Black ready to get the conversation back on mission. "Since the start of the op we've had an APB on Adam Johnson and Brian Campos. Other than your interactions with Adam, we've had no sightings of either of them. We searched Brian's home and Vernon Oil's headquarters. We've sent agents to interview the CEO on his ranch, but so far he's been of no help. There are many small airports and private airstrips throughout Texas and both Brian and Adam have pilot's licenses so they have a lot of options to avoid discovery."

"Adam's parents are in Houston?" Jill asked. "Have you made contact with them? Are they caring for Adam's children? Does Adam or Brian have other family in this area or in Texas?"

"Agents have visited Adam's parent's home with a search warrant," said another person in the room. "There was no sign of him or the children. The parents were shocked by our allegations, and said they had last spoken with him and the grandchildren at Stacy's funeral. So our guess is he is running with the children."

"Great, so we'll have to worry potentially about keeping three children safe when we confront Adam," Agent Black noted.

"Brian Campos seems like more of an enigma," noted another command post member. "We searched his home this morning and came away with nothing. It looked as sterile as one of those long term stay hotels with no family pictures anywhere in the house. We have no record of his being married or having children. We're hoping to get something out of our interview with Vernon's CEO."

"Are Mexican authorities cooperating with us?" asked Chief Swanson. "Do we have any information on Mexican residences for these two?"

"They're cooperating with us but remember they also cooperated with the U.S. over the capture and imprisoning of El Chapo, so take the cooperation for what it's worth," replied Black and looking around the room asked, "Dave, what did you learn about property in Mexico? Do Brian or Adam own any?"

"They both own large complexes in the city of Culiacán, a city considered to be the home base of the cartel," Dave replied. "We'll get cooperation from local authorities but likely they'll warn Campos and Johnson and they'll be long gone by the time a "raid" is made. The economy is booming in that city with the flow of narco money south and the cartel is not viewed negatively by the average citizen."

"So do you just give up on locating these two men?" Jill asked.

"They'll end up on a Most Wanted List and be prevented from re-entering this country," replied the agent. "We still have a fair amount of work to do to unravel their operation, and shutting it down so the moment we stop surveillance, the chemical transportation stays closed. While we don't have Brian or Adam, we do have about fifteen other narco criminals, their tanker trucks, and all chemical assets under wrap."

"Agent Black, some new information has just come in from the agents at the Vernon CEO's house. He was asked if he knew of any other properties the two of them owned and he gave us an approximate location about one-hundred miles west of here that they had all visited. Using Google Earth we were able to identify the ranch. The CEO may not be any good with oil, but he has a great memory for ranch layout, and outbuildings."

"Let's dispatch a team there now," replied the Agent and within ten minutes there was a convoy of law enforcement officers heading to the address at speeds of ninety miles per hour.

"Agent Black, one more thing, the CEO mentioned that a small plane was kept in one of the outbuildings. The CEO doesn't fly and described the plane as too small for him to fly in although it did have four seats."

"Let's contact the FAA and see if we have any small planes that took off from the coordinates mentioned," replied Agent Black. "Since it's a private landing strip and they're criminals, I'm sure that no flight plan was filed. So we'll need to trace them on radar. If they get across the border, they're gone. We'll dispatch a military helicopter from El Paso, but since we think there are three children on board we have to be careful with what we do."

The room was animated with discussions and preparations. One of the agents said, "Regional Air Traffic Control Houston has a blip on their radar screen that they think matches the plane we're looking for. It's about thirty minutes from the border of Mexico. Mexican authorities on their side have a helicopter approaching their border and we have a copter approaching from the west. FAA has advised the nearest landing strips for a major operation are El Paso International and Horizon Airport in El Paso. Of course Mexican authorities could follow the plane in their airspace to Juarez International Airport. We have permission to follow the plane into Juarez air space, but no farther into the interior of Mexico."

Another voice called out, "Agents have arrived at the ranch and there is a lone Hispanic female by the name of Sofia Torres.

She says she's the kid's nanny and Adam left with the three children about forty-five minutes before we arrived."

"Damn," replied several people in the room.

"She also said the other man is coming back to pick her up in about three hours. She, Adam, and the children will be driving from Juarez to Culiacán over the course of the next couple of days."

"I don't think he'll be coming back for her," replied Agent Black. "I have word that both the Mexican and the military helicopters have the small plane in sight. They are attempting to establish communication with the plane."

Chapter Twenty-Eight

"Crap."

"What?" asked Adam and then he saw what Brian was looking at.

"Perhaps it's a joint Mexican-U.S. Training exercise that we just happened to get close to. I'll pretend I don't see them."

Shortly the U.S. copter pulled abreast of the small plane and gestured for them to land. Brian pretended he didn't understand them. Would they really shoot them down? Brian took the tactic of ignoring them. Then they held up a sign that said Channel 8 in English and in Spanish. Brian knew this meant that they wanted him to turn his headset to that channel for a conversation. He didn't think he could maintain stupidity and the most basic of pilot lessons would have included training on the air channels.

He switched to the specified channel, then said in Spanish, "I am just a Mexican citizen returning home." Maybe denying that he knew English would give them the time they needed to cross the border. Not that the Mexican helicopter would help. He was entering a touchy area. The border area was controlled by his cartel, but farther into the city, the Juarez cartel had control and wouldn't lift a finger to help them escape.

A voice came back in Spanish, "We are requesting that you land immediately by order of the United States Drug Enforcement Agency. There is an airport on your right that has been cleared for your approach."

Brian looked over at Adam and let loose a string of cuss

words. Fortunately the plane was so noisy that the kids couldn't hear the words in the back seat. "What should we do?" Then he had a brilliant thought.

"I have a parachute in the back and I'm pretty sure I can aim to land on the Mexico side of the river and the helicopter will follow me to the ground, but I know all the narco tunnels in that area so I should be able to escape. You can continue on piloting the plane, if the Mexican copter tries to communicate with you just stall them long enough to get beyond the city and they'll leave you alone after that. Tell them that you have three kids on board," Brian said as he was moving about his seat getting ready to change places with Adam, reaching for and snapping his parachute into place.

The tricky thing about the maneuver would be closing the door after Brian jumped out and keeping the plane steady with the wind and weight changes. The only alternative was to ask his oldest kid to close the door but he wouldn't put him at risk. Seconds later the men were in place and with a muttered 'good luck' and 'Vaya con Dios', Brian jumped out of the plane at 3,000 feet, almost the minimum requirement to deploy a parachute and survive. Adam struggled to get the door closed quickly and control the plane. He could hear his middle child crying in terror, but there was nothing he could do at the moment.

He looked out the window and Brian was right; the helicopter was following him to the ground. Good, thought Adam, he and the kids would make it to their new home. The maneuvers that he and Brian just executed took the small plane away from where the Mexican helicopter was hovering and with any luck Adam would have just enough speed to outrun it since it didn't look as powerful or menacing as the U.S. copter.

He looked at his gauges and the fuel was good. He knew a

little about helicopters and thought he could outrun it with speed eventually; he was likely about ten miles per hour faster. It could match him for altitude so there was no reason to waste time gaining or losing elevation. He'd been to Juarez several times and would avoid crossing into the flight path for their main airport. If he skirted the border, he would look for a private landing strip where he could park the plane and catch a ride to a car rental agency. Fortunately in his dealings with the cartel over the years he had become fluent in Spanish and he had enough cash and a gun to buy himself and the kids out of any situation. He looked out the back of the plane and he could see the copter falling further behind him. Southeast was not the direction that would get him close to his home, but eluding capture was his biggest priority. Another half an hour and he could no longer see the copter and it was time to turn inland toward the city of Chihuahua. He knew it to be a large city and it was thirty to sixty minutes away. He would dump the plane, pay cash for a car, and follow a series of highways home to Culiacán. He'd have to find a new nanny for the kids as Sophia was likely in custody of the DEA or some federal agency. He looked back at his kids and they were all asleep. The unrelenting noise of the small plane did that to people. He wondered how Brian was doing on the ground. Adam owed him big time for devising their escape plan.

Brian jumped out of the small plane and immediately opened his parachute. He looked up and watched the American copter change course to follow him to the ground south of Juarez. Growing up in the cartel, he was well aware of the supply routes and tunnels between Mexico and the United States. He was certain he could control his parachute to land on the Mexico side, and then disappear underground. The river was one to two hundred yards wide at this point, so they would be able to see him land, but he planned to quickly disappear before any police showed up from the Mexican side.

He landed hard as the parachute had barely had enough time to slow his descent to ground down. He released the parachute cords, and then rolled everything up as the copter hovered above the middle of the river. He looked around him for the telltale signs of a tunnel entrance. It could be a big wad of tumbleweed that never moved with the wind, or a certain rock formation, or one of the other signals used over the years to mark tunnel locations in the barren ground. He knew this region was like a gopher habitat at a zoo; it was full of rabbit holes to hide in. After a quick scan, he thought he had two possible options. He needed to be quick about it as the copter was moving menacingly slow across the river towards him. They were probably trying to get permission from Mexican authorities to land and make an arrest.

He ran for a still tumbleweed, pulled up a small door latch hidden by the weed, and dropped inside using his cell phone flashlight to light his way. He hoped this tunnel went back toward town as he had no desire to go across the border to America. He moved in as fast a pace as he could through the low ceiling, narrow walled path. Ten minutes later, to his delight, he popped up inside an empty house. A quick search of the house gave him nothing useful, so he was out the door and walking toward Juarez. There were a fair amount of trees to provide cover as he slowly made his way on foot back to town. It might take him a day or so to get there, but with success at evading arrest, he'd be willing to walk a year. He just needed to slip across the border to kill that Jill Quint. You didn't cause trouble for the cartel and get away with it, he thought angrily.

Chapter Twenty-Nine

It was mid-day in the command post and Jill had been awake for thirty-six straight hours. She hadn't stayed awake this long since her year as an intern and resident during her medical education. She actually felt pretty good and thought her brain was still in high gear. It helped that they were hearing about the action going on in El Paso and now south of the border. While they were working on chasing Adam Johnson and Brian Campos in the plane, she had been using the feeds given to her to locate which warehouse and oil wells the four tanker trucks visited. Not exciting work like chasing a plane, but her contribution would close down a major chemical precursor pipeline and she had to be satisfied with that so far.

She still wanted to be in on the questioning of Adam Johnson if they caught him, but she suspected that by the end of the day, there would be no further reason for the Dallas PD to retain her as a consultant. She'd exchanged a few texts with Nathan and knowing that she was sitting in a police station working had almost eliminated his anxiety level about her.

"We have a visual on the suspect plane," called out the agent monitoring the helicopter dispatched from El Paso. Just as Agent Black was about to ask a question, he held up his hand so he could listen to whatever was being said. After a pause he added, "An adult male departed the plane with a parachute, the plane has crossed into Mexican airspace and now our Mexican copter is following it. Our helicopter is following the parachute to the ground."

After another pause, "The man folded up his parachute and retreated through a tunnel on the Mexican side of the river. Based on the pictures we provided them, the parachutist was Brian Campos. Sir, they lost him."

He interrupted Black again with a hand up and then added, "The plane continued southwest and was able to outrun the helicopter. It appears they've lost both suspects."

"Are Mexican officials searching for Brian Campos?" Black inquired.

"Yes, but they aren't expecting any success. There're too many places to hide."

"Can we track Adam's plane?"

"We're tracking it by radar. Normally that would be nearly impossible to identify a small plane but since we followed it all along, we'll know where it flies."

"Do we know its range and speed?"

"We can make an educated guess and based on the plane's direction in the last fifteen minutes we believe it is heading to the Chihuahua airport. There are some smaller cities with airports that he could head to, but it would be far easier to walk away from the plane in a big city. Although, there's been no sighting of the children, we believe they are with him, and that will make it harder on him to stay hidden."

"Will Mexican police help us?" Jill whispered to Castillo.

"Yes, they should get him."

Black overheard Jill's question and said, "Mexico has a long history of cooperating with the United States on a criminal apprehension for a suspect with Adam Johnson's alleged crimes. I fully expect to have him in the El Paso office of the DEA this evening."

"He belongs to Dallas PD, he'll be in Dallas tonight," Castillo replied. "Murder is a higher crime than drug trafficking. We get first interview rights."

Silence reigned in the room, and Jill injected her opinion though no one asked for it, "We suspect Adam Johnson of marinating blueberries in arsenic, then baking a blueberry muffin for his wife. This is a very pre-meditated murder. His wife was a nurse giving a presentation at a conference when she passed out at the podium and then physicians in the room and later paramedics and even a hospital were unable to bring her back to life. She was the mother to those three children likely in the plane with Adam. This is a heinous crime and he needs to be taken to Dallas."

Castillo looked at her briefly and gave her the slightest nod of approval.

Agent Black stared at Jill and she stared right back at him. Then he said, "A compromise, we'll take him to the Dallas office of the DEA and you folks can interview first."

That was indeed a compromise that Castillo agreed with. The Dallas DA could charge Adam with first degree murder while the DEA held him and continued their investigation into the actions of the cartel and their chemical distribution network.

"Let's catch the bastard first, then we can fight over jurisdiction issues since he should be charged with drug trafficking in Odessa and attempted murder of Dr. Quint," noted Detective Guerrero.

The agent monitoring the plane's trajectory said, "It appears he's headed toward the city of Chihuahua. There's a major airport there as well as an executive airport. Police are in place at each airport to apprehend Adam and his children."

The room went to silence waiting for the next report from the agent. Jill was thinking about the attempted murder charge.

Somehow she had forgotten the terror of facing down Adam while he held a gun and had forgotten that his actions had amounted to attempted murder. At least if they couldn't nail him for Stacy's murder, they surely had enough evidence on the attempted murder charge.

Five minutes later he said, "The plane is in the approach pattern for the main airport. Air traffic control will direct the plane over to an area where the police are waiting inside a terminal."

The room reverted to quiet conversations among colleagues as they waited for word that the Mexican police had Adam Johnson in custody. U.S. officials were in the air and expected to arrive within half an hour at the airport to extradite Adam back to the United States. A female agent would take the children and a call would be made to the two sets of grandparents to look for immediate family to take care of the kids.

Twenty minutes later, the agent announced that Adam Johnson was in Mexican custody and U.S. officials were expected soon to take him into custody and fly him and the children back to Texas. There was an additional report that police from Juarez had been unable to locate Brian Campos. Given his long ties to the drug cartel, he might easily hide for a long time. The DEA would continue to hunt him, but there was a good feeling in the room related to Adam's capture and the discovery and closure of the chemical pipeline.

The discussion in the room turned to organizing the interrogation that would take place that evening. They were meeting in Dallas and if after the interview it appeared that they had no evidence connecting Adam to Stacy's murder, then the DEA would be free to return with him to Odessa for prosecution. Castillo and Jill would return on the DEA plane to

271

Dallas along with several agents and representatives of the Odessa police and district attorney. Fortunately the airport was in Midland and Jill had time to gather her belongings and meet them at the airport. Given their lack of sleep over the past thirty-six hours it would have been dangerous for them to drive back to Dallas that afternoon. The flight from Chihuahua to Dallas was about two hours and there would be a brief legal proceeding on both sides of the border to get him sent north.

Castillo and Jill planned their interview strategy on the plane ride. Jill lacked experience in interviewing but she had all the forensic details in her head that might be used to trip him up. Adam's legal representative was meeting them in Dallas. So there was nothing to stop them from starting the interview tonight. Upon arrival, they were joined by an assistant district attorney to round out the team.

Finally, six hours after his capture that day, Adam arrived in an interview room in Dallas police headquarters. His attorney met with him first and then it was Castillo and Jill's turn with lots of other personnel watching the interview through the one-way window. The conversation started once all the legal rhetoric was out of the way.

"Where were you two days before Stacy's murder and who can verify your whereabouts that day?" Castillo asked.

"I was in Odessa at work," Adam replied looking puzzled. "I did a lot of field testing of our oil rigs, so my co-workers saw me in the morning when I arrived and then again later in the afternoon when I returned. Do you want their names?"

"We looked at the transportation cameras around Odessa for that day and we found no record of you behind the wheel for a large chunk of the day. In fact we have record of your journey to the Midland airport, where you filed a flight plan to land at the Dallas Executive airport. We checked the cameras in

Dallas and there is evidence of you behind the wheel of a rental car," Castillo replied. "Let's try this again, where were you that day?"

"I must have mistaken the day you mentioned. I had to fly into Dallas for a meeting of petroleum engineers so I took my own plane to get there."

"Where and when was the meeting?"

"It was eleven in the morning two days before Stacy's death and the meeting was at the Dallas Convention Center."

"So if we pull the tape of the meeting, you're saying that we'll see you on the tape," Castillo said.

"I had to leave and use the bathroom," Adam replied. "I had a bit of the stomach flu, so I might not be there at the time of the filming."

While he was talking, Jill was accessing the films from the convention center folks. They had a sophisticated security camera system because of the expensive trade shows that occurred inside. Using her facial recognition software she tracked Adam out of a conference room and into a men's bathroom. Minutes later he left the bathroom wearing the uniform of the maintenance guy. She turned her laptop over to Castillo who watched the feed and nodded.

"Mr. Johnson, what you meant to say was that you went to the bathroom to change your appearance and then walked toward the hotel that Stacy would be staying in the next day," Castillo corrected. "Let's see what happens after you leave the bathroom."

Jill had been sorting the video footage and on camera after camera they tracked his progress to the door outside of Stacy's future room. Then they traced back into the bathroom where he changed back into his convention suit and he re-entered the engineering conference. At the end of the meeting, he hit the same bathroom and changed this time into the room service outfit. Originally when Jill had run the footage, her software had said there was a possible match but not a confirmatory match. With this additional footage, it would be excellent evidence that Adam had opportunity.

On advice of his attorney, Adam had no response to the footage. So they changed tactics and asked him about the ugly cookie jar that Mexican officials had tagged for evidence when they searched the plane. They found it inside one of the kid's suitcases. The crime lab texted Castillo that it was positive for arsenic.

"We have evidence that you removed what appears to be a cookie jar from your house before your attempted murder of Dr. Quint," Castillo said while Jill gave Adam her best fierce look. "Our lab has confirmed that it's positive for arsenic. Your wife died from eating blueberries marinated in arsenic and you possess that substance. We questioned some other people who said you were known to bake, so it was well within your capabilities to create the muffin that killed your wife. What's wrong? Did she catch you driving a transport truck around town and threaten to expose you?"

"No comment," replied Adam Johnson who had been slowly losing his confidence as he heard the evidence piling up against him. He was a smart man and he had to know they had enough evidence to convict him of multiple felonies and violations of State and Federal laws.

Despite several more hours of questioning with alternating personnel, they got nothing more out of him related to Stacy's murder or the chemical transportation scheme. There was such a wide array of circumstantial and factual evidence that they likely had enough to convict him if he never said another word.

Jill walked out of the police department near midnight.

Castillo gave her a ride back to the hotel and she would fly back to California in the morning. She played a key role in the collection of evidence that would nail the coffin on Adam Johnson for multiple crimes. It was the first time she ever turned on a client and it didn't feel good. In fact, nothing about the case felt good. Brian Campos got away, Adam hadn't admitted he killed Stacy. His kids had lost both parents. She was getting deep in the pity party. The only thing she felt good about was shutting down the chemical operation; it was solely her investigative skills that uncovered the operation.

She got her room key from the front desk and headed up to her room dead tired, dragging her suitcase behind her. She couldn't wait to fall face first onto the bed. She inserted her room key and opened the door, she had her shoulder holding the door open, one hand on the luggage pull and the other inside her purse about to drop her room key. Then she smelled a man's cologne and her hand slipped farther into her purse for the bug spray. The light switch was inside the room but she pulled out the bug spray and leveled the nozzle toward a six foot five inch target and moved her hand in slow motion across the entrance to her room. For a second her mind flashed to what a mess she would have to clean up before she went to bed.

By the third second, she heard a gasp followed by a man's scream, then her own in response. She flicked the light on and found Brian Campos, she thought, on his knees, his hands covering his eyes as he moaned. She speed dialed Castillo and told him to return to her hotel room, that she thought she'd disarmed Brian Campos. She moved closer to the man and sprayed him again near his eyes. Doors opened down the hallway and she could hear people coming; she yelled at the first person to call hotel security immediately. She heard sirens outside as well, as Castillo raised the alarm to come to her aid.

Two minutes later, the first police officer arrived on the heels of hotel security.

"Ma'am, what's going on here?" said the officer taking the bug spray out of Jill's hand.

"When I entered my room, this man was waiting for me. I smelled his cologne and sprayed him with bug spray before he could harm me. Then I resprayed him to keep him down until help arrived."

Castillo arrived at a run, happy to see Jill unharmed. He had a sliver of sympathy for Brian Campos as he was quite blinded by the bug spray and was in such pain that he was incoherent. They had to call paramedics to treat the man as it seemed that he had contact lenses that had accelerated the damage done by the bug spray. His eyesight would be impaired for a while. Within twenty minutes, Castillo had the situation wrapped up and Brian Campos was taken away to the hospital for clearance and then he'd be booked into jail.

"My lieutenant thought my reasoning for hiring you was about the strangest she ever heard. Now, she'll have to eat humble pie. You made a great target to catch a lot of bad people in the State of Texas," Castillo said with a grin. "By my last count, I think it's Jill Quint twenty points, bad guys zero."

"Now that I've done all your work for you, rounding up the Texas most wanted criminals in two cities, I'm heading home to my peaceful vineyard in California. I'm sure I'll have to come back for their trials since there were murder attempts on me, but if you have a witness statement or anything else for me to sign, just send it to me."

"It's really been a pleasure working with you Dr. Quint. I wouldn't be surprised if the department called upon you again to consult; you have some unique skills and attributes and you think on your feet. Thank you on behalf of the city of Dallas and the State of Texas."

Jill was always embarrassed by praise and she was so dead tired, that if Castillo said many more nice words to her, she'd cry. She was thrilled to see the hotel security guard return to the room ready to assist her elsewhere to sleep for the night. After a handshake from Castillo, and an elevator ride to another floor she crashed onto her new bed ten minutes later. What an amazing thirty-six hours, Jill thought as she settled her face on the soft pillow.

Epilogue

Two weeks later, Jill and Nathan hopped aboard the private jet sent by Henrik Klein for the friends to enjoy the long weekend together in Germany. In three hours, they would touch down in Green Bay for Marie, Jo, and Angela to join them on the luxury jet complete with its own attendant. The seats reclined to flat so they had the most comfortable ride to Europe ever.

They arrived for a late dinner at Henrik's estate. Plied with wine from the Rhine Valley, a fireplace and the companionship of friends, it felt like one of those moments when all was right in the world. Nathan urged Jill to relay her stories of the bug spray and soon Jo and Angela's eyes were hurting from the thought of chemicals adhering to their contact lenses.

Nick would be arriving from Amsterdam in the morning and they were all going to watch an elite Belgium police force try Henrik's obstacle course after he toured them around his newly planted vineyard. He'd added additional traps since they last saw the course and they would be entertained by the training exercise. Later, they were going to several wineries to sample the wine and cheese of the region. The next day Henrik had arranged a brewery tour for Angela, who was more partial to beer as well as an Oktoberfest party.

Henrik and Marie seemed to be getting along so well that Jill could see a blossoming romance even though they were worlds apart. Henrik had the financial resources to make it happen if he so desired and since he was such a nice friend, she would love to see Marie paired with him.

While they were together, the four women finished their plans for their upcoming vacation to the United Kingdom. When Henrik learned of their itinerary, he consulted his calendar and found he'd be in Edinburgh the same day they would. It was the technology capital of Scotland and he was doing a presentation, so they made plans for dinner.

Yes, Jill thought, she was lucky to be enjoying this moment. Thinking back to a few of the dangerous circumstances in which she'd found herself in Texas, maybe she'd take this weekend to think about her future and if she should continue to put her life and sometimes that of her friends at risk. Maybe she should be a vintner full time and moonlight with a few crime labs to supplement her income until the winery could fully support her. Maybe she would just do autopsies but no longer offer any investigative services, but that would cut into the vacation funds her friends were now enjoying. She hated to be pessimistic, but one day her luck would run out. Should she quit now to ensure that she would be able to have moments of bliss like she was having at the moment? Only time would tell.

ABOUT THE AUTHOR

Discover "Vials", "Chocolate Diamonds", "A Breck Death", "Death On A Green", and "A Taxing Death" also written by Alec Peche.

A 7th book is a work in progress for this series.

Connect with me: Friend me on Facebook
http://facebook.com/AlecPeche

Find me on Twitter @AlecPeche

www.alecpeche.com

email: vials@alecpeche.com